JUST FOLLOW THE INSTRUCTIONS

Becky grabbed the book. "*Handbook of Practical Heroics*?"

"Check it out. It's all there. What to wear, what to bring, when to go. Armor, weapons, plans of attack, swordplay techniques. Complete instructions for penetrating fortresses and dispatching Evil Overlords. Discount coupons for lodging and restaurants."

"Kevin, this is insane."

"No, look at this." Kevin grabbed the book and started leafing through it, showing her the chapter headings. "Okay, so when the villain is holding the heroine at knifepoint on the edge of a waterfall, and the hero comes swooping down on a vine and snatches her away, did you ever wonder where the vine came from? Well, this tells you. And here's a bit about knocking a guard unconscious with a single punch to the jaw. And look at this! It even shows how to jump through a plate-glass window without getting a single scratch . . ."

Heroics
for Beginners

John
Moore

ACE BOOKS, NEW YORK

This is a work of fiction. Names, characters, places, and incidents either are the product of the author's imagination or are used fictitiously, and any resemblance to actual persons, living or dead, business establishments, events, or locales is entirely coincidental.

HEROICS FOR BEGINNERS

An Ace Book / published by arrangement with the author

PRINTING HISTORY
Ace mass market edition / September 2004

Copyright © 2004 by John Moore.
Cover art by Walter Velez.
Cover design by Rita Frangie.
Interior text design by Julie Rogers.

For information address: The Berkley Publishing Group,
a division of Penguin Group (USA) Inc.,
375 Hudson Street, New York, New York 10014.

ISBN: 0-441-01193-4

ACE®
Ace Books are published by The Berkley Publishing Group,
a division of Penguin Group (USA) Inc.,
375 Hudson Street, New York, New York 10014.
ACE and the "A" design
are trademarks belonging to Penguin Group (USA) Inc.

PRINTED IN THE UNITED STATES OF AMERICA

10 9 8 7 6 5 4 3 2 1

To my friends
in the Fandom Association of Central Texas

Before attempting to penetrate the Evil Overlord's Invincible Fortress, the practical hero will seriously examine the option of maintaining a safe distance and picking him off the ramparts with a long-range weapon.

—*HANDBOOK OF PRACTICAL HEROICS*
BY ROBERT TAYLOR

Dark gray clouds scudded against the moon. It was totally overcast when Thunk started out, but the sky partially cleared, and when the bright moon came out, it illuminated the Fortress of Doom and striped it with black-and-gray shadows. Thunk stayed motionless in one such shadow, thrown by a chimney, with his feet braced against the steep slope of the slate roof. Voices wafted from below, from the heavily guarded doorways. More guards, armed and armored, could be seen pacing across the gates, leaning out the windows, or standing at the parapets. Thunk the Barbarian waited. To pass the time he pulled an india rubber ball from his pouch and practiced grip-strengthening exercises. He flexed the muscles in his forearms and wondered if it was time for a new tattoo.

When the moon darkened once again he allowed himself a derisive smile. For a man of his skill and experience, the seemingly impregnable fortress had posed little challenge. Soldiers walked the streets of the nearby village, but they had taken little notice of him. He did not find anything odd in this, despite the fact that a tall man with massive shoulders, dressed in barbarian leather and furs, and carrying a huge sword engraved with cryptic runes, usually attracts at least a second glance. The trail up to the Fortress was also guarded of course; but he had bypassed that, using his expert climbing ability to go directly up the cliff. He wasn't surprised that the cliff edge was unguarded. No doubt they considered the sheer face unscalable. There remained the smooth stone walls of the Fortress itself, and a skillfully thrown rope had solved that problem. Then from atop the wall, a convenient cast-iron drainpipe provided access to the roof. An easy job. Not much of a challenge to a man like Thunk.

Now he removed an iron grating that provided access to a ventilation shaft. The grate wasn't even bolted down but just slid into a groove in the shaft housing. It was amazing how often the fools who built these castles forgot to secure the ventilation shafts. Anyone would think they'd know better by now.

Once inside he replaced the grating and sat back, listening. All was silent on the roof. Reassured, he slid back the cover of his dark lantern. The shaft, wide enough for even the broad-shouldered barbarian, dropped away into darkness.

Something, however, obstructed his view. He lowered

the lantern into the hole. A faint thin odor of burning lamp oil filled the shaft. Four broad steel bars stretched across the opening. But not all the way across, and at one end they were set into a rotating cylinder. It looked for all the world like a turnstile.

Thunk leaned forward for a closer look. It *was* a turnstile. Neat letters had been painted above a narrow slot. "Ventilation Shaft Entrance: 2p." Puzzled, Thunk reached into his pouch and extracted a tuppence. He dropped the coin into the slot, then drew his sword. Carefully, he touched the blade to the bars. The cylinder rotated. The bars swung down against the wall of the shaft. He shrugged, replaced his sword in its scabbard, and slipped through the open gate.

He left the lantern at the turnstile, braced his feet against one side of the shaft and his back against the other, and carefully and quietly worked his way down. His sword dangled from his belt, the point swinging gently. It was an easy descent, for he'd had plenty of practice at this sort of thing. Thunk had lost count of the number of impregnable fortresses he had penetrated by climbing through a ventilation shaft. True, Thunk would also be the first to admit that counting was not one of his strong points, but it was still a lot of shafts.

The opening above him grew smaller, the light from the lantern grew fainter, but presently Thunk could make out a dim glow beneath him. He had dropped nearly sixty feet and was well into the interior of the castle. A few feet later he reached the bottom of the shaft, which ran horizontally in four directions. The glow came from a square of glass set into the side of the shaft. Behind it was a candle. Below the glass was a small metal plaque. Thunk lay down in the shaft and put his nose nearly against it, barely able to make out the etching. It showed a vertical shaft descending against a black background and branching out into four horizontal shafts. At the intersection was a small dot, with an arrow pointing to it. The arrow was labeled "You Are Here."

Thunk had plenty in the way of physical courage and a good deal of native cunning, but not much of a sense of humor. He grunted and unsheathed his sword, keeping it pointed in front of him. It was obvious now that he had descended into a trap. A trap set by someone who *did* have a sense of humor. Not a clever sense of humor, mind you, but some wise guy had made the attempt. Thunk looked at the entrances to the four shafts and debated which one to take. All of them, he suspected, would turn out badly. He considered climbing back up the shaft and forcing his way through the turnstile. Then he looked at the glass plate and the lamp.

Someone had to light the candle. Someone had to replace it when it burned down. There must be a door in back of it, one that led into the castle. He peered through the glass. Yes, in the back of the alcove he could see the edges of an access panel. The Barbarian Swordsman hesitated not a moment before reversing his sword and smashing the hilt into the glass plate.

Immediately the shaft began to fill with gas.

Thunk's instinctive reaction was to draw a deep breath and hold it. But it was already too late to avoid getting a lungful of gas. His nostrils filled with a faint, opium-like scent, his ears filled with the hissing of a gas valve. And just before he lost consciousness he heard something else. It was far away and very faint, barely audible under the gas noise. But he was sure he heard the sound of evil laughter.

* * *

There were fairy-tale kingdoms, twenty of them, clustered on the edge of an ancient and primitive land, a land of magic and mystery, where crystal waterfalls dropped from icy peaks and wild beasts skulked in hidden glens, where castles guarded the cities and wishing wells dotted the countryside. It was peopled by lords and ladies and knights and scholars, by wizards and witches and bandits and intrepid travelers who were always told that yes, it really was safe to drink the water in any of the Twenty Kingdoms but to be on the safe side you might want to boil it first, or just stick to beer and wine. Not all of the twenty were actually ruled by kings. Some were ruled by queens and a few were more or less constitutional monarchies. But all of them were definitely fairy-tale kingdoms.

Now fairy tale is a rather broad definition. Here, it does not refer to the children's storybook type of fairy tale, populated by cutesy talking neutered animals. In the Twenty Kingdoms the cartographers filled the blank spaces on their maps with the warning, "Here Be Dragons." The cartographers weren't kidding around. And the dragons didn't talk either.

But neither were they the gruesome and grim sort of fairy-tale lands, describing the kind of place where wicked stepmothers not only killed their children but boiled them into soup and served it up at royal banquets. Oh sure, there were evil villains and awful crimes, but they weren't the norm.

It is more the romantic type of fairy tale that is being referred to here, for the Twenty Kingdoms were lands of gallant knights and elegant ladies. Lands where polite discourse and courtly manners were interspersed with fiery speeches and deadly duels. Lands of dramatic gestures and passionate romances. Real romance, that is. Heartfelt love. Tender emotion. Devoted adoration. Caring. Sensitivity. Not that hot, sexy, bodice-ripping sort of romance that was so popular in the more decadent kingdoms. There was none of that. No.

Well, okay, there was *some* bodice ripping. But, really, most of it was consensual.

And years ago, in one of these fairy-tale kingdoms, a man named Eric Timberline ascended the throne of Rassendas. He was a fair and just ruler. He maintained a powerful army, but thanks to clever diplomacy and alliances he managed to avoid war. He kept the roads in good repair. He improved the schools. He discriminated against all ethnic groups equally. Eric was a good king, but he was not called King Eric the Good. There already was an Eric the Good of Calvados, so King Eric of Rassendas became known as Not-Eric-the-Good-the-Other-One.

Needless to say, he didn't care much for this nickname. It seemed to imply that if he was not Eric the Good, then he was Eric the Bad. He could see it coming. All it would take would be one lazy historian, and he would be down in the books forever with an unwanted nickname. He was determined to stop it. For a while he involved himself in the Rassendas court system, hoping to earn the name of Eric the Just. But he didn't have the devious mind necessary to succeed at law. A number of churches hinted that, for an appropriately large donation, they could arrange for him to become Eric the Pious. This was entirely too sleazy for him. His worst idea was to seduce a large number of women, in the hope of getting a name like Eric the Sexy. His advisors warned him that this plan had a high potential for backfiring. Eric didn't listen, but he fell in love with the next woman that hopped into bed with him, married her, and forgot the seduction scheme. Eric the Philanderer was not the reputation he was looking for.

It was the merest chance that solved his problem. One bright sunny day, while riding through the city, he looked in a shop window and saw a pair of spectacles with smoked glass lenses. King Eric dismounted and handed the reins to an assistant. He went into the shop. The spectacles, he was informed, were designed for explorers who had to cross sun-beaten deserts or glaring ice fields. King Eric bought a pair. He tried them on. He liked the way they made him look. He liked them so much, in fact, that he took to wearing them all the time, even at night. And a few months later he discovered, to his delight, that he was now being referred to as Eric the Totally Cool.

Prince Kevin of Rassendas was a long way from home, and he was thinking of his own reputation. It is when you are away from home, surrounded by strangers who know little of your past achievements, that your reputation becomes important. If his father was Eric the Cool, and Kevin was simply Prince Kevin, did that mean Kevin was not cool? It is disconcerting for a young man to think that his father is cooler than he is. That's not what fathers are for.

"Kevin the Good," he murmured to himself. "That would be bad. Kevin the Bad. That would be good. Kevin the Nice would be the worst."

"Beg pardon, sire?" said his valet.

"The hot babes don't go for nice guys," explained Kevin. "They think they're boring. Girls like bad boys. They think bad guys are exciting."

"Yes, sire."

The Prince of Rassendas carefully adjusted his cuffs, flicking an imaginary speck of dust off the lace. His expression, when he looked at himself in the mirror, was perhaps a trifle smug. Light brown hair flowed over the carefully starched pleats of his collar and tumbled about his shoulders.

His strong hands adjusted the satin waistcoat over his hard, flat stomach. The dark cloth of his trousers draped smoothly down long, straight legs to meet the highly polished black calfskin of his boots, breaking just above the silver ornamental spurs. Prince Kevin cut a dashing figure, and he knew it. With great precision, he twisted a lock of hair around his finger and let it fall over his forehead. In doing so, he saw, behind his own reflection, his valet approaching with a piece of folded silk.

"Will you be wanting your diplomatic sash, Your Highness?"

Kevin considered it. "I think not, Winslow. Makes the whole thing seem a bit too mercenary, don't you know?"

"It *will* be a marriage of convenience, sire."

"Yes, but no sense rubbing the fact in the girl's face. May as well maintain a pretense of romance, however thin it may be." He saw a cloud pass over his valet's face and turned away from the glass. "You disagree?"

Winslow did his best to sound neutral, but his look of fatherly concern was plain to see. He hesitated before speaking, his gray eyebrows drawing together. "Sire, I realize your father wants the match very much, but I have a concern, arising from my longtime—erm—service."

"Friendship, would you say?"

Winslow permitted himself a small smile. "Yes, sire. That is, I cannot feel honest enthusiasm at the betrothal of yourself and Princess Rebecca. From all accounts she is quite unsuitable in temperament."

"A cold-hearted bitch, I believe is the term."

"Um. Yes, sire. Even her own people call her the Ice Princess."

"Well, maybe she'll warm up to me." Kevin turned back

to the mirror and gave his cuffs one final tug. "Come, Winslow. We mustn't keep the court waiting."

"Certainly, sire." Winslow put the scarlet sash away. "Will you be wearing your court sword this evening?"

The Prince reflected on this. "Logan is quite the martial hero, isn't he, Winslow?"

"Yes, sire. I expect him to be in dress uniform, with full miniatures."

"And he'll have a sword, of course. No, no sword for me. We mustn't try to outshine him at his own game. Nothing that smacks of the military. Just a cane, I think."

Winslow brought him an ebony walking stick, topped with a gold knob, and helped him fasten his cape around his shoulders. The valet himself was dressed in plain dark blue trousers and a jacket with the Rassendas crest on the pocket, the standard uniform of the Rassendas court. The two men set off down the long corridors of the Castle Deserae. They had been guests here for several weeks and had started to become familiar with its many rooms and multiple staircases. It was to be a busy night, and the broad hallways were bustling with visitors and servants. The Prince greeted as many people as he could by name, including the servants, and acknowledged the rest with easy smiles. He was pleased to notice how the castle's staff treated Winslow with respect.

"A good sign, I think," he told him in a low voice. "Those in service always know what's up before the gentry, don't you think?"

The older man nodded. "Very true, sire. The fact that the other valets are showing deference to me indicates we are certainly still in the running."

"How many are here?"

"There are four other potential suitors, Your Highness, counting Lord Logan."

"Hayward didn't show?"

"His lordship was taken ill, sire."

"Not seriously, I hope. I'll send a note tomorrow. What about Monty?"

"The rumor is that Prince Montcrief is about to announce his own engagement."

"Lady Allyson?"

"So they say."

"Good for him. About time, I should think. Those two have been making puppy eyes at each other for half a year now. All right, so that leaves me, Logan, Raymond, Harkness, and Bigelow.

"Yes, sire. But the word below stairs is that you and Logan are the only serious contenders. The nobility of Deserae still favors Lord Logan, but popular opinion seems to be swinging your way."

"Those old guys always back the military. Well, keep your ears open, Winslow." They descended another broad staircase, standing aside to let two women in wide gowns pass. Kevin picked up the thread of conversation again. "Truth to tell, Winslow, this isn't just politics. I personally would like to have this match with the Princess."

"Why is that, sire?"

"Well for one thing, she's really beautiful."

"Every princess in the Twenty Kingdoms is beautiful, Your Highness. It is one of the unexplained mysteries of our land. I have never seen an unattractive princess."

"Okay, but she's also about my age. I mean, look what happened to Prince Frederick. The family refused to let him marry until he was thirty, and then he was betrothed to a six-year-old girl."

"That was ten years ago, sire. Now he is the most envied middle-aged man in his kingdom."

The two men turned into a wider and even more crowded hallway. They followed the current of people to their destination but paused at the entrance to the grand ballroom.

A twenty-piece orchestra was playing at full volume, but the conversational hubbub still rose above the music. A thousand candles, each flame reflected a hundred times more from gleaming crystal chandeliers, filled the massive ballroom with a bright golden glow. Within the crowd a constant glitter of reflection dazzled the eye, as necklaces of diamonds, rubies, and emeralds flashed from the ladies' necks. From the men's shoulders swung capes of silk, velvet, and fur. All of Deserae's nobility, and the cream of its merchant population, flowed around the room in a large, slow circuit, shaking hands, chatting, making introductions, forming into knots and groups and cliques, then breaking up again to join the main flow, like a stream flowing into a circular pond. Servants bearing silver trays of canapés and full wineglasses smoothly entered the whirlpool, and other servants with empty trays exited just as smoothly. And in the center of the flow were the four other men who had traveled from their respective countries to compete for the hand of Princess Rebecca.

"Bigelow, Raymond, Harkness, and there is Lord Logan," said Kevin, looking over the crowd. "That's him with Lord Hepplewhit and Baron Ashbury. He brought along some of his Black Guards. Bigelow left his entourage behind, I see. Did our other diplomats reply to my message, Winslow?"

"Yes, sire. You received a note from their excellencies Berry and Wainright this morning."

"And what did it say?"

"It said that Deserae is proud of its orchards but produces little wine."

"Good. What else?"

"Principal employment lies in sheep and lumber. Not surprisingly, most of the manufacturing is in wool cloth and carved wood. They also weave flax. And there's some tin mining."

"Sheep," said Kevin reflectively. "Hmmm. Okay, I may need you. Wait for me here."

He gave his invitation to the doorman, who announced him—not that anyone was listening, or could hear above the music and the chatter. It took the better part of an hour for Prince Kevin to reach the center of the room, for every step meant another round of greetings, bows, handshakes, and exchanges of pleasantries. The Prince never wavered from his course, although to the other guests it appeared that he had no direction at all, but merely by chance the press of the crowd had nudged him into the royal center. Indeed, he seemed almost surprised when he turned around and found himself facing Prince Bigelow.

"Samuel," he said, bowing slightly. "Good to see you again. You're looking well."

"As yourself, Kevin." Bigelow did not bow or smile. He was a good-looking young man, a little heavyset but powerful, normally quite friendly and personable. Three weeks ago he had been considered a solid choice. Now he was tired of the whole game and ready to go home. The Lords of Deserae had narrowed the field to two. Bigelow was sufficiently well informed to know he was out of the running.

"Raymond, Harkness," said the Prince, shaking hands with each of them. Raymond was a thin, weedy sort, with a scraggly beard, who always seemed to be daydreaming. He had never been a serious contender and was probably just there for diplomatic reasons. He had a glass of wine in each hand and a pipe in his mouth. Prince Harkness had wide blue eyes and long golden hair, and every adolescent girl in the kingdom thought he was absolutely adorable. But he was also three years younger than Kevin and two years younger than the Princess. Kevin knew the Princess objected to marrying a younger man.

Which left Logan of Angostura, son of the Lord High Chancellor and a general in the Angosturan army. He was tall, even taller than Kevin, who was by no means short. Square-jawed, muscular, with broad shoulders—and the epaulets on his jacket made them seem even broader. He normally traveled in the company of highly trained commandos called the Black Guards. Black Jack Logan, his men called him. It was easy to see why. He had black eyes and black hair, cut short to keep the curls under control, and a thick and precisely trimmed black beard. Brighter-than-regulation gold braid covered the sleeves of his black wool uniform, and a double row of medals stretched across his left breast. He wore a collarless shirt with a black silk cravat knotted around his neck, in the military style, and he wore a military sword. His greeting to Kevin was curt, and the dislike showed plainly in his face. Logan had made it clear from the start that he wanted this marriage, and he regarded each competing suitor the way a soldier regards the enemy, as an obstacle to be destroyed or circumvented by the most expedient means. Prince Kevin, for his part, gave no indication that he was in a competition at all. He gave the soldier a cheery smile and respectful bow.

"As I was saying, the proper disposition of troops along the border is paramount in the defense of a country like Deserae." Logan had been discoursing on military preparedness. He picked up the thread of conversation again. "You don't want to station all your forces on the outposts. Especially in mountainous terrain like yours. You want to keep troops where they can be rapidly shifted to cover breakthroughs. If you stop them in the passes, they'll only pull back and try again. To destroy an enemy's army, you have to lure it onto the plains, where you can maneuver."

Bigelow looked bored. Harkness had his eyes on a girl in a low-cut gown. But two members of Deserae's ruling council were following Logan's words carefully. Baron Ashbury was white-haired, elderly, and stout, and Lord Hepplewhit was white-haired, elderly, and thin. "Lord Logan has been telling us of some of his victories," Ashbury explained to Kevin.

"Of which he has many," Kevin said. "Your reputation has spread even to my own country, Lord Logan." Logan barely acknowledged his words.

"I was thinking that his is the sort of leadership we need in Deserae," said Hepplewhit to Kevin. "Consider our situation. Bordering on the frontier, we get all sorts of nasties coming over the mountains. And our location makes us a temptation for other countries with an eye to expand."

It was true. Deserae had a strategic location between two major rivers, and the easiest pass through the northern mountains ended at its border. "Rassendas has many experienced generals. My father, of course, is eager to form a treaty of mutual defense with Deserae. Under the right circumstances." Kevin added this last bit offhandedly, not making a point of what those conditions were. Logan glared at him anyway.

"Wine, yes, thank you," said Bigelow. He was talking to

a white-jacketed steward, who proffered him a tray. He swirled the glass of deep purple liquid and tasted it. "Good wine, this."

"Imported from Rassendas," said Hepplewhit, as each of the other men took a glass. "You don't care for it, Lord Logan?"

"It is adequate for cooking, perhaps." Logan put his glass, barely tasted, back on the tray. "I'm afraid that the wines of Rassendas cannot compare to the full-bodied wines of Angostura. Like many of the products of Rassendas, they tend to be immature and weak."

There was certainly insult in this. The group fell silent, a small pocket of quiet in the surrounding conversational hubbub, waiting to hear how Kevin would respond. Bigelow especially let his eyes flick to Kevin's waist, noted that the Prince was not wearing a sword, and gave a speculative glance at the heavy knob of his walking stick. Logan's Black Guards leaned forward. But Kevin answered cheerfully enough. "Can't argue with you there. I don't know much about wine—don't really care for it myself."

"You prefer beer?" said Bigelow.

"Beer's all right, Sam. I really prefer cider, when I can get it."

"Cider? Really?" Ashbury pushed forward. "Prince Kevin, you must try some of our ciders." He grabbed Kevin by the arm and led him across the room. "You're a cider man, eh? I myself have extensive orchards on my estate. I supply many of the breweries in Deserae. In all modesty, I must say that my ciders are—well, I'll let you decide for yourself."

"You have orchards? Really?" Part of the crowd, seeing the Prince leave, followed them.

"Oh yes. Apples, cherries, plums, pears—now here."
Ashbury let him out a side door, into an antechamber where
a number of barrels were stacked. Stewards were filling
glasses and setting them on trays. The Baron ran his free
hand over the barrels. "Ah, here we go. This is one of mine.
We keep the best for ourselves and ship the rest. And the
King, of course. We supply the King with our best and sell
the rest. Now, wait until you taste it. Waiter! A clean glass
for the Prince, if you please."

"Oh, not a glass," said Kevin. "I always think cider
tastes best when drunk from an honest wooden mug."

There was a murmur of assent from the gathered men.
"Quite right," said a tall man, moving up from the back. He
had close-cropped gray hair and waved a wooden stein
above his head.

"Lord Tripple," said Kevin.

"A mug of cider, that's what the Prince needs. Grindsey,
where's that mug I brought—ah, here we go. Here you are,
Timberline. Put your lips to this."

He shoved a wrapped object into Kevin's hands. Kevin
unwound the cloth cover and examined it carefully. It was
a wooden tankard, carved from oak in deep relief, then in-
laid with cherry, walnut, rosewood, and curly maple. The
elaborate hunting scene pictured on the side held at least
two dozen figures, so delicately fashioned that a distinct
expression clearly showed on each tiny face. "This is beautiful. Really a work of art."

"Tut," said Tripple. "A modest enough little gift, I assure
you. It's always a pleasure to meet a man who appreciates
fine wood. I can't tolerate metal tankards—they set my teeth
on edge. Now my wood-carvers—they did the doors of our
chapel, you must stop by and see it—did this all out of local
woods. I keep a wide selection of hardwoods growing on my

land. Cut one down, plant two more, that's the key to careful forest management."

"Let me put some cider in that for you," said the Baron, passing it to a waiter.

"Excuse me, my lords," said a steward. They all looked at him. "I beg pardon for interrupting, my lords, but His Majesty the King was most insistent that our guests be presented."

"Of course," said Lord Tripple. He motioned for Kevin to follow the steward, then took up a pace behind him. Baron Ashbury waited until Kevin's tankard was full, then fell in step with Lord Tripple. Back in the Grand Ballroom, Kevin saw Raymond waiting before a pair of large French doors that fronted a small balcony. Bigelow appeared out of the crowd dragging a reluctant Harkness, who had a string of young women trailing him like a wake. The three men gazed outside with a sense of weary duty. Kevin came up beside Lord Hepplewhit, giving him an inquiring look. Hepplewhit stepped to one side, allowing Kevin to see out a neighboring window. Sixteen feet below were the castle's front gardens. Quite a crowd had gathered there. Kevin estimated it was over a thousand people.

"Commoners from the city," said Hepplewhit. "And the surrounding villagers. They're all eager to see the men who are courting the Ice . . ." He cleared his throat. "Yes, our beloved princess. There's been a lot of excitement over the past few weeks. So much visiting royalty in town, and a wedding coming up. The city has been abuzz with gossip. His Majesty decided to open up the gardens for this evening. If you could each step out and wave, perhaps say a few words?"

Lord Logan was already outside. "I'd be delighted," said Kevin.

"I'm sure you know the drill. They just want to see you

lads. You know, something to tell their friends and children. Some of them have come a long way."

"The Princess is popular with her people?"

"Oh yes. Well, I wouldn't say popular. But admired, in a way. His Majesty, of course, is regarded with great respect by the commoners. And he returns that respect."

Bigelow examined Kevin's tankard. "Clever of you to bring this along, Kevin."

"Why is that, Sam?"

"Well, no princess wants to marry a man with an ugly mug."

"Can't argue with that."

Logan finished speaking. Kevin couldn't hear the exact words. He could tell from the tone that the speech was aggressive and militaristic. The crowd gave him a round of applause.

Bigelow took his place on the balcony. Logan stepped inside. "Tiresome rabble," he said.

"I quite agree," said Harkness. "There's something a tad degrading about having to pander to the great unwashed."

"Well, *noblesse oblige,*" said Raymond. "We all have our roles to play." They watched Bigelow speak. He was generating laughter from the crowd.

"There are some good-looking babes out there, though." Harkness flipped his hair back.

"I should think they'd have better things to do with their time then to pry their noses into our affairs," said Logan. He looked around irritably. "Where the hell has Timberline got to?"

Bigelow had just stepped inside. He waved a hand toward the balcony. "He's down there."

"What!" said Logan. There was a round of polite shoving and shuffling as all the suitors, except Bigelow, sought to get

out onto the small balcony. Tripple, Ashbury, and Hepplewhit crowded behind them. Logan was the first to reach the
balustrade and look down. "Now what is he doing?"

Left to himself in the ballroom, Bigelow smiled. "Working the crowd," he murmured. "Working the crowd. You
know," he told a waiter, "I believe I'll have a mug of that cider
myself."

Winslow hurriedly followed Kevin into the garden.
The Prince of Rassendas was already surrounded, almost
lost to sight in the press of people. Winslow noted with
appreciation that they had cleaned up and were wearing
their best clothes—apparently entering the Royal Gardens
counted as a special occasion. Kevin was wading through the
crowd, slapping the backs of the men, squeezing the hands
of the women, patting the heads of the children. Thankfully,
no one actually gave him a baby to kiss, although Winslow
was sure the Prince would kiss one if he had to.

It was something he had learned from his father. Winslow
had been there to hear it once. The King of Rassendas had
been in his dressing room. "No monarch can rule effectively
without the respect of the people," he told the young prince.
"Nor can the Lords. You can't lead them against their will.
Get support from the bottom, and the Lords will go with the
crowd."

Kevin nodded. King Eric had gone back to trying on
black turtleneck sweaters. "How do you think these look
with my shades?"

It was clear that the Prince was following this strategy
now, garnering support from the bottom up. And it seemed
to be working. Everyone the Prince touched left with a
smile. "He seems a right good sort," one florid-faced man

told Winslow. "I think he'd make a fine husband for our princess."

"Yes, I think so, too," the valet replied. He pushed his way toward the Prince, finally getting close enough to hear Kevin speak with a man in a rough leather jacket.

"Came all this way to see a prince," the man was saying. "I told her not to expect too much, but she insisted. I thought you'd be up on the balcony. I told her we'd just be waving to you from a distance. Now here you are, and she won't say a word." He looked over his shoulder. "Come on now, Emma darling. Don't be rude. Come out and say hello to His Highness."

Hiding behind the man's leg was a small girl. For a moment she peeped out from under his coat, offering a tentative smile, wide dark eyes, and hair tied back with a new ribbon. Then she ducked behind her father again. The Prince got down on one knee, so his face was almost level with her own.

"She gets shy, sometimes," said the man, stroking her hair. "Then once she gets to know you, she's a regular little chatterbox, she is." He gently pushed the girl out in front of him. "Emma, show His Highness what you brought."

Reluctantly, the girl came forward, and Kevin could see she was holding a small, earthenware crock in her tiny hands. The top was covered with a piece of clean cloth, tied around the rim with string. Suddenly she thrust it at the Prince, and as soon as he took it, she turned back to her father and buried her face in his jacket.

"It's mint jelly," said the man. "She made it herself. With a little help from her mum, isn't that right, Emma?" The girl hugged him tighter and made no reply. "We thought we'd be leaving it for you. Didn't think we'd actually be talking to you."

"Thank you, Emma. I love mint jelly," said the Prince. He stood back up. "Especially with my favorite meal, roast lamb."

"You like lamb? I raise sheep myself."

"Really?" said Kevin.

And here Winslow noticed that the man was wearing a shearling jacket and the pin of a minor guild official. It was the sort of thing that the Prince would pick up on immediately.

"As a matter of fact, Your Highness, our annual guild picnic is coming up. Now if you like roast lamb . . ." He suddenly looked uncomfortable. "Of course, no doubt you're used to eating fancy foods, but if you'd care to drop by and say a few words . . ."

"I'd be delighted. Here." He brought Winslow forward. "Winslow, pencil me in for a guild picnic." He turned back to the sheepman. "Give the details to my man here, and we'll see if it can be arranged. Good-bye, Emma."

The girl looked up briefly and gave a tiny wave.

"The picnic is next Thursday," the man told Winslow. "At two . . ." He paused thoughtfully. Winslow made a mental note to set out wool clothing for the Prince and rehearse him on his speech "Sheep Raising, the Foundation of a Strong Economy."

When he caught up to Kevin again the Prince was talking with a woman who spun flax. Her husband raised flax, her daughters spun it, and her uncles wove it. They were planning a large family reunion. Kevin promised to stop by. Winslow made a mental note to set out linen clothing and rehearse the Prince on his speech, "Flax Cultivation, the Foundation of a Strong Economy."

Kevin continued to work the crowd, collecting more gifts of jams and preserves, hand-knit scarves, sweaters,

gloves, mittens, baskets of fruit, carved wooden cups and
bowls, and even a wooden flute. All of which were passed
on to Winslow to carry. By the time they reached the edge
of the gardens, the valet had his arms full and gifts stacked
up to his chin. Kevin decided they had done enough. The
other suitors were finished speaking. They had left the balcony, while the crowd below was thinning out and going
home. The two men slipped through some bushes to follow
an empty path back to the castle. Kevin stopped to take
some of the heavier parcels from Winslow. When he turned
back an old woman was standing in the middle of the path.

"Beware, Timberline," she said. "Beware of the *man in
black.*"

Kevin sighed. "Oh great, a soothsayer." He shifted his
parcels. "That's all we need right now."

They could barely see her in the darkness. It was the
rasp in her voice that gave the impression of great age, a
whispery sound like coarse sandpaper on soft wood. She
wore a dark cloak with a hood, and her features were hidden in shadow, but when she held up a crooked finger, the
moonlight gleamed off bone white skin. "Beware, Prince
Kevin of Rassendas," she repeated. "Beware . . ."

"Of the man in black. I got it the first time," said the
Prince. "Sorry, but I've never been impressed with seers
and soothsayers. Save your sooth for another sucker. I
don't believe anyone can predict the future."

"I knew you were going to say that. Beware the man . . ."

"Yes, yes. You all give the same vague, useless warnings
that could mean anything. 'Repent, for the End is Nigh. Beware the Ides of March. Watch out for the Man in Black.'
Now what good is that? There are men wearing black clothes
everywhere. Why can't soothsayers ever be specific?"

"About six-foot-two, fourteen stone," said the old woman

promptly. The words were not loud, but they were clear and definite. "Brown eyes, dark hair parted on the left, small mustache and pointed beard. Likes his tea with lemon biscuits. Two lumps, no milk."

Kevin wasn't expecting a reply like this. "That could still describe a lot of people."

"Slightly chipped upper left canine tooth. Small tattoo of a spider on the back of the right hand."

"Um, that's still . . ."

"Third button of his waistcoat will be missing."

"Okay, okay, I get the picture." Kevin moved closer. Now he could see the woman was bent and hunched over. "And just when exactly is this mysterious encounter supposed to take place? I don't suppose you could . . ."

"Five days from now," said the old woman. "A few hours past midnight. It will be chilly. Wear a sweater."

"Chilly? It's the middle of summer! And just what am I supposed to beware of?"

"Goodness, you're a picky one. What is it? You want quatrains? I'll give you quatrains. Pay attention." She cleared her throat, rolled her eyes up until the whites showed in the patented, spooky prophetess manner, and rasped out:

> *"You shall not defeat the man in black*
> *That which you seek, you won't bring back*
> *The guards will falter in the attack*
> *And you will . . . you'll . . . um . . . what's another word that*
> *rhymes with black?"*

"Snack," said Kevin.

"Heart attack," said Winslow.

"She already used attack."

"Oh, right. Sorry."

The woman was leafing through a pocket-sized rhyming dictionary. "Can't read a word in this moonlight. I'll have to get back to you."

"No hurry. Listen, lady, if you could really see into the future, you wouldn't be standing in the King's garden at night making predictions. You'd be cleaning up on short-term investments."

The old woman suddenly straightened up. "Good Lord!" she rasped. "That reminds me. I've got to see my broker. What with the market so uncertain and the change in interest rates . . ." She turned, took two steps off the path, and disappeared into the shadows. But from the darkness she called back once more. "Just beware, young Timberline. Beware of a tall man with dark hair, hypnotic eyes, a scarred face, an evil smile, and an insane laugh. Oh, and a pinkie ring."

"Wait!" said Kevin. "What's going to happen to interest rates?" He followed her off the path and looked around. The lights from the castle windows fell on an empty garden. The old woman had vanished.

He returned to the path. His valet had been watching all this over his stack of parcels. "What did you make of that, Winslow?"

"I must say, sire, that the seers here in Deserae certainly give value for money."

"Yeah. Nonsense, of course. Did you happen to catch all of it?"

"I'm afraid that all I can remember now is to beware the man in black."

"Yeah." The Prince frowned. "Didn't she say he had a beard? It's got to be Logan, right? A man in black?"

"Perhaps not, sire. It's hard to judge color in the lamplight. I think His Lordship may be wearing dark navy."

"I think it's black. Of course, everyone in the city knows

I'm competing with Logan, so that's not much of a prophecy. It just convinces me that they're all a bunch of frauds."

"I quite agree, sire. Still, Your Highness, it would have been nice . . ." Winslow hesitated.

"If she'd talked more about her investments?"

"Yes, sire."

"Forget it, Winslow. Let's go eat."

They returned to the castle. Back inside, it was easy enough to find servants to care for their parcels. By the time the two returned to the Grand Ballroom, it had mostly emptied into the Banquet Hall. It was filled with long tables and seats with velvet cushions. But no one was sitting yet. They were all standing behind their chairs, waiting for Princess Rebecca to arrive. Between the guests, waiters were filling glasses, setting out baskets of rolls, and relighting any candles that had gone out. Candlelight gleamed off highly polished silver cutlery. New tapestries, of burgundy-and-gold cloth, draped the walls. A string quartet was playing chamber music. Kevin sent Winslow off to dine below stairs and took his place on the dais, alongside the other guests of honor. Bigelow nodded at him when he returned, then murmured an aside. "So we get to meet the Ice Princess at last. At least I'll get a look at her before I leave town."

"You've never seen her?"

"If my old man had his way, we'd never see our betrotheds until the wedding day. Bad for discipline, he thinks. He's a bit old-fashioned. I take it you have seen her."

"I did some diplomatic work here last summer," said Kevin. Bigelow was smart enough to recognize this as a nonanswer. He shrugged it off.

The suitors gathered on a raised platform, all on one

side of a table, an assortment of Deserae's nobility on the
other side, and Lord Hepplewhit at the foot. (In their pur-
suit of the Princess, Deserae's custom was that all suitors
were considered of equal rank.) Kevin was placed between
Bigelow and Harkness, and across from Lady Tripple. She
gave him an encouraging smile. The seat at the head of the
table was empty, as were the chairs on either side. Hepplewhit talked with Raymond, while keeping half an eye on the
clock. A door opened in the side of the Banquet Hall, and
Princess Rebecca entered, preceded by two of her ladies-in-
waiting and followed by two officers of the guard. The music
stopped. As one man, Logan, Harkness, Bigelow, and Raymond leaned slightly forward.

When a man looked at Princess Rebecca, the first thing
that registered on his mind was an impression of curves.
Curves that moved. Curves that swayed. Curves that flowed
and rolled like waves on a tumultuous sea. Curves that
shifted and slid under her clothes, making the fabric strain
and stretch and hug her flesh at one spot, then suddenly rip-
ple away to find a new curve to caress. A woman might notice the curves also, but she would also notice that the blond
hair was tied up in a severe bun, the pale skin of her face
showed only a trace of makeup, the blue eyes were every bit
as cold as her reputation, and the lips, when she looked at the
assembled suitors, were set in an expression of seemingly
permanent disdain. Men did tend to notice these things,
too. Eventually. It usually required three or four looks—
sometimes as many as nine—before the average male could
raise his eyes to Rebecca's face at all. She was, in truth, just a
little bit on the heavy side. But the extra weight had been distributed well. Her waist was narrow, so the extra padding on
her hips and breasts simply exaggerated her hourglass shape.

"My God," murmured Bigelow. "To think when my

father mentioned the mountains of Deserae I thought he was talking about the countryside."

"Shush," said Kevin. "Be nice." Rebecca's dress was of a lightweight watered silk, sky-blue to match her eyes, and thin enough to reveal that there was nothing to conceal. No wire or whalebone supported that lush figure. It was all girl.

The Princess and her entourage reached the table and stopped. One of the officers stepped forward and pulled out her chair. She sat down, looked around the room, and nodded. The two ladies-in-waiting took their seats on either side of the Princess. There was a great rustle of skirts as the rest of the women in the Banquet Hall sat down. The men remained standing until Hepplewhit gave the toast to the King. The music started. Hepplewhit sat down. Everyone else sat down. The officers withdrew. Conversation resumed.

A waiter with a tureen and a ladle appeared between Bigelow and Kevin. "Soup, sir?"

"Just dump it in my lap," said Bigelow. "It will take my mind off what I'm missing."

"Beg pardon, sir?"

"Nothing. Just a joke. What is this, turtle? Yes, I'll have some soup. What do you think, Timberline?"

"The turtle soup here is always good."

"I mean the Princess, you twit."

Kevin gave her an uninterested glance. "A pretty girl."

"Dammit, man, are you giving up or what? Look at Logan hanging over her every word. You're going to have to lay the charm on pretty thick if you don't want to lose out."

"Lord Logan can pitch woo to the Princess all he wants, but it will help him not one jot. It is her father that needs to be persuaded. And the King will act on the advice of the Council of Lords. Those are the people who need to be convinced."

"Well, that's true. But it can't hurt to get the girl on your side. I'll discuss the subject in my after-dinner speech."

"It's your turn to speak tonight?"

"My topic will be Large Breasts, the Foundations of a Strong Economy."

"A perennial favorite."

Rebecca was already in conversation with the other men. "I understand, Raymond, that you consider yourself something of a poet."

"Indeed, Your Highness. In fact, I have composed a poem in your own honor. Would you do me the favor of listening to it?"

"No. And you, Harkness. I'm told you are a student?"

"I am at university, yes."

"And do you study something useful?"

"Geography, Your Highness."

"I approve of that. There is so much about the globe that remains unknown. Perhaps you can fill some of those gaps in our knowledge. When you become an adult. Personally, I cannot abide an idle man. And you, Lord Logan?"

"I am far from idle, Princess. I am a man of action. I am in charge of my country's defenses, and I have devoted myself to keeping Angostura secure. As you are no doubt aware, for some time we suffered from . . . disturbances, both from within and without. I am pleased to say that I have resolved those difficulties."

"Commendable of you, I'm sure. Samuel Bigelow, many of my friends are looking forward to hearing you speak."

"I appreciate that, Your Highness. But are *you* looking forward to it?"

"I am not. And you, Timberline. How do you occupy your time?"

"In idleness, Your Highness."

As a conversation stopper, this served very well. Bigelow frowned at him and give a tiny sigh of exasperation. The rest of the table fell quiet. Lady Tripple raised her eyebrows. The ladies-in-waiting looked at Kevin with interest. Rebecca put down her spoon, cocked her head, and eyed Kevin severely. Kevin calmly took another spoonful of soup.

"Is that so, Prince Kevin?"

"Indeed yes, Your Highness. It is clear to me that most of the world's problems are caused by the inability of men to sit quietly in a room and do nothing."

"That sounds like a quotation."

"It is, although I fear I cannot remember the source."

"What nonsense!" said Logan.

"Do you find it hard work, this program of doing nothing?"

"It can be quite an effort sometimes, particularly when the situation cries out for dramatic action. But I persevere, for I believe that a man of my position should set a good example for others."

"Hmm. I can respect the perseverance, if not the intention. So many men would be unable to stick to a rigorous program of inaction." Princess Rebecca fixed her cold, clear eyes on Kevin and studied him for what seemed like a long time. The rest of the table watched them both. Kevin calmly finished his soup. "Prince Kevin, you intrigue me." Suddenly, the Princess stood up. The rest of the room began to rise also. She motioned for them to remain seated. "Honored guests, please enjoy your dinners. Prince Kevin, we will continue our discussion in my salon at eight o'clock. Do be prompt." And with that she swept out.

There was a strained hush at the table for a long moment, the kind of feeling you get when you are expecting a violent thunderstorm, but the clouds pass over without letting go.

It lasted until the waiters came to set out new plates. Harkness was the first to break the silence. "If I were married to that girl," he said to Raymond, "I would give her a sound spanking."

"Would that do any good?"

"It would do me a world of good."

" 'Prince Kevin, you intrigue me,' " repeated Bigelow. He clapped Kevin on the shoulder. "Congratulations, old boy. You threw away the opening pawn, and she responded to your gambit. Good luck to you."

"I'm sure we'll have a pleasant conversation," said Kevin noncommittally.

Logan said nothing. He just stared at Kevin with dagger eyes.

Thunk the Barbarian propped himself up against a tree, breathing in short gasps, for the pain in his chest was too great to allow deep breaths. On the brighter side, the pain in his ribs was less than the pain in his legs. Which was less than the pain in his head. "Heroism," he told himself, "consists of hanging on one minute longer." His father had taught him that, and he was sure his father had been quoting someone else, perhaps his own father. He never learned the source of the quote, but he did learn the lesson. Being a barbarian hero meant more than fighting and drinking and rescuing underdressed babes and wearing a necklace of wolves' teeth. It meant . . . it meant . . . well, it meant hanging on when you couldn't hang on any longer. It meant fighting when your arms were too weak to lift a sword. It meant ignoring cold and heat. It meant going without food or sleep or booze if that's what it took to get the job done. It meant satisfying an underdressed babe even when you were too tired—not that he'd ever had that problem—besides, he'd been drunk.

And it meant taking another step when you couldn't move a muscle. And when you couldn't take another step, you crawled.

He took another step.

And then another. He'd been taking another step for days now. He'd lost track of the days, and his vision had gotten pretty dark and it was hard to focus. Now it was night. There was a full moon out to light his way. How long had it been night? He didn't remember the sun going away. But there was the moon, and there were plenty of stars out. And there were lights on the horizon that weren't stars. Lights of the city. He headed that way.

He was walking on the road. During the day he left the road to shake off his pursuers, and at night he got back on. Now it was night, and he was back on the road, even though he couldn't remember finding it. He didn't like that. He was Thunk the Barbarian, and he didn't run away from anyone. They ran away from him. A hero died fighting. His father had died fighting. Granted, he had been fighting in a tavern over an unpaid bar tab. It was still fighting, though. But Thunk remembered he had something important to tell the King. That was all that counted.

The city was ahead. There were taverns in the city. He told himself he'd have a drink when he got there. And clean up some of this blood. And then he could sleep. Yes, drink and sleep. Right after he saw the King.

The next time he stopped, he told himself he'd only rest long enough to get his strength back. But his strength wasn't coming back anymore. It was ebbing away, and he was running out of time. He knew now that he couldn't stop again, that the next time he stopped he would stop forever. He'd have to keep walking.

And then crawl.

He pushed himself away from the tree with both arms and took an unsteady step forward. And then another. And another. He was walking in the woods again, amid oak and alder and beech. And lots of other trees he couldn't recognize. Trees with flowers. When he broke out of the trees he could hear music. And hear voices. There were bushes, with paths in between. People were walking along the paths, men, women and children. He realized that he wasn't in a woods, he was in a garden. Ahead he could see the castle, the large lighted windows, and the shadows of the people dancing behind them. He aimed himself in that direction, at the biggest window, with the lights and the music and the dancing and the people.

And staggered on.

When a wise old sage tells you not to let a magical talisman fall into the wrong hands, take him seriously. Do not laugh it off until the object is stolen and the Forces of Evil are unleashed.

—*HANDBOOK OF PRACTICAL HEROICS*
BY ROBERT TAYLOR

Prince Kevin stopped at the door of Princess Rebecca's salon, which was lacquered in a light pink with a seafoam green frame. The brass lock plate was intricately engraved with flowers and curlicues. It looked very feminine. He adjusted his lapels and cuffs, and said, "What time is it, Winslow?"

"When we passed the clock above the stairs, sire, it was ten minutes past the hour."

"We're early," said Kevin. He turned and strode briskly past the door. His valet followed him to the end of the hall, where the Prince found a mirror in a gilt frame. He stood there critically inspecting the ruffles in his collar.

"Beg pardon, sire." Winslow was a little out of breath. "Did the lady not say to be there at eight o'clock and to be prompt?"

"Yes, but girls' time is different from guys' time. If you get there on time, you catch them when they're still putting on their makeup, and that flusters them. Then they think you're stupid for not knowing you're supposed to be late. Better to give them more time."

"If you say so, sire." Winslow was doubtful. He had served the Prince for many years, but only recently had His Highness begun dating, and back in Rassendas, the girls came to him. This was an unfamiliar situation.

"Let's take a look." He strolled unhurriedly back down the long hallway, pausing to look at a few paintings that adorned the walls. They were mostly of the royal women, for this was the wing of the castle where Deserae's queens and princesses traditionally had their suites. As yet, there was no portrait of Rebecca. He looked for a painting of her mother. Before leaving Rassendas, his father had given him an additional piece of advice. "If you find out what her mother looks like, you'll know what the Princess will look like in twenty or thirty years. Or maybe as little as fourteen years, in some of the more rural kingdoms. So look for a portrait of her mother. On second thought, don't look for a portrait of her mother. Sometimes it's better not to know."

Kevin had treated these words of wisdom with the same weight and gravity that all young men give to advice from their parents. "Dad," he said, "are you aware that there's a dead mouse on your chin?"

"I'm growing a little beard. You don't like it? Everyone else thinks it looks cool."

Going from portrait to portrait, with Winslow beside him, he eventually reached the pink-and-green door again.

This time he rapped on it three times and waited. There was no answer. He looked at the bottom of the door for a sign of light. There was none. He shrugged. "Maybe I'm still too early."

"Perhaps, sire, you are too late, and she got tired of waiting."

"I don't think so." The Prince tried the handle and found the door was unlocked. "Well, I've been invited. Winslow, wait for me outside this door. Do not leave. On no account are you to let anyone in. Do you understand?"

"Yes, sire."

"See you later." He turned the handle and opened the door halfway. Inside it was dark. He turned back toward his valet and gave him a questioning look. Winslow could only shrug. Kevin slipped inside and shut the door carefully and quietly behind him.

Inside, the room was not quite black, but the only light came from the moon shining through a pair of open French windows and a few tiny red dots in the fireplace, the last embers of a dying fire. Faintly, the sounds of the ball still wafted in the air. Kevin waited for his eyes to become accustomed to the gloom before moving forward. He didn't wait long enough. Almost immediately he hit his shin on a low table. "Ow!" Kevin was annoyed now. "Becky! What are you doing?"

A girlish giggle sounded just behind him. Kevin whirled, reached at the air in front of him, jumped forward, and banged his other shin on yet another table. "Dammit, Becky!"

He felt the lightest of touches on the back of his neck. This time he was quicker. He spun, grabbed—and felt a pair of warm, moist lips pressed against his own, firm breasts squeezed against his chest, and the curve of a smooth, bare bottom beneath his hands. These sensations held for but a second. Then in an instant the body squirmed from beneath his arms, and with almost magical swiftness the girl's laughter sounded across the room.

Kevin moved toward the sound, coming up against a sofa and climbing over it. Very faintly, he could see an outline of pale skin glowing in the moonlight. Or thought he could—the outline seemed to fade away as he got closer, and suddenly he felt a hot, wet, female tongue slide into his left ear.

"Ah!" He swung his arms wide and brought them together in a bear hug, clasping them around—empty air. A moment later he felt a pair of soft arms wrap around him from behind, the front of her thighs press against the back of his, and her delicate fingers stroke his chest. She kissed his neck and faded away, and once again he heard a giggle. This time he was sure it came from near the fireplace.

"How does she do that?" Kevin asked himself, starting toward the laughter and getting tangled in a chair. He gave it a kick. It hit something else and he heard a clatter as things he couldn't see, but did not doubt were expensive and delicate, were knocked to the floor. He swore under his breath. Then he discerned a candlestick in the dim light. He grabbed it. Carefully he carried it to the fireplace, lowered the wick to the grate, and blew on an ember until the wick came to a tiny flame. It was all he needed. He stood up once more, and in the soft glow of candlelight, he finally beheld the Princess of Deserae.

She was clad in a loose velour dressing gown. Her hair was still tied in a tight bun, her arms were folded sternly across her chest, and her lips were pressed into a thin straight line. She was standing at the door to her dressing room, as if she had just walked in to investigate the noise. Her eyes swept over the disarranged furniture, pausing on an overturned vase, and a fallen statuette. She said nothing, but looked at Kevin with cold disapproval.

The Prince gave his head a small shake, as if to clear it. "Becky, weren't you naked just now?"

Becky's lips twitched. She tried to hold the severe expression, but her eyes, suddenly filled with merriment, gave her away. "Prince Kevin! Are you suggesting that I, the Princess of Deserae, would let a boy into my rooms while in a state of dishabille? I am shocked, absolutely shocked, that you could ask such a question. Really, what kind of girl do you think I am?" She lowered herself onto a settee and patted the space next to her.

Kevin reached it in two leaps. He slid up next to her. "I think the Princess of Deserae is a tease."

Becky bounced out of her seat and onto his lap. "Just a flirt." She wrapped her arms around his neck and breathed into his ear. "There's only a thin line between being a flirt and being a tease."

"Yeah, and you're about six leagues on the other side of it." He held her tight and kissed her. This time it was a long kiss, slow and deep, and her mouth met his with enthusiasm. When they finally broke away, he asked her, "How am I doing? Any news?"

"You're doing great." Becky flicked a stray strand of hair out of her face. "Oh, the Baron is so pleased that you liked his cider. That was absolutely inspired. He has a lot of influence with Daddy."

"Mmm." Kevin stretched out on the settee and pulled Becky on top of him. "We can't get overconfident though. My feeling is that the Council as a whole still leans toward Logan."

"Yes, but don't forget their wives. The ladies are coming to your side. And you can bet they whisper in their husbands'

ears." Becky sat up. She let her robe fall open and gave a little shake, enjoying the way Kevin's eyes involuntarily followed the motion. "Oh, and that bit with the little girl in the
garden tonight—the women loved it. That story is already all
over the castle."

"She was a cute kid. Kiss."

Becky kissed him again. Then suddenly she broke away,
laughing.

"What?"

"I was thinking about dinner. 'I am a student of idleness,' " she mimicked. "Where do you come up with lines
like that? Did you see Logan's face? I had to leave the table
to keep from laughing out loud."

"I'm glad you did. One smile from you, and those guys
would be head over heels in love. I'd never get rid of them.
I know what I'm talking about. One smile is all it took for
me."

"What a charmer you are, Kevin. Will you always talk
to me like this?"

"Alas no. After a while I'll run out of the good stuff and
begin repeating myself. Remember which lines you like
best, so I can use them again."

"I'll start taking notes." She snuggled in his arms for another round of kisses. "Oh, I have something to show you."

She took the candle, lit a table lamp, then crossed the
room and took a magazine from a wicker basket. Bringing
the candle back to Kevin, she shoved the magazine into his
hands. "This is so great. It's this month's *Teen Princess*
magazine. Have you read it?"

"*Teen Princess*? Gosh no, I've been meaning to . . ."

"Check this article."

"Black Velvet!" Kevin read. "In a Hot New Look for Cold
Winter Nights."

"No, the other page."

"Has Your Prince Come? Find Out Now with the *Teen Princess* Quiz!"

"See, the idea is that you and your boyfriend take the quiz together. Then you add up the score, and if it's high, you know you're right for each other."

"I am *not* taking the *Teen Princess* quiz."

"I knew you'd say that. So I took the quiz for both of us, choosing the answers that I know you would have chosen."

"Uh-huh."

"And then I did the same thing for each of the others. Raymond, Bigelow, and Logan. I skipped Harkness because he's too young." Becky leaned over him and ran her finger down the column of printed questions. "And guess what? You scored the highest!"

"Good, good. Who came in second?"

"Lord Logan, of course."

"Of course? Why do you say *of course*?"

Becky looked at him out of the sides of her eyes. "Well honey, you have to admit he's really good-looking."

"What? He's old! For God's sake, Becky. He's over thirty!"

"And he's so tall. And he's very muscular. Look at his arms."

"Becky! Are you trying to make me jealous?"

Becky suddenly looked coy. "Why, Prince Kevin. *Are* you jealous?"

"Of course I'm jealous." Kevin tossed the magazine aside. "So there's no need to make me more jealous. It's just throwing fat on the fire. A fire that's already burning for you."

"Oh, you're so poetic." Becky kissed him again, then, just as Kevin was really getting into it, pulled away. "Wait,

I have something else to show you. Stay here." He remained seated while she went back to her dressing room. But once there, she turned and paused with her fingers on the door handle. "I bought this for our wedding night, but I'm just going to give you a sneak preview now."

"You're already buying clothes for our wedding night? I guess you're pretty confident."

"I have faith in you, darling. You'll win them over. I'll work on Daddy from my side. And I'll keep giving Logan the Ice Princess treatment. Maybe that will discourage him." Becky's voice came through the door, which was still partly open. "Now this is very naughty, so you'll have to remember your promise. I'm the Princess, after all. There are some things I just can't do until we're married."

"Well, you can't do what we've been doing either." There was a mirror just on the other side of the door. Looking at it, Kevin caught a few fleeting glimpses of creamy skin.

"Yes, but there are some things I *really* can't do. Now remember."

"I remember."

"Are you looking at me in that mirror?"

"Of course I am. That's why you left the door open, isn't it?"

"Oh you." Becky sounded exasperated. But she made no effort to close the door. "Go put on some music. I just got some new disks. They're under the settee."

The Prince lit another candle and slid a wooden case out from under the couch. It held a stack of perforated brass plates. He selected one, carried it over to the panharmonium, and put it on the turntable. He found the crank on a shelf underneath the machine. He wound the spring and closed the cover. From the speaker horn came the soft sounds of a light waltz.

"That's nice," said Becky from her dressing room. "Oh, I can't wait until we're officially engaged and can go out together. Won't it be nice to go to a concert? Or a ballroom?"

"Sure," said Kevin. He thought of the last date he'd had in Rassendas. He and the girl had managed to sneak away from the palace, away from the prying eyes of servants and courtiers. He had taken her to a dark, smoky club on the bohemian side of town, where a trio of musicians was playing, and the candles were set in old wine bottles with straw covers. They had just ensconced themselves in a corner booth when the King, with his shades, beard, and black turtleneck, and carrying a clarinet, came to jam with the band. The crowd loved it. Kevin's girlfriend was impressed. "Wow," she had said. "Your father is totally cool." Kevin had sourly agreed.

Now the gentle notes of the panharmonium floated through the room, out into the soft night air. Almost concealed by the music was a whisper of breath. Becky had blown out one of the remaining candles. The other she had placed in the room behind her, so that when Kevin turned, he found her silhouetted in golden light. The nightgown she wore was little more than a translucent film, almost transparent in fact, a glossy sateen that hung from her shoulders on two thin spaghetti straps, baring everything above her nipples. What remained below was tight in all the right places, and where it was loose, enough light showed through to outline the figure beneath, letting his mind fill in the erotic details. She paused long enough to give Kevin a good look, and when she was sure she had created the maximum impact, she removed two pins from her hair and gave her head a gentle shake. A waterfall of golden curls cascaded over her soft shoulders and down to the middle of her back. She let him drink in this sight also, then said, "Well, what do you think?"

"Can't talk," said Kevin. "I'm trying to keep from swallowing my tongue."

"Maybe I can help." She fitted her body to his and found his mouth with her own. Together they circled the room in a slow dance, his arms around her waist, her arms around his neck, clinging together while the panharmonium tinkled its way to the end of the disk. Even when the music stopped they didn't separate but stood close together. Becky rested her head on Kevin's shoulder and firmly moved his hand from her thigh back up to her waist. A gentle breeze came in through the window and caressed her hair. She smiled as Kevin patted the stray tresses back in place. He looked at the spaghetti straps of the nightgown and considered pushing one off her shoulder, wondering if the whole nightgown would slide to the floor, leaving her naked in his arms. Or would it just slide down on one side, leaving one breast bare? Would she get angry with him? Probably not. He decided to risk it. He kissed her deeply, and, while her tongue was in his mouth, he gently pushed a strap with one finger.

Becky opened her eyes and screamed.

He pulled back, but she grabbed him and held him tightly. "Kevin!" she whispered hoarsely. She spun him around so he was facing the open windows, the draperies waving slightly in the gentle wind, and the white marble balcony stained with a puddle of dark liquid. "Blood!"

Winslow heard a scream, kicked the door open, and ran into the room, stumbling over furniture right and left. The Prince and Princess were on the balcony, each with a candlestick in one hand, both kneeling next to a prone figure. It was lying in a pool of what was quite unmistakably blood. He stopped at the windows. The Prince looked up and spoke sharply. "Winslow!"

"Yes, sire."

"There are glasses and a decanter on the sideboard. Pour a large brandy."

"Yes, sire."

"And drink it yourself. Then sit down."

"Yes, sire."

Becky was holding a mirror to the man's lips. "He's dead."

"Who is he? Do you know him?"

"It's Thunk the Barbarian," said Becky. "He's a professional hero. Daddy sometimes hired him for troubleshooting. You know, dangerous missions for the kingdom."

"He's been tortured." Kevin held the candle over him, looking at the array of fresh bruises and recent scars. "Someone worked him over pretty badly."

"Oh, poor Thunk. It must have been terrible."

"What was he doing?"

"I don't know."

"Well, he's beyond feeling any pain now. Winslow, alert the castle guard."

"Wait!" Becky clutched the front of her nightgown. "I can't be seen like this. I have to change clothes." She ran back to the adjoining room, closing the door firmly behind her.

That nightgown is ruined, Kevin thought irrationally. He stood up. *So are these trousers.* The knees were soaked with blood. It all seemed so unreal—the dead man, the moonlight, the drapes blowing gently in the French windows, the girl in the bloody nightgown—like some sort of gothic novel.

He went back inside. Winslow was still sitting, eyes

closed, hunched over, his hands on his stomach, as though nauseous. Kevin poured a brandy for himself and sat down next to his valet. He put a hand on the older man's shoulder. "Are you all right?"

Winslow opened his eyes and gave a half nod. "I'm sorry, sire."

"Nothing to be sorry about."

"In my own mind, I've often pictured myself as one of those imperturbable valets that you hear about. The sort who always know the right thing to do and are never at a loss for words. I suppose I've never really achieved that. Still, I thought I was a good man to have around in an emergency. But this was so . . . unexpected . . . and grotesque. All the blood!"

"He looks pretty bad all right. And to see him suddenly, at night, would have given anyone a turn. Don't worry about it. You're still a good man to have around in an emergency."

"Thank you, sire."

"And Winslow, about Becky . . ."

"The Princess Rebecca, sire?"

"The Princess. Not a word to anyone about what you saw."

"Of course not, sire."

"I mean it. Not to anyone. Not below stairs either."

"I understand. Sire, if you don't mind my asking, how did you—I know you move fast but—how is it possible— the Ice Princess?"

"You remember last year, when Dad sent me up here for a diplomatic visit with Berry and Wainright?"

"Yes."

"Well, I met Becky and—I won't go into the details, but

we kind of really liked each other, and we've been secretly exchanging letters. Also, I've been coming up here . . ."

"When you said you were going on those fishing trips?"

"Yes. She's in a difficult position, you've got to understand. The marriage is a very big thing. There's all sorts of politics here, and she's not supposed to play favorites."

"You can count on my discretion, sire."

"Good man." Kevin sipped his brandy. "We've been planning this evening for a long time. You think this will put her out of the mood?"

Winslow managed a weak smile. "I fear so."

"Ah, well. There will be other evenings."

Winslow suddenly pointed. "He moved!"

Kevin looked. Thunk's body was still. He was about to tell his valet that the moon was playing tricks with his eyes when he saw a finger twitch. "Winslow, get a doctor. Becky!"

By the time she reached him, clad in a loose dress and with her hair back up, Winslow was already gone, and Kevin was kneeling by Thunk's side. The barbarian's eyes were open now, and he seemed to be trying to speak.

"Just take it easy," said Kevin. "Help is on the way."

Becky grabbed a pillow and slid it under Thunk's head. The barbarian was opening and closing his fist. She spotted his sword on the edge of the balcony.

"He wants his sword." She took it by the handle and brought it back. "Is this what you wanted, Thunk?" She put it in his hand. "Does he think someone is chasing him? Thunk, you're in the Castle Deserae. You're safe now."

"You're going to be okay."

Thunk managed to shake his head. Blood bubbled from his lips. Kevin bent his head low. "Stop him? Did you say stop him? Stop who, Thunk?"

Thunk lay still a long moment. He closed his eyes. Then he opened them again and, with a final, convulsive effort, thrust his sword into Kevin's hand. "In ten days," he gasped, and this time the words were very clear. "In ten days the kingdom will . . ." And then he was really and truly dead.

Becky looked at Kevin. Kevin looked at Thunk, then at the bloody sword in his hands, and then at Thunk again. "Dramatic exit."

"I think," said Becky. "That there are things Daddy hasn't been telling me."

> Before setting off on a heroic adventure, it is wise
> to practice climbing scaffolds and trellises until you
> can do so WITHOUT dropping your sword.
>
> *—HANDBOOK OF PRACTICAL HEROICS*
> BY ROBERT TAYLOR

It was not immediately, nor the next morning, but the day after, that Kevin was summoned to see the King. In between had been a time of much activity. No public announcement was made of Thunk's death. The army, however, was placed on alert. Furloughs were canceled, and soldiers began drifting from their homes back to their barracks. Weapons were inspected. Bridles were repaired, and horses were reshod. New socks were issued to the infantry, a dead giveaway that a long march was coming up.

Officers, in uniforms of ruby red twill cloth, buff leather straps, and gold braid, stalked the corridors of Castle Deserae. Official couriers, dispatch cases under their arms and the insignia of the silver whippet on their breasts, raced up and down the staircases. The Council of Lords met in an emergency session with the King. Ambassadors and diplomats questioned Kevin repeatedly, asking him to describe every detail of the evening with Thunk. Then they pulled their cloaks over their shoulders and held quiet, furtive conversations in the doorway. Berry and Wainright, Kevin's seniors in diplomatic service, sent long, coded messages back to Rassendas. Princess Rebecca remained in her rooms. Harkness and Raymond were discreetly informed that they were out of the running and hustled on the way back to their respective countries with as much haste as could be mustered without seeming rude. Sam Bigelow made his farewells to Logan and Kevin, then mounted his horse and rode off on his own schedule. If he noticed anything was amiss, he gave no sign of it.

Once he had told his story, Kevin was pretty much out of the loop. He decided to stick with his original schedule. In the morning he ate breakfast at the Merchant Seaman's home, where he visited with elderly sailors, followed by morning tea with the Deserae Ladies' Baking Society. After judging the contest for fruit tarts, purchasing a vast quantity of them, and handing out the prizes (embroidered doilies), he proceeded to City Hall to have lunch with several members of the city council. In the afternoon he found himself surrounded by schoolchildren when he went to visit a house that was being quarantined for scarlet fever. The children remained outside the gate, while the Prince stood in the garden and called out cheerily to a small, serious boy standing at an upstairs window. He gravely told the Prince that he was going to become a pirate, as pirates did not have to learn how to spell. The Prince said that the spelling tests teachers gave these days were much too hard, but what could you do? Piracy, they agreed, was the only option. The conversation terminated with the arrival of a delivery wagon, which distributed the aforementioned fruit tarts to the household and surrounding children. Returning to the castle, he declined to dress for dinner and instead asked for a cold plate to be sent up to his room. It arrived along with a silver tray, which held the summons to the King.

King Calephon of Deserae prided himself on being a practical man. He had told Kevin so when Kevin arrived, three weeks previously, to "officially" court Becky. "Deserae is a small country," he had said. "We're rich in resources, but they're not well developed yet. We have neither the finances nor the manpower for constant warfare, yet we occupy land that others want. Our survival depends on strategic alliances. Do you see where I'm going with this?"

"I think so, sir."

"Rebecca's a fine girl. A king couldn't ask for a better daughter. A daughter who understands that she has a role to play. She knows her responsibility. She'll marry whomever I and the Council of Lords choose for her, regardless of her own personal feelings. Do you follow me?"

Kevin wasn't sure that he had. Was this a warning? Did the King already know that he and Becky were in love? He sent a message to Becky as soon as he could, but she had no more clue than he did. They had decided to assume their secret was still secret and act that way.

Now he looked at the note and passed it to Winslow. "Good news," his valet said.

"You think so?"

"Surely the King will wish to discuss your engagement to the Princess."

Kevin took the note back, folded it, and tapped it thoughtfully against his front teeth. "I don't think so, Winslow. When the announcement comes, it's going to be something

official, from the Council of Lords, with a lot of flourish and
fanfare." He unfolded the note and looked at it again. It was
a simple appointment with the King's "C" scrawled at the
bottom. "Not a page ripped out of his Day by Day calendar
with the daily golf joke at the top."

"Good point, sire."

The next morning he dressed with particular care,
knowing that he was representing Rassendas, wearing his
diplomatic sash and a blazer with his crest of office. The
summons was not to the throne room, but to the vast
chapel in the west wing of the castle. Kevin arrived a little early, taking time to admire the beautiful stained-glass
windows, the marble floors, the intricately carved pews
and pulpit, and the complex artwork that covered the
walls and ceiling. The ceiling of the Sisyphean Chapel
was famous throughout the Twenty Kingdoms. At one end
Prometheus reached down to give the gift of fire to
Man—the other end showed Eurydice descending into
Hades. The center of the painting encompassed the whole
panoply of classical gods. As always, painters were at
work. A good portion of the room was blocked by scaffolding. The masterpiece was so big, and the pigments
used so delicate, that no sooner was the last section finished than the first one had to be retouched again.

"To tell the truth, all I really wanted was a light sky-
blue, with perhaps some gold trim."

Kevin started at the sound of a voice. He turned to find the
King standing behind him. He came to attention and bowed.
The King waved him off casually and continued, "Then
somehow, I got in a stupid argument with the contractor over
the difference between off-white and eggshell." Calephon
gestured at the scaffolding. "I had no idea there were so
many different shades of white. Then we got sidetracked

onto interior design. One thing led to another, and before I knew it, I had agreed to all this. Ridiculous, really." He strolled down the length of the chapel. "I should have listened to Rebecca's mother. 'Beige,' she said. 'Paint the ceilings beige.' She said that all the time. Damn good idea."

"Yes, sire."

"This way, Timberline." The King had his office not far from the chapel. It was a square, high-ceilinged room lined with beautifully carved bookcases. The floor was padded with a thick carpet that spread outward from an elaborate and truly enormous desk. A person with an eye for security might also notice that the room had no windows and one small door, accessible only by a narrow and easily defended hallway. When Kevin entered the King dismissed his other visitors and shut the door firmly behind them. "Come on in, Timberline. Whiskey there in the decanter. Pour yourself one if you want it."

"No, thank you, sir."

"We need to talk, Timberline. Private. Face-to-face. I've got something to say to you. You have a decision to make. Some things have to be said in person. You know what I mean?"

"Yes, sir."

"Good. I want you to look at this." The King walked over to one of the bookcases. He selected a volume called *History of the Draconian Empire* and slid it partway out of the shelf. Then he stepped back and waited. Nothing happened. He slid the book back into the shelf and then out again. Still nothing. Finally, he pulled the book out completely, peered in the space behind it, and put it back again.

Kevin stood by patiently. The King went to his desk, extracted a note from the second drawer, and studied it. *"The Seven-Minute Despot,"* he muttered, as he went back to the wall and pulled out an entirely different book. A section of bookcase slid back a crack and stopped.

The King took off one of his shoes and gave the shelf a hearty whack with the heel. The section slid back more to reveal a hidden alcove. The King buckled his shoe back on. "It sticks sometimes during damp weather."

"Right."

"Now then," said King Calephon, straightening up, "what do you see in there?"

Kevin peered into the hole. It was about a yard square and perhaps a foot deep, lined with iron plate and firebrick. It look extremely secure. At first glance it appeared to be empty. Kevin picked up an oil lamp and examined it more carefully. "I see nothing, sir."

"Exactly. It's been stolen."

This bit of noninformation obviously invited questions, and it was a great temptation at this point to play the smart-aleck and remain silent. But the King looked grave, so Kevin said the lines that were clearly expected of him. "What was stolen, sir? And by whom?"

"An Ancient Artifact. Stolen. By Lord Voltmeter. 'He Who Must Be Named.' "

"Beg pardon, sir?"

"Lord Voltmeter is He Who Must Be Named. For some reason it's considered dangerous to use personal pronouns with regard to Voltmeter. Don't ask me why. Some sort of local superstition. Anyway, he's an Evil Overlord."

"Ah," said Kevin. "One of those guys."

"Yes. As if we didn't have enough troubles. Deserae tends to attract Evil Overlords. They like the mountainous terrain. Crumbling castles perched atop dramatic crags, mist-filled valleys, isolated villages. Plenty of spots out there that are perfect for an Evil Overlord to set up shop. Some years they're just thick as thieves along the passes. During the summer anyway. During the off-season they tend to head for the islands."

"Right."

"They're all dangerous, of course, but usually we can defeat them without too much trouble. Unfortunately, Voltmeter presents a different case. He stole the Ancient Artifact. Not him personally, of course. No doubt some highly accomplished professional thieves stole it for him. I won't go into the details, but it was spirited right from under our noses and out of the castle."

"Was it insured?"

"Yes, but we still have to pay the deductible. Anyway, the money isn't the problem. The problem is that the Ancient Artifact is a source of tremendous power." The King handed Kevin a thin booklet. "Here, take a look at the owner's manual. You see what I mean?"

Kevin flipped through the booklet. It was full of numbers and cryptic abbreviations. With warning messages. Lots of warning messages. He couldn't follow any of it except the title. "Ancient Artifact Model Seven," he read aloud.

"The most powerful there is. Hot stuff, they told me. The latest model."

"I thought it was an ancient artifact."

"It is. Practically brand-new, too."

To cover his confusion, Kevin read from the booklet again. "Clean your Ancient Artifact with soap and water, then polish with a soft cloth. Do not use ammonia-based cleaners."

"Dulls the finish," said the King. "The point, Timberline, is that Voltmeter has become far more dangerous than your ordinary Evil Overlord. The Ancient Artifact gives him the power to put his Diabolical Plan into action. He's got to be stopped, and stopped quickly."

"What is his Diabolical Plan, sir?"

"We don't know. But we know he has one. All Evil Overlords have a Diabolical Plan and any Diabolical Plan Voltmeter comes up with is bound to be a goody. Thunk spent his last breath trying to warn us."

The King walked back to his desk and took a seat behind it. "I didn't want the public to be alarmed, so I tried the quiet approach first. I sent Thunk off myself to steal the Ancient Artifact back. That didn't work, and now Voltmeter is forewarned. Now we go in with military force. And that's where we need your help."

"Happy to oblige, sir."

"Good, good. Naturally, as soon as you arrived to court my daughter, we ran a background check on you. You're quite an exceptional young man. And your record of military service is particularly impressive."

"Thank you, sir."

King Calephon opened a dossier in front of him and flipped through the pages as he talked. "Nothing but compliments from everyone we spoke to. Exemplary performance, they all said. The highest recommendations. Your superiors rated you as the most capable young officer they'd seen in that position in years. Frankly, Timberline, you're just the person we need in a time of crisis like this."

Kevin the Capable? It wasn't great, but the Prince thought he could get used to it. "I'm at your service, Your Majesty."

"Excellent." Calephon reached for a second dossier. "Now, Lord Logan will be leading the attack against Lord Voltmeter's castle. He'll need horses, arms, food, supplies . . ."

"Excuse me, sir. Did you say Lord Logan will be leading the attack?"

"Yes, of course. And I must say we were damn lucky to have him here at this time. This sort of frontal assault is right up his alley."

Kevin had that feeling you get when you are walking on a frozen lake and one foot suddenly goes through the ice. "Um, I rather thought that you were asking me to . . ."

"Supply officer. Logistics and supply, that's where you put your time in, wasn't it? 'If you want a top-notch supply officer, Timberline is your man.' That's what they all said."

"Yes, yes, I'm very flattered, but if you could give me a force of men, I'd much rather join the assault."

"Have you ever led an attack on a fortress, Timberline?"

"Well, no but . . ."

"Have you ever led a force of any kind?"

"Not per se, but . . ."

"This is not the time to break in. Logan is an experienced and accomplished general, and he'll be in command. He'll also call on his own forces from Angostura to supplement our troops."

"If it's troops you need, Rassendas can supply them."

"Voltmeter is originally from Angostura, it turns out, so Angostura is taking a special interest in the case. You'll have to wait for another battle."

"I don't have to lead an attack, sir. Just put me in the lines. Indeed, it would be an honor—um—yes, an honor to serve under Lord Logan's command."

"You will. As a supply officer. I'll be honest, Timberline. Right now our supply system is a complete muddle. If you could just get it straightened out, we'll be in your debt."

Kevin gritted his teeth. "I'll do what I can, sir."

"Good, good. I suspect my daughter will be less than pleased. I got the impression she rather likes you."

"I'm glad to hear it, sir." Kevin wondered if it was too late to accept a drink.

"Or at least that she doesn't care for Logan. But I'm sure she'll get used to him. Her mother got accustomed to me, after a while."

"Sir?"

"Yes, we'll announce it tonight." The King closed the dossiers and tossed them negligently to one side. "For recovering the Ancient Artifact, and thus confounding Voltmeter's Diabolical Plan, Lord Logan is to be awarded Rebecca's hand in marriage. The Council of Lords was quite insistent. So was Logan himself. Not that I had any objection. It's the traditional thing to do."

Both feet broke through the ice this time. "Sir! Your Majesty!" Kevin grabbed the front of the desk. "I really must protest!"

"I understand your disappointment, Timberline. I know you put quite a bit of effort into this match. I have to say that I didn't think much of you when you came here, but you showed yourself to be quite a worthy candidate over the past few weeks. But my word, Timberline, you're a diplomatic sort. You of all people should know how these things have to be done. I can't give a man command of our army, send him off to storm an Invincible Fortress, then deny him the right to marry my daughter. Wouldn't look right at all. Surely you see what I mean?"

The Prince was having trouble focusing. Images of Becky swam up before him, her face, her eyes, her long hair gleaming in the candlelight. He put a hand to his head and knocked over the whiskey decanter. Steadying it, he tried to put his confused thoughts into words. "Your Majesty—

I have to tell you—your daughter—Rebecca—Rebecca and I . . ."

The King leaned back in his chair. "I know what you're feeling, Timberline. It's tough to lose a girl like Rebecca. And these things seem so important when you're young. But you'll get over it. Here, here's something that will help you. Go and take that book off the shelf there. The one by Taylor."

Kevin looked around, still a little unsteady. He saw the shelf that the King was pointing to and took the first book off it. He read the cover aloud. "*Handbook of Practical Heroics,* by Robert Taylor.*"

"Hmmm? No, not that one. The one next to it."

Kevin put the first book under his arm and pulled out the second one. The shelf immediately rotated to reveal a chamber filled with gold bars. He ignored them and read the second title. "*Handbook of Practical Fly-fishing?*"

"That's the one. We've got some excellent trout streams here. When this is over, take a few days and go fishing. It's a great way to relax. Gives you a chance to sort out your thoughts, ponder over life, and put things in perspective. I do it whenever I can get away."

Kevin dropped the book on the desk. "Please, your Majesty, you must reconsider. There are issues here that I need to explain."

The King came around the desk and put his arm around Kevin's shoulders, gently but pointedly steering him to the door. "No need to explain anything, Timberline. Believe me, a few days with a rod in your hand will help you forget about Rebecca. There are plenty of other fish in the sea. Another thing I learned from fishing, ha-ha." And with those words his office door closed firmly, and Kevin found himself once again in the narrow corridor.

He stalked through the hallways of the west wing, back

to the castle's main entrance. In his mind he turned over the events of the past days. Fly-fishing? Was the King of Deserae some kind of nut? What kind of loon thought you could cure a broken heart by fishing? His depression gradually faded away, to be replaced by anger. Who were these people that treated their daughters like prize cattle, to be auctioned off or given away as gifts? It was demeaning. It was inhumane. Girls should be allowed to make their own decisions. God knows they couldn't do any worse than their parents. By the time he crossed the center of the castle and found the east wing he had worked himself into a fury. Logistics! Did they really think he was going to help Logan so the man could marry Princess Becky? What kind of chump did they think Kevin was, anyway? Help his rival? Ha! As far the Prince of Rassendas was concerned, the Kingdom of Deserae was on its own!

He kicked opened the door to his rooms, shut it behind him, slammed his book on a table, and yelled at the top of his voice, "Winslow!"

His valet opened the door from the bedroom. "Yes, sire?"

"Pack up. We're leaving. Now."

Winslow appeared about to say something, but he looked at Kevin's face and thought better of it. He disappeared back into the bedroom.

"No, wait. Winslow!"

His valet came back out.

"Summon a courier. I need to send a message to Dad. Rassendas is filing a diplomatic protest."

"Sire?"

"After inviting us to bid for the hand of Princess Rebecca, Deserae is terminating the contest. I'm going to demand that they proceed as originally planned. Get Berry and Wainright in here. I'm going to need their help on this."

Winslow said nothing. He simply pointed to the desk, and when he saw that it had received Kevin's attention, he quietly retreated back to the bedchamber.

The desk held a buff envelope, tied with string and sealed with the mark of the Rassendas Diplomatic Corps. Inside was a second, smaller envelope, with a note from Wainright saying that it had just arrived by fast courier, and the contents were for Kevin's eyes only. The second envelope bore the seal of the King of Rassendas.

Kevin opened a pot of ink, got out a fresh sheet of foolscap, and began work with his cipher key. It took some twenty minutes to decrypt the message, which eventually laid out like this:

IM LIKE HEP TO YOUR FEELINGS MAN AND KNOW YOU
DIG THE PRINCESS BUT IMPORTANT TO MAINTAIN
GOOD RELATIONS WITH DESERAE AND ANGOSTURA SO
STAY COOL MAN I LIKE VOLUNTEERED YOUR SERVICES
TO CALEPHON OKAY BEST OF LUCK LOVE DAD

Kevin crumpled up the decoded message and threw it into the fireplace. "If he ever asks me to call him Daddio, I'm gonna put my foot down." He found an armchair to slump into and put his head in his hands. Eventually he looked up and found himself staring at the book on the table. He stood up and examined it. It was small, with a soft leather cover, the right size to slip into a hip pocket. The front and back were blank, but the title was embossed in gold along the spine. It was the *Handbook of Practical Heroics*. He had left the King's office with the book still under his arm.

He took the book back to his chair and started leafing through it, scanning the pages, slowly at first, then more quickly, with gradually mounting excitement. An hour later he carried the book to his desk, got out another sheet of foolscap, and began making notes. The pages fluttered beneath his fingers. By the time Becky arrived he had a plan.

She brushed past Winslow and fell straight into Kevin's arms, putting her face against his shoulder and immediately bursting into tears, so for a while he could do nothing but hold her until the sobs ran down and she was able to talk. "Oh Kevin, I am so, so sorry."

"You have nothing to be sorry about." He stroked her hair. "It's not your fault."

"I came straight here as soon as Daddy told me. I tried to talk to him, but he wouldn't listen."

"Same with me."

"Then I went to the Council of Lords. But they wouldn't talk to me either. I have to marry Logan. There's no way out of it. Unless Lord Voltmeter kills us all. And you really can't plan a wedding around something like that."

"You don't have to marry Logan. We can elope."

Becky straightened up. "Kevin! Do you really mean it?"

"Absolutely." He gave her waist a quick squeeze. "You love me, don' t you?"

"Of course." Her face was streaked, but her eyes were shining. She took his handkerchief from his breast pocket and blotted the tears.

"Pack a few things, and we'll take off for Rassendas tonight. I'll have a coach waiting. I'll think of some sort of story to tell Dad, and by the time he sends a courier here and back to check it out, we'll be married and done with it. We can even get married in the royal chapel, so you'll still have a royal wedding."

"Tonight? No, that's impossible!"

"Why? Do you have other plans?"

"No, but . . ." Becky moved thoughtfully to the couch

and sat down. "Kevin, everyone is watching us. We can't leave when the country is threatened. The people will think we're running out on them. There would be panic. Maybe rioting and looting. The army will lose morale—that could be dangerous for Deserae."

"Hmm. Yes, you're right." Kevin sat down next to her. Reflexively, she edged over into his lap. "We'll have to wait until Logan gets the Ancient Artifact back. Becky, you'll have to stay here until then."

"So will you, sweetie. You need to stay and help outfit the troops."

"Yeah, right. I'm going to help my rival so he can win my girl? Not hardly."

"Kevin, if you leave the kingdom now, it will look like you're running away from danger. There's no way I can marry you if you appear to be a coward. The people will never stand for it."

Kevin picked her off his lap and set her back down, so he could pace back and forth while he pondered this. Damn, he thought. She was right again. "No. No, this is a really bad situation. If we get married before Logan gets the Ancient Artifact, then it's kind of a gray area. Everyone will be angry, people will say we shouldn't have done it; there will be all sorts of high-level retribution, but there will be no way to undo it, and we can talk our way out of real trouble. That's what eloping is all about."

He sat down on the couch, leaned his head back so he was staring at the ceiling, and put his arm around Becky's shoulders. "But Becky, if I stay and help with the attack, that's tantamount to agreeing to the whole stupid plan. Once Logan has the Artifact—well—from a diplomatic point of view, you belong to him. I'll be nothing but a double-crossing scoundrel who seduced away a hero's bride. It's the sort of thing that countries go to war over. Hell, Logan *will* go to war over it. He loves that stuff. If you and I get married after the attack, Logan will mobilize Angostura's army and march on Rassendas."

"Can Rassendas defeat Angostura?"

"Sure. We would kick their butts. But Becky." Here Kevin paused and thoughtfully nibbled her earlobe. She gave a little shiver. When he spoke again his voice was very soft. "But Becky, people will die. No matter who wins, soldiers will die because of our love. It's not the sort of foundation we want to build a marriage on."

Becky pulled away. Her eyes began to well up with tears again. "Then I'm trapped. I will have to marry Logan. There's no honorable way out of it." She sniffed. "I guess I'm lucky that he's such a hunk."

"What!"

"Um, I'm just trying to look on the bright side."

"Yeah, well don't get your hopes up, because you're not marrying Logan." He jumped to his feet. "Winslow!"

The door snapped open before he got to the second syllable, as though his valet had been standing just on the other side, listening. "Yes, sire?"

"Bring my saber." Kevin turned back to the princess. "Start planning our wedding, my love. I'm going to get the Ancient Artifact back myself."

The problem, as Lord Voltmeter saw it, was that he had plenty of evil but not enough lord. True, he had an honest right to be called Lord. He'd purchased the title. It came with a decaying manor house and some boggy salt marsh on the coast of Angostura. Centuries ago it had been adequate grazing land, but the area had subsided and now grew little more than mosquitoes. Voltmeter visited it once, to check the names on the tombstones against the title search. You couldn't be too careful about something like that. There were a lot of crooks around.

The upgrade from Lord to Overlord was justified also. There were plenty of lords who knuckled under to Voltmeter, either because of blackmail, debts, threats, or a combination of all three. His mercenary army was the largest and deadliest private force in the Twenty Kingdoms, while his evil minions had infiltrated every seat of government. His criminal activities kept the gold rolling in, while leaving a grisly trail through five countries. His competitors were mostly dead.

And the Evil part of the title went without saying. Yes, Voltmeter was hated and feared throughout the continent. But it wasn't enough.

Voltmeter finished signing the papers on his desk and waited until his Chief Minion left his office. Then he threw open a pair of shutters. Thick gray mist swirled around the Fortress of Doom, and a cold rain pattered on the sill. A handful of forlorn birds huddled under the eaves. Lamplight spilled onto the ramparts below his window, where his mercenary guards, clad in oilskins, patrolled in the wet and fog. The light gleamed on his black silk shirt and reflected off his gold pinkie ring. His Lordship ignored the rain and sat on the sill, stroking his beard thoughtfully.

No, it wasn't enough. Money wasn't enough anymore. And he didn't want just the kind of power that money could buy. Any rich merchant had that. Granted, Voltmeter was an evil, crooked merchant, but when you faced it, that difference was only a matter of degree.

His goal was legitimate rule. He wanted to go beyond stealing, swindling, and extorting. He wanted to tax. That was the ticket. Brutal, repressive taxation could crush your subjects far worse than any simple theft.

And he'd had enough of secretly torturing his enemies to death, deep in some private dungeon. He wanted to flog them publicly, then hang them. Better still, haul them into court on phony, trumped-up charges until they were bankrupt and disgraced, then release them to live out their shattered lives. Ha! You couldn't do that when you were a criminal.

And hiring a regiment of criminals and cutthroats, no matter how brutal, just didn't compare with riding into a city before your own army, *a real army,* with banners and horse-drawn artillery and full-dress uniforms, parading before a sullen, conquered people who had been forced to come out and wave flags. That was power. The way Voltmeter saw it, anyway. He didn't want to be a Lord. He wanted people to *lord over.*

The world is full of megalomaniacs who aspire to positions of power. The good news is that most of them never achieve it. At best, they merely get to abuse their apprentices and perhaps send their children to bed without supper. A lucky few will succeed as tax collectors, and fewer still may reach assistant headmaster at some public school. But in places like Rassendas, and Angostura, and Deserae, the real authority was in hereditary positions. You couldn't buy them. You couldn't earn them. You had to be born into them, or at least born into the class that was appointed to them. That was not such a bad thing. When power went to the eldest heir, there was a pretty good chance that the man who inherited it would not be a complete lunatic. Whereas when men competed for positions of power, it was generally acknowledged that the ones who got it were invariably the ones who could least be trusted with it.

Men like Voltmeter.

A short knock sounded on the door. Voltmeter started from his reverie. "Yes, Valerie?"

A slim young woman slipped inside. She had long black hair, bloodred lipstick, and fingernails that were sharp enough to field dress an elk. Her heels were high and her clothes were tight and she walked with a sway to her hips that was almost snakelike. There was the usual hesitation, a brief imbalance, as she came under the Overlord's spell, but she was used to it and recovered immediately. "Excuse me, my lord." Her voice had a husky sound, as though she had spent too many evenings in smoke-filled taverns and burned her throat too many times with cheap liquor. "The dungeon is getting rather full. Stan suggests it is time for another round of executions."

"Ah. Whom did we get in the ventilation shaft this week? Anyone good?"

"Just the usual, my lord. A couple of traveling salesmen, a Jehovah's Witness, and a pair of children selling cookies."

"Buy two boxes of Thin Mints and kill them all."

"Yes, my lord."

The girl swiveled out. Voltmeter watched her leave with appreciation. Being a master criminal had its advantages, not the least of which was that you had hot, kinky babes like Valerie working for you.

Now where was he? Voltmeter tried to pick up his previous train of thought. Ah, yes. Acquiring power. Once in a while, a kingdom would end up being run by a decent, compassionate man who abhorred war and violence. The kind of man who thought that conflicts could be solved by diplomacy and negotiation. At first glance, it might seem that men like these would be pushovers for an Evil Overlord. But no. Nice guys invariably had the sense to install brutal killers—men like Lord Logan—to head up their armies. Their defenses were often well organized. So there was no easy answer there either. Overthrowing a kingdom was a long, bloody, and expensive process.

Or rather, it had been.

Voltmeter smacked one fist into his palm and gave a short laugh. It was a harsh laugh, an unpleasant and chilling sound, and the men on the ramparts looked up and gripped their weapons more tightly. The Overlord pulled the shutters closed. He stood in the center of the room, his head thrown back in silent laughter, his arms raised above his head, his fists clenched in that famous, overly dramatic gesture known to theatre students everywhere as "milking the giant cow." Yes, it was hokey and clichéd, and Voltmeter knew it, but he loved doing that gesture anyway, the quintessential stance of a man mad with power. He practiced it several times a week.

In private, of course. He wasn't ready to do it in public, yet. But he had the Ancient Artifact. Soon his army would be ready. Soon they would be invincible. They would break out from their fortress in this isolated valley, they would conquer kingdom after kingdom, and Voltmeter would be there at their head. Eventually he would subjugate the entire world. He would show them what the words "Evil Overlord" really meant.

Then he would milk the giant cow.

Prince Kevin was not stupid. Under normal circumstances, that is. Indeed, the people of Rassendas tended to look upon him with a certain self-congratulation, pleased that this time around they'd gotten themselves a sensible heir to the throne, a solid young man with a good head on his shoulders, not one of those idiots who too often result from upper-class inbreeding. His parents, his relatives, his tutors, his coaches, the various levels of court authorities, and the gossip columnist for the *Rassendas Herald* all agreed: the Prince of Rassendas was a smart cookie. That, of course, was before Kevin fell in love.

Love makes all men fools, goes the adage, and the adage is correct. Any man who has been in love can confirm this; any man who has not been in love yet should consider himself forewarned; every woman who intends to make a man love her should be prepared to lower her expectations regarding his intellectual prowess. Prince Kevin was no exception to the general trend.

He thought he was, mind you. Kevin knew all about love, and he was prepared for it. Sure, he still felt that empty ache whenever he and Becky were apart, but that was okay. He knew the cause. Yes, he had developed a tendency to find meaning in the lyrics of pop music, but he was able to recognize those thoughts as asinine. "And so what," he told himself, "if I've just compared her smile to a sunrise? So what if every single goddess on the chapel ceiling reminds me of her. I've got it under control. I can stop acting like this anytime I want to."

He was wrong, of course. He didn't know it, but he was badly under the influence, and it was love that convinced him his plan was not every bit as idiotic as it appeared to be.

"What?" said Becky.

"You heard me. With a fast horse I can get to the Fortress of Doom in three days, ahead of Logan."

"Logan will have mounted troops also."

"Logan isn't ready to leave yet. He may not be ready for days. I can leave immediately and ride faster. I'll have at least two days, maybe more, to get into the castle, defeat the Evil Overlord, and return with the Ancient Artifact.

"Kevin, what are you talking about? The marriage is set. Daddy already promised me to Lord Logan."

"No, he didn't. Think about it. He promised you to the man who could recover the Ancient Artifact. Those were his words, and we're going to hold him to them."

"And you're going to attack a fortress? All by yourself? Do you have any combat experience?"

"I did my time in the military. I know a few things."

"You were a supply officer!"

"I went through basic training, the same as everyone else."

"Oh, that's just great. You're going to get killed."

Kevin gave her a steady look. "Life without you would not be worth living."

"This is not the time to lay sentimental nonsense on me, Kevin Timberline of Rassendas! You can't just waltz into an Invincible Fortress and slay Lord Voltmeter. Thunk tried it, and look what happened to him! And he was a professional hero, an experienced Evil Overlord–slayer. It takes years of training to do something like that, plus twelve hours of hands-on experience before you can solo. What the hell do you know about slaying Evil Overlords? You don't know a damn thing!"

"I don't have to. I've got a book that tells me everything I need to know. Your father, uh, loaned it to me."

"What book?"

"It's on the table there. It was written by a guy named Robert Taylor."

"Robert Taylor?" Becky stood up and her voice rose into a screech. "What does fly-fishing have to do with all this!"

"Not the fly-fishing book. He wrote another one. Look at it."

Becky grabbed the book. "*Handbook of Practical*

Heroics?" She flipped back the cover. It opened to a flyleaf. "Other books by Robert Taylor:

Handbook of Practical Fly-Fishing

Handbook of Practical Gardening

Handbook of Practical Antique Refinishing

Handbook of Practical Dragon Slaying (with Holly Lisle)

Handbook of Practical Burn and Wound Dressing"

She looked up. "Oh yes, this sounds very practical."

"Check it out. It's all there. What to wear, what to bring, when to go. Armor, weapons, plans of attack, swordplay techniques. Complete instructions for penetrating fortresses and dispatching Evil Overlords. Discount coupons for lodging and restaurants."

"Kevin, this is insane."

"No, look at this." Kevin grabbed the book and started leafing through it, showing her the chapter headings. "Look, you know the heroic legends. You've heard the ballads. You've read the histories and maybe you've seen some heroic epics in the theatre, right?"

"Yes."

"Okay, so when the villain is holding the heroine at knifepoint on the edge of a waterfall, and the hero comes swooping down on a vine and snatches her away, did you ever wonder where the vine came from? Well, this tells you. And did you ever wonder how the hero always manages to get there in the nick of time, not too late or too early? It's right here. And here's a bit about knocking a guard unconscious with a single punch to the jaw. I might have to study that some more. And look at this!" Kevin was getting excited now. He held the book up for her to see. "It

even shows how to jump through a plate-glass window
without getting a single scratch!"

"Oh, give me that." The Princess snatched the book away.

"Becky, don't you love me?"

"It's *because* I love you that I'm not going to let you get
killed on my behalf. Aside from love, think also about our
responsibility. Do you understand what will happen to the
relationship between Rassendas and Deserae when your
father finds out that my father allowed you to go on a suicide mission?"

"Neither of them will know a thing until it is all over.
I'll pretend to be sick. All my meals will be sent up here.
Winslow will stay behind to fend off visitors and keep the
charade going. Winslow?"

His valet entered the room, bearing a scabbard with the
Rassendas crest stamped in gold upon the leather. "Your
sword, sire."

"Thank you." Kevin buckled it on. "You were listening
to all this?"

"Yes, sire."

"To maintain the illusion that I'm still here, you'll have
to eat both my meals and your own. We want to send back
empty plates. So order light meals for us both."

"Yes, sire."

"Winslow," Becky interrupted, "talk him out of this. He
trusts your judgment. Do you really think Kevin can fight it
out with an Evil Overlord?"

The valet cleared his throat. "His Highness has . . . done
well in several tournaments."

"Tournaments! That's it, I've heard enough." Becky
shut the book with a snap and flounced toward the door—
and the princess was a woman who did not flounce lightly.
"This ends right now. I'm telling Daddy, and I'm going to

tell him to stop you. I'm sorry, Kevin, but it's for your own good."

"Okay," said Kevin contritely. "You're right. It is a stupid idea. I'm sorry, Becky. I'm a fool to think I could ever be a hero."

Becky stopped with her hand on the door. She turned back toward him, her face softening. "Oh, sweetie, you're not a fool. It's very brave of you to want to attempt this. I know you're very heroic. It's just that this isn't the right time for you." She sat back down next to him and took his hand. "You don't have to prove yourself to me, Kevin. I just want you to be careful."

"You're right. I hope you and Logan will be very happy together. I can't stick around for your wedding, though. It would just be too hard to bear."

A tear welled up in the corner of Becky's eye. "I understand, sweetie."

"I'll just have to go back home and marry Angela."

The tear evaporated like a snowflake in a baker's oven. "Angela?"

"Lady Angela Graydove. Some girl Dad wants me to marry."

"Your father wants you to marry Angie?"

"Oh, you know her?"

"We prepped together. Tall, skinny, flat-chested. Couldn't play field hockey worth spit."

"I haven't met her myself, but Dad did say she was slim. A nice smile, long blond hair . . ."

"Oh, so her hair is blond now?"

"And a beautiful singing voice, Dad said."

"Beautiful voice? High and squeaky is more like it."

The Prince shrugged. "As I said, I haven't met her. But Dad really liked her singing. He went on and on about it."

"Squeak, squeak, squeak, all day long. Like a rusty iron hinge."

"I don't have any choice in the matter. He went through a lot of trouble to set this up, especially on short notice." The Prince took the message from the desk and passed it to Becky. Since it was still encrypted, it meant nothing to her. He pointed to the royal signature.

"I can't go against my father's wishes," he continued sorrowfully. "Dad thinks he's doing me a big favor. I guess I'm just in the same position you are."

"I've got it!" said Becky. "We'll go together. I'll be your comic sidekick."

"Say what?"

"It's here in the book. Here, let me find it again." Becky started flipping through the pages. "Every hero needs a comic sidekick."

"Becky, you can't be a comic sidekick."

"Why not?" Becky found the page she was seeking. "Look, there's a whole chapter on comic sidekicks. Girls can do it."

"Not you. It's too dangerous. And besides, you're not funny."

"Of course I am."

"No, you're not. Try it. Say something funny."

"Well . . . of course I can't think of anything right now! Anyway, the comic sidekick doesn't have to be funny. She can just feed straight lines to the hero. So I would say, 'Well, Kevin, tell me about your brother.' And then you say something witty."

"I don't have a brother."

"It was just an example."

"If I don't have a brother I don't have anything witty to

say about him, so I don't need a comic sidekick. Thunk didn't have a comic sidekick."

"Thunk had *plenty* of comic sidekicks!"

"And what happened to them?"

"They didn't *all* get killed."

"I bet they did. The comic sidekick always gets it first. I bet that's in the book, too. Let me see."

Becky moved the book out of his reach. "I'll just go with you to the nearest village. Then I'll go drinking with the locals and learn vital information that will help you penetrate the Invincible Fortress. That's what comic sidekicks do best. I've been to nightclubs, and let me tell you, there's plenty of comedians that never do anything funny. They do prop comedy, slapstick, song parodies, improv—stupid stuff like that. Besides, I have large breasts. If worse comes to worst, I'll let something fall in my cleavage. That's always good for a cheap laugh."

"No, no, and double no. Becky, I am not going to lead you into danger. It's out of the question. You either stay here, or I go back to Rassendas."

Becky folded her arms and pouted. Kevin waited silently. Eventually she said, "Oh, all right. I'll help cover for you with Daddy. But I'm only doing this to save you from the awful fate of marrying Lady Angela."

"And I appreciate that." He watched her walk away. "Wait, where are you going?"

Becky stopped at the door. "To see the King. I told you."

"Don't I get a farewell kiss?"

The Princess looked around for Winslow. With impeccable timing, the valet had discreetly disappeared again. "Well, okay. But only for a minute. I've got things to do."

It took more than a minute. But eventually Becky left,

and Kevin closed the door carefully behind her and bolted it. Almost immediately the bedroom door opened, and Winslow reappeared.

"Am I packed, Winslow?"

"Almost, Your Highness. And sire?"

"Yes, Winslow."

"It is my understanding that your father *loathes* Lady Angela Graydove."

"Does he? I'll have to remember that. I'm off now.

Do not let the Evil Overlord's beautiful assistant lure you into a trap. Keep your libido in check until the mission is completed.

—*HANDBOOK OF PRACTICAL HEROICS*
BY ROBERT TAYLOR

An undercurrent of excitement ran through the Fortress of Doom. Valerie could feel it as she walked the corridors. The guards and minions moved quietly but briskly, talking in low voices. The mercenaries were checking extra bowstrings out of stores and honing their swords, putting the final edge to already sharpened steel. In the evenings she could find them darning socks or oiling their boots, preparing for the march on Deserae's capital. No official announcement had come down from Lord Voltmeter yet, but everyone knew he was almost ready to put the Diabolical Plan into action.

It was a race against time. The King of Deserae obviously knew of the threat to his kingdom—that's why he had sent Thunk the Barbarian to assassinate Voltmeter. And now that Thunk had failed, Calephon's next step would be to lay siege to the Fortress of Doom. That could get bloody indeed. Rumor had it that Lord Logan would be leading the attack. No one was looking forward to that.

Unless . . . Valerie smiled at the thought, her bright red lips forming a sensual curve. Unless Lord Voltmeter completed his Diabolical Plan first. Then the Fortress of Doom would truly be an Invincible Fortress.

The beautiful brunette flipped her hair back over her shoulders. She walked quickly and naturally, despite the fact that she was wearing over-the-calf boots with towering spiked heels. It had taken months to learn how to walk in them, but that was part of the job of being the Evil Assistant to an Evil Overlord. Like her carmine lipstick, and the leather bustier that hugged her slim torso. It wasn't an official uniform—not exactly—but people expected an Evil Assistant to dress like an Evil Assistant. Gingham didn't work at all, and white lace was absolutely out the question. Black leather was the only way to go.

She slapped her palm thoughtfully with her riding crop and resolved to speak to Lord Voltmeter about it. He wanted to change the dress code, demanding that she wear something less extreme. She needed to explain to him why that was a mistake. It was difficult to maintain a high standard of evil. Even Stan, who'd taken a minor in Evil Studies at Angostura University, knew that it was easy to backslide into niceness. When you want to be taken seriously, she planned to tell His Lordship, you have to dress like a professional. If the Plan was this close to completion, it was no time to lose your momentum.

The slap of the riding crop made a crisp counterpoint to the click-click of her heels on the stone floor. The ring of

keys on her studded leather belt jangled slightly. She slowed
and approached the central chamber with caution. More than
a few times she had found herself gasping as she approached
the door, as though she had been running up a long staircase,
unable to catch her breath. She thought at first it was a poi-
son gas, and had looked in vain for signs of smoke or vapor.
Nor did she ever smell anything out of the ordinary. Now she
was sure it was something magical and not just the power
Lord Voltmeter used to control his subjects. That was completely different, just a simple protection spell. This new
thing, this feeling that her lungs were empty and couldn't be
filled, had something to do with the Diabolical Plan. And
with the alchemist whom Lord Voltmeter had kidnapped.

That had been a good gig. The old man had been wary,
and he was too valuable simply to bop on the head and wrap
in a sack. Evil Assistant Valerie had lured the elderly
scholar into Voltmeter's clutches. It was part of her job and
a good example, she planned to tell him, of why she needed
to dress for her role.

She turned a corner, onto the broad hallway that led to the
central chamber. There were no windows here. She paused
to test her breathing and to let her eyes adjust to the flickering lamplight. The walls were bare of decoration. The floor
was scratched and scored from the heavy machinery that
had been dragged across it. The toe of her boot found a chip
of stone and kicked it off into a corner. Once across the hall,
standing in front of the entrance to the central chamber, she
tested her breathing again. It was normal. Slipping the riding
crop under her arm, she pushed with both hands on the massive oak door that guarded the Diabolical Device. It opened
only a crack before she heard Voltmeter's laughter.

There was a thin line, Valerie had been told, between genius and madness. Lord Voltmeter, she had always known,

was about sixteen leagues on the wrong side of that line. You could tell by his laughter, a baritone hooting that sounded like an owl with whooping cough. It gave even her the shivers, and she was in the evil business herself. Oh sure, all Evil Overlords cultivated mad laughs. You couldn't be an Evil Overlord without a mad laugh. But in truth, for most of the others it was just an affectation. Voltmeter had a laugh that was truly insane.

And mingled with his laughter were the moans of the kidnapped man.

Valerie decided to put off her complaint until another time.

The shadows were lengthening when Kevin Timberline, Prince of Rassendas, stopped his horses. He was at the top of a mountainous pass, and walls of tangled wood rose on either side of him, the heavy timber interlaced with fallen limbs and sealed with thick, thorny brush. Behind him a narrow track, sparsely dotted with wildflowers, skirted around the side of the mountain, followed a long ridge of rock, then disappeared among deep green pines. In front, the pass opened up into a shallow valley, carpeted with thick, lush grass. A broad stream cascaded down from the mountains, fed a water mill at the far end of the valley, and ran through the center of the pastures, to exit somewhere beneath Kevin's feet. Sheep, goats, and cattle grazed on the lower slopes. The upper slopes were forested. Opposite the pass a cluster of shops sheltered at the base of a broad cliff, and above them, the sheer walls of the Fortress of Doom cast an umbra over the thatched roofs and cobbled streets.

Kevin was relieved. He had set out from the castle days earlier with two fresh mounts and a packhorse, switching

horses to keep up a steady pace. It had been a long hard ride.
One of the horses had thrown a shoe, and several times he
had taken a wrong turn in the unfamiliar country and had to
backtrack. With each delay his nervousness grew, for he was
nagged by the fear that some other hero would get to the Invincible Fortress before him, dispatch the Evil Overlord, and
carry Becky away. So when the Fortress finally came into
view, when he was able to see for himself the armed guards
that paced its ramparts, to note the fearful looks that the local farmers gave its rough black stone, to actually feel the
evil presence that emanated from the dark towers and filled
the valley with a sinister atmosphere, his mood improved
greatly. There was little doubt that dark horror still lay
within the Fortress of Doom. The cows especially were a
giveaway. Any other valley this charming would have con-
tented cows. These were the most disgruntled cows Kevin
had ever seen, constantly looking over their shoulders at the
Fortress and mooing under their breath.

He gave the reins a shake and cheerfully guided his
horse into the valley. There were no signs along the road,
but his map labeled the cluster of buildings as the Village
of Angst. Kevin found a stable for his horses and carried
his saddlebags into a hostelry that identified itself as
Muldoon's Inn of Despair. It consisted of a half dozen
rooms over a typical country tavern, a place framed in
rough wood, smelling of old cheese, new sawdust, pickles,
and smoke. It was only late afternoon, but the tavern was
doing a good business already and starting to fill up. Farmers and tradesmen were rubbing elbows at the bar, drinking
ale from tankards. Other guests were sitting at small tables,
sipping wine from glasses. Muldoon's appeared to be the
social center of the village. A pretty barmaid, her hair in
braids and wearing a kirtle, was working the taps. She

brought Kevin a tankard of ale, then returned with a bowl of pottage and soused pork.

The Prince had left his flashy court clothes behind. He was dressed in a nondescript gray traveling cloak, plain soft-sided boots, and a slouch hat. He looked like any other wanderer, but the barmaid gave him a curious look. Kevin was not surprised. It was unlikely that anyone here would recognize the Prince of Rassendas—his signet ring was in his pocket, and he wore no badge of office—but his horses came from the royal stable, and horseflesh of that quality was bound to attract attention. There was no way to avoid that. When an older man, wearing an apron, entered from a back room, the barmaid whispered to him. The man wiped his hands and sat down at Kevin's table, introducing himself as Henry Muldoon, owner of the Inn of Despair. The Prince offered to buy him a drink. Muldoon got right to the point. "Come about the Fortress, have you?"

Kevin showed neither concern nor surprise. He allowed that the Fortress was interesting.

"Thought so. It's been bad business ever since Lord Voltmeter moved to Angst. We've been expecting the King to take action for some weeks now. We've had a terrible time of it, what with the goings-on at the Fortress of Doom."

"Lord Voltmeter, you say? Hmm. At least he followed your naming conventions."

"Oh, he didn't name it. The old Castle of Doom was already there. He just expanded it and built it up into an Invincible Fortress."

Kevin reflected on this. "The Castle of Doom in the Village of Angst. The Inn of Despair. I sense a trend."

"That's right," said Muldoon. "Across the street is the Foreboding Market and down by the stream is the Melancholy Mill."

"I take it there's a reason for all these depressing names."

"The tourists love it."

"They do?"

"Yes indeed. We get a lot of artists and poets coming to take a holiday in the mountains. You know, your existential types. They like to do a little fishing, a little climbing, hike through the woods, contemplate suicide." He jerked a thumb back toward a corner booth, where two men in paint-spattered smocks were talking over a carafe of white wine. "German expressionists. They really go for the depressing stuff."

"Uh-huh. Okay, so what about this Evil Overlord? Is there anything about him that you care to tell me?"

There was sudden silence throughout the tavern. Kevin looked around the room. The other patrons avoided his eyes. They glanced nervously at the doors and windows and pulled their cloaks closer around themselves. The young barmaid hurried over. "Don't say *him*," she whispered. "Say Lord Voltmeter. Lord Voltmeter is He Who Must Be Named."

"Um, right," said Kevin. "Lord Voltmeter. He Who Must Be Named. Sure. I'll remember that. And the Fortress of Doom?"

There was more silence while the men at the bar gave each other questioning looks. "It's a foul place," said one of them at last. He stared hard at the murky depths of his tankard. "And Voltmeter's an evil man."

And then they all started talking.

Once they got started, they had a lot to say. It was a good half hour before Kevin could cap his ink bottle, wipe his pen nib on a crust of dry bread, and motion to the barmaid to refill his mug. "Okay," he said, consulting his notes. "To sum it all up, the main reasons you hate Lord Voltmeter are because the tower he added to the Invincible Fortress ruins the view, he lets his dogs bark all night long, sometimes he doesn't take in his trash cans for two or three days after pickup, and because he tortures, enslaves, or kills every villager he can get his hands on. Is that about right?"

The townspeople exchanged glances. "Well yeah," said Muldoon. "I mean, you didn't say to list them in order of importance."

"No, that's fine. Anything else you can tell me?"

Someone spoke up. "There's that alchemist he kidnapped."

"Alchemist?"

"A professor of alchemy at some fancy university," said Muldoon. "Mercredi was his name. He said he came up to do a little fishing. And then Voltmeter's henchmen grabbed him and dragged him away, right out of this very inn. Oh, it was a terrible thing. They carried him up to the Fortress, and no one has seen a trace of him since. Terrible, terrible."

"Sounds awful. The poor guy. It must have given all of you quite a shock."

"Well, he paid for his room in advance. But I was letting him run a tab at the bar."

"That's when the real horror started," said the customer with the big pewter tankard, the one who had first spoken up. He had been standing at the bar. Now he pulled up a chair and sat next to Kevin. "After Voltmeter grabbed that alchemist fellow."

"All right, Pete." Muldoon shook his head. "Let's not get into that again."

"I tell you it's true!"

"What's true?" said Kevin.

Pete leaned over the table. He held his hands apart and brought them together, squeezing an imaginary balloon. "Lord Voltmeter made the air disappear."

"Of course."

"He did! I was taking my goats up the cliff trail. You know, letting them get some of the sweet grass up on the cliff. We were getting close to the walls." Pete paused, trying to add dramatic tension to a story that was not, after all, particularly dramatic. "Anyway, it was getting dark, kind of twilightlike, so I didn't figure they could see me from the fortress. And then all of sudden, I couldn't breathe."

"It's a steep trail," said Muldoon. "You were out of breath, Pete."

Pete made an angry motion, as if to slam his tankard on the table. Before it connected with the wood he thought better of the idea, looked into the bottom, and drained it in a gulp. Then he slammed it on the table. "I wasn't out of breath," he snapped. "I've been climbing that trail my whole life."

"Which has been fifty-two years. You're getting old."

"My goats aren't old. Some of them are just kids."

"You said you couldn't breathe," prompted Kevin.

"Right. But I wasn't out of breath, not that way. I mean, there was nothing to breathe. My lungs were working fine, but the air was gone."

"Maybe a touch of hay fever?"

"No, no, my head wasn't stuffed up. I'm telling you the air was gone. I turned and ran back down the trail, and at the bottom I was breathing just fine, even though I had been running."

"When was this?"

"About a fortnight ago."

Kevin pondered the information. The barmaid came over, set a mug down in front of Muldoon, and took Pete's tankard. "Fill you up again, Pete?"

"Yeah. Thanks, Cherry."

She looked at Kevin. "You ready for another?"

"Hmmm? Yes, please." Kevin made a few more notes. Muldoon bent his head around and tried to read them.

"So," he said, after deciding that Kevin wrote too fast for him. "Don't believe you gave your name, traveler."

"Timberline," said the Prince, looking at Muldoon carefully. The man gave no sign of recognition, nor did any of the other customers.

"Well, Mr. Timberline. I expect that you're working for our King."

"You could say that."

"I thought so. And you came here to survey the Fortress. I figure you're some sort of scout for the army. An advance man, I think they call your type. Or maybe a spy."

"Maybe a bit of all three," said Kevin, smiling.

"I thought so. Sometimes they send a Hero to slay an Evil Overlord, but it's obvious you're not a hero."

Kevin frowned. "Oh really?"

"No surprise to us, of course. As I said before, we've been expecting the King to send an army. You don't fool around when you're dealing with someone like Lord Voltmeter. Troops, and plenty of them, that's the way to go. The word is that Lord Logan will be leading the campaign." Muldoon watched Kevin carefully when he said this.

Kevin was noncommittal. "Is that what they say?"

"Not talking, are you? Well, I guess I shouldn't expect you to. Not if you're Logan's advance man."

"I'm not," said Kevin shortly.

"Oh, I do hope it's Lord Logan," said Cherry, from the bar. "He's supposed to be very handsome. And so tall. And covered with muscles."

"He's not so tall."

"I'm going to see him. I'll travel to the city. I have an aunty there who said I could stay with her."

"You're going to see him?"

"In the parade. There's sure to be a parade after the wedding. When he marries our Princess."

"I don't think that's a certainty."

"Oh yes, there's always a parade. Logan and the Princess will travel the streets in an open carriage. We'll throw flowers, and they'll wave to us," Cherry went on dreamily. "It will be beautiful. All the girls think Logan is a total hunk."

"Just get the beer, will you?" snapped Kevin.

The barmaid looked hurt. "What's your problem?"

"Of course, there's still that other chap," said Pete. "The one from Rassendas. They say he's a crafty one."

Prince Kevin the Crafty? Kevin rolled it over in his mind. It didn't sound quite right.

Cherry came back and slammed a mug in front of him. Ale sloshed over the side.

"War is a terrible thing," said Muldoon. "The death of so many fine young men, the women and children left behind. And the crippling injuries. Sometimes the injuries are even worse than death. Terrible, terrible."

"True," Kevin said. "And then there is the devastation that accompanies a prolonged siege. The destruction of crops and forests, pollution of the streams, the potential for epidemics, the possibility of lawlessness and looting, all that can happen when large groups of soldiers are camped in one spot for months. We can only hope it won't come to that."

"All those soldiers buying beer?" Muldoon got a dreamy look on his face. "No, hopefully our peaceful valley will not have to suffer from a long military encampment. Thousands of men getting drunk on my beer. Perhaps tens of thousands. Buying beer from me. And ale. And my wine, cider, and brandy. That would be terrible."

"Buying my milk and cheese," said Pete.

"My bread," said someone else.

"However," continued Muldoon, "if the King does choose to get rid of Lord Voltmeter, you may assure him that the Village of Angst will do its part. We know where our duty lies, yes sir. Why, we've been hard at work already, preparing for the arrival of the military."

"I'm sure," said Kevin. "Hard at work raising prices, you mean." He pointed to a corner of the room. A half dozen freshly painted signs, stating OFFICERS ONLY, were stacked against the wall.

"Oh, don't let those mislead you," said Muldoon quickly. "Everyone is welcome here at the Inn of Despair. I'll put up a tent for the enlisted men. That reminds me . . ." He called back to the bar, "Cherry, when you're done watering that wine, don't forget to add more saltpeter to the sausages."

"Sure thing."

"Voltmeter's up to something terrible," said Pete. "My story is true, and Voltmeter's behind it. The King has to do something."

"His Majesty is on top of the situation." Kevin thought for a minute and decided to let slip some information, to see how the villagers would react. "He knows that Lord Voltmeter has an Ancient Artifact."

"Which model?" said Pete instantly.

"Um, a model seven."

The room fell silent. Pete and Muldoon raised their glasses thoughtfully and took tiny sips. Even Cherry stopped wiping the bar and stared.

"What?" said Kevin. "Does everyone know about these things except me?"

"A model seven is bad," said Muldoon. "Very bad. And dangerous. That is not good news. The model seven is a very powerful Ancient Artifact."

"I've heard that."

"Although, in my opinion, still not as good as the old model three," said Pete. "Now *that* was an Ancient Artifact."

"The model three kicked ass, all right."

"I rather liked the model six," said someone.

"The model six was for wimps," someone else objected. "It was just a model five tarted up with extra chrome."

"I like chrome. And it handled better than the model five."

"Oh, like that's supposed to be impressive? Now, if you want an Ancient Artifact that really packs a wallop . . ."

"Yes, well thank you," said Kevin, excusing himself. He slipped out the front door and looked toward the Fortress. The sun was setting behind its walls, and the Fortress showed as an ominous black mass against a backdrop of pristine mountain peaks. He could understand why the villagers hated it. He judged there were still several hours of daylight left and decided to get a closer look. Going back to the stable, he signed out his freshest horse and soon found the trail that Pete had spoken of. It was more a narrow road than a trail, wide enough for two or three men to walk abreast. It was cobbled with stones that had once been rough but had worn smooth over centuries of use. They made the horse's shoes ring. The road switchbacked up the cliff face, ending at a tree-studded escarpment; but for the most part it was in full view of the Fortress walls. Kevin reflected on this, then turned his horse onto the path. Actually penetrating the Fortress would have to be done at night—the book described all the standard methods of getting in—but it wouldn't hurt to do a reconnaissance in daylight. If Voltmeter's men questioned him, he could tell them that he was lost, or that he just came up for the view.

In fact, he didn't need to tell them anything. The trail led right to the walls of the Fortress of Doom, ending in front of a single, intensely heavy door, covered with black iron plates. It looked quite formidable. Even the small bronze plaque reading NATIONAL REGISTER OF HISTORIC FORTRESSES seemed forbidding. Two guards, armed with pikes and armored with mail, barred his way. Up on the wall, more guards with cocked crossbows looked down. Above flew Voltmeter's flag, a banner showing crossed thumbscrews on a bloodred field. Kevin stopped his horse and swept off his hat. "Good evening. Is Lord Voltmeter in?"

"We're closed," said a guard.

"Closed?"

The guard stepped aside to reveal a wooden sign, posted on the wall in back of him. He jerked a thumb at it. It said, FORTRESS OF DOOM and underneath OPEN MON TO FRI, 9:00 A.M. TO 4:00 P.M.

"Sorry," said Kevin. "I thought it was open late on Fridays."

"That's only for the holidays. During the summer we go back to normal hours."

"You'll have to come back Monday," said the second guard. "And don't try sneaking in, either. All the entrances are heavily guarded at all times by elite soldiers."

"Like ourselves."

"Right," said the second guard. "Except . . ." And here he paused to wink at the first guard. "Except for the main ventilation shaft."

"That's right," said the first guard, smirking back. "Every door and window is locked, barred, and guarded. But not the ventilation shaft."

"How disappointing," said Kevin. "Still, it's a nice view. Do you mind if I have a look around?"

"Not at all," said a guard. He pointed along the wall. "The ventilation shaft is that way."

"Thanks." Kevin followed the direction the guard was pointing, past a sign that said, LOCKED OUT? TRY OUR EXTENDED HOURS. VENTILATION SHAFT OPEN UNTIL 10 P.M. He turned a corner and was out of sight of the guards. Even the ones up on the ramparts seemed to have disappeared. Ahead of him was a small courtyard, walled on three sides, with another sign that read VENTILATION SHAFT. FREE VALET PARKING MON–WED. An iron drainpipe led to the roof. Kevin looked it over carefully.

"Ventilation shaft," Kevin murmured to himself. "Hmmm."

He turned his horse back to the village and thought about this, riding slowly, letting the horse pick its own way in the gathering dusk. By the time he reached the inn, he was pretty sure he could get into the Fortress. He looked up at the massive shape hanging over the tiny hamlet, its black walls blotting the stars from the clear sky. He smiled. It would just take a little bit of planning, a little luck, and a few pieces of equipment that he could get in the village. He left his horse at the Stable of Sorrows and went back into the tavern.

Becky was waiting for him.

She was sitting in the corner, wearing breeches and some sort of brown leather jerkin that laced up in front, over a man's wool shirt, and on her head was a peaked green forester's cap with a feather in it. She was studying a small book, hunched over the table with her elbows on the rough wood. Scattered in front of her were half a dozen cups, of various sizes, most of them untouched. Kevin pulled out a chair and sat down across from her. She appeared not to notice him. "Becky, what are you . . . ?"

The Princess held up a hand to silence him.

He waited while she continued to study the book with furrowed brow. Finally, she closed it, looked up, smiled brightly at him, and said, "Okay, so a rabbit and a priest walk into a bar. And the bartender says . . ."

"Becky, what are you doing!"

"I'm telling a joke. I decided to be your comic sidekick after all. I got this book of jokes out of the castle library. By the time I got back you were gone. You ride really fast, you know. It was all I could do to keep up with you."

"You're not my comic sidekick! You're supposed to be at home, oiling up your father. That's what we agreed on. And why are you dressed like this?"

Becky leaned over the table and whispered, "I'm a boy."

"What?"

"It's the standard practice. Whenever a girl goes on an adventure, she binds her breasts and tucks her hair under a hat so she looks like a boy. You know, so ruffians won't bother her. It's in all the books."

"You bound your breasts?"

"Right. I wrapped them around with linen cloth to push them in, then cinched it up tight across the back. It took a lot of cloth."

"I can imagine."

"And I borrowed this darling little hunting cap from one of the valets. Isn't it the cutest thing? All the hunters wear them. It has a hawk feather."

Kevin was still staring at her breasts. Far from suppressing them, the bindings had pushed them up and together, giving a supercleavage effect that strained the front of her shirt and drew his eyes like a compass needle toward a lodestone. He made himself look away, at Becky's face, but that view was equally enticing. A fringe of blond ringlets peeped out from around the edges of the cap, shimmering in the candlelight like a golden halo. With her bright blue eyes and sweet smile, the effect was absolutely angelic. Kevin felt himself slipping into a erotic fugue. With great effort he forced down the hormone surge and gestured at the table. "Becky, what are all these cups?"

"The men here have been buying me drinks."

"No kidding. Now, if they think you're a boy, why would they all be buying you drinks?"

Becky counted the cups on the table. "Um, maybe they're just really friendly here?"

"I'm sure. Go back to the castle and wait for me. I have to do this alone. There's a certain etiquette to these things. The prince is supposed to risk his life to rescue the princess and save the kingdom. The princess is supposed to clasp her hands to her bosom and look at him with shining eyes."

"Like this?"

"Um, right. You've got it exactly." Kevin gripped the edge of the table. Hormone levels had now spun past Maximum on the dial and were extending into Dangerous Overload condition. "Maybe not so much of the clasping the hands to the bosom part."

"Okay, now listen." The Princess tapped her book. "This is a good one. A traveling salesman stops at a farmer's house and asks if he can spend the night. But the farmer has a daughter who . . ."

"I've heard it. Becky, I want you to go home right now. I'll be back soon. Just wait and do—um—whatever princesses do in their spare time."

"We hang out in seedy princess bars. And it's a tough

crowd, let me tell you. Sometimes a fight breaks out, and then there's teeth and tiaras flying everywhere."

"I'm sure there's nothing meaner than a pack of princesses. Now go and find one. I don't need a comic sidekick."

"You need this, I bet." Becky reached into her handbag and pulled out a thick sheaf of paper, bound in pasteboard. She swept her arm across the table, carefully pushing the cups to one side, and laid the file down.

"What is it?"

"The dossier on Lord Voltmeter. From Angostura military intelligence. Logan had it brought over by special courier. He read it to his officers. When he looked like he was through with it, I grabbed it and sneaked it out of the castle. I thought it might help you."

Kevin had to admit this was good thinking. "Let's take a look at it."

"Voltmeter has only been Evil Overlord for a couple of years. Before that he was just an Evil Lord, of course, and an Evil Burgomaster. He actually started out in Angostura as an Evil Schoolteacher."

"What could be evil about a schoolteacher?"

"Pop quizzes."

"Oh, right." Kevin leafed through the file, reading the pages quickly. "Yes, I see what you mean. Look at all this. Pop quizzes on Monday mornings, extra homework on weekends, essay questions, and no partial credit for math problems. The man is a fiend."

"Somewhere along the way he picked up some magic power. He inherited some money and bought a spell that makes him invincible in single combat. Or at least really hard to defeat. Or something like that. They're not sure. And he's been working his way up the ranks ever since."

Logan's intelligence people had done a good job. The

dossier was very complete. As Kevin read it, he became more and more discouraged.

The Evil Overlord was athletic. He was skilled with the sword and the crossbow, and reputed to be a formidable boxer, violent and aggressive. He excelled at science, math, and double-entry bookkeeping. He didn't drink or smoke, and only gambled on sporting events that he fixed himself.

Voltmeter was unmarried. He had joined his local Evil Singles Club (listing his interests as "candlelit dinners, long walks on the beach, and vivisecting small furry animals") and even organized their annual ski trip, but this was mostly for the networking opportunities. He invented a torture device and sold it to King Bruno of Omnia. It didn't make much money but won several design awards. All through this period there had been a stream of vicious murders, violent armed robberies, and a steady increase in wealth. Then he started building his organized crime syndicate—illegal gambling, prostitution, smuggling, protection, life insurance, and home remodeling. But as with all evil overlords, no one dared speak a word against him, or those that did died mysterious deaths. The Angostura Ministry of Investigation had him on their top ten list of "People We Would Rather Not Mess With." The Masters of Malice—an evil overlords professional society—had given him their Mephistopheles award, and there was talk of voting him into the Evil Hall of Fame in Erburg.

Kevin concealed his dismay. "He can't be all that tough," he told Becky. He spread out some of the papers from the dossier and stared at them thoughtfully. "It says here it took him three tries to get from Evil Lord to Evil Overlord."

"He's from Angostura, don't forget. Their certification test is a lot tougher than ours."

The barmaid appeared. "You two doing okay?"

"I'll have a glass of wine," said Becky.

"The *good* wine," said Kevin. Cherry glared at him, but came back with a glass of nonwatered wine.

"I'll need a room," Becky told her. "Could you arrange it with the innkeeper?"

"I've got a room," said Kevin.

"Then I'll need another room."

"I was thinking we could share a room," said Kevin, trying to keep the hopefulness out of his voice. "Because, you see, you're disguised as a boy, and it would be more convincing if . . ."

"Two rooms," Becky said firmly. "Two *separate* rooms."

"Nice try, stud muffin," Cherry told Kevin. She went off to find Muldoon, who booked Becky into a room next to Kevin's, and did it without comment. Kevin folded the papers back into the file and carried Becky's bags in from the stables. He set them down on the bed. Becky reached for one and unbuckled the straps.

"Don't leave yet," she said. "I have to show you something. Turn around."

Kevin dutifully turned his back. There was a rustle of clothing behind him. When he faced her again, she was wearing one of the more spectacular pieces of lingerie he had ever seen—and the Princess Rebecca was a girl whose closet was by no means bereft of sexy underwear. Even the Prince, who was rarely at a loss for words, needed a few moments to collect his thoughts. Finally, he said, "Becky, what *is* that?"

"Do you like it? It's a chain-mail bra."

"It's certainly something else."

"Taylor recommended it."

"He did?"

"Uh-huh." She reached back into the bag and pulled out

her own copy of *The Handbook of Practical Heroics,* where she had a page turned down. She read aloud, "Insist that your comic sidekick wear body armor before going into a dangerous situation. And while you're at it, it isn't a bad idea to get some for yourself." So I stopped at this cute little boutique before I left the city and bought this. I was going to get something for you, but I didn't know your size."

The Prince was squinting in the candlelight, trying to decide if he could really see her nipples through the links or if it was just his imagination. "It looks good, Becky, but I don't think that it was really designed to be functional body armor."

"No?"

"It looks more like a costume for a barbarian swordswoman."

"Oh." Becky thought about this. "I guess that explains the fur bikini."

"They sold fur bikinis?"

"I'm going to keep this anyway. I think it will be functional. It seems pretty well made."

"You won't need it because you're not getting into a dangerous situation. You're father would kill me if he found out I took you into the Fortress of Doom with me." Kevin paused, then said, "Did you buy a fur bikini?"

"The comic sidekick watches the hero's back when he goes into the Invincible Fortress. Taylor said that, too."

"You're not my comic sidekick. Are you wearing the fur bikini now?"

"Kevin! Of course I didn't buy the fur bikini. It was a thong. There was nothing but a little strappy thing up the back."

"Is that a problem?"

"Certainly it is! Thong underwear is lewd, perverted, disgusting, lascivious, and immoral."

"Oh. Well, I just wondered . . ."

"And I don't think I look good in it. How are we getting into the Fortress of Doom?"

"Don't you listen? *We* are not going. And you said yourself that the comic sidekick just hangs around the tavern and picks up information from the locals."

"Did I say that? When?"

"Back at the castle."

"Are you sure?"

"Yes," said Kevin definitely.

"And you're going to hold me to that?

"Absolutely."

"Then," said Becky, "you're conceding that I am the comic sidekick in this mission. Now then, a man goes into a doctor's office and says, 'Doctor, I've got this terrible pain. And the doctor says . . .'"

"All right." Kevin knew when he had been outmaneuvered. He thought fast. "Okay, Becky, you can be the comic sidekick. But you're going to have to wear real body armor. A breastplate and metal shoulder guards at the very minimum. I'll wear some, too, if it makes you feel better."

"Where are we going to get plate armor?"

"There's a whole Fortress full of armed and armored soldiers. They must get it from somewhere. I'm sure there will be an armory in this village, if only to serve the Fortress. It probably has some sort of depressing name. I'll take you there tomorrow."

Becky looked at him suspiciously. "Kevin Timberline, do I understand that you are offering to take me *shopping*?"

"Right," said Kevin, thinking hard. "Yeah, I'll take you

shopping for armor and, uh, I'll hold your purse while you're in the dressing room."

This was too good an offer for Becky to turn down. She wrapped her arms around Kevin and rewarded him with long kisses before turning him out of her room for the night. The next morning she eschewed her boy's disguise and dressed for a shopping trip, paying particular attention to her hair and makeup. Cheerfully, she presented herself at Kevin's door. But when she knocked on his door, there was no answer. The Prince had left the building.

When it becomes necessary to penetrate the Evil Overlord's lair, remember to dress appropriately for the occasion. Despite tradition, leotards and a cape are not practical. Neither is full evening dress. Standard-issue military fatigues will usually do the job quite nicely.

—*HANDBOOK OF PRACTICAL HEROICS*
BY ROBERT TAYLOR

The Fortress of Doom had a long and dubious history that began, oddly enough, not in the Village of Angst but some forty miles to the south, in a town called Rockhadden. Four hundred years previously, the kingdom of Deserae had not yet come into existence, and the area instead was comprised of three duchies, one of which was ruled from Rockhadden. The Duke of Rockhadden built a fine castle there, where he lived and died, murdered in his own bed by—yes—an Evil Overlord.

Lord Riddance himself led the charge up the stairs, his

sword in one hand and a torch in the other. He stepped aside, though, to let a pair of burly guards demolish the door with sledgehammers. The Duke was in his nightclothes, sitting up in bed, reaching for his spectacles, when the Overlord pushed through the splintered wreckage. Two quick thrusts, and it was all over. Riddance surveyed the scene with satisfaction. Blood soaked the bedclothes where the Duke and his wife lay, a single white hand protruding limply from beneath the scarlet sheets. Riddance wiped his sword on a pillowcase and slipped it back into its scabbard. His two bodyguards stood by quietly. They had accompanied His Lordship into the bedchamber, but had stepped aside to let Riddance have his moment of dark triumph. Now there came a knock at the door. Both guards drew their swords. One of them opened the door.

The Overlord's Chief Minion entered, bearing a clipboard and a worried look. He stopped in front of Lord Riddance. One hand came up to nervously adjust his spectacles.

"The deed is done, Cameray," boomed Riddance. "And I am the ruler of Rockhadden. Our years of plotting and scheming have come to fruition." He gestured at the bed. "Savor this moment, Cameray. Revel now in our moment of triumph."

"Um, yes, Your Lordship." Cameray tugged at his spectacles again. "Um, there is the question of the Duke's heirs."

"I want them killed, Cameray. Don't let them escape. You know how it is. You can't throw them in prison—they always escape eventually and raise an army to overthrow you."

"Yes, my lord, but . . ."

"Kill the infants, too. They're the most dangerous. Some maid or laundress spirits the infant heir out of the

castle and hides him in the forest to be raised by woodcut-
ters, and decades later, when you think you're safe, he learns
his true identity and zap! It's uprising time."

"Actually, my lord . . ."

"And here's the part I really hate. When some Evil
Overlord tries to raise the heir as his own son, thinking he
can bring him up to be evil. It never works. The kid turns to
the path of goodness and righteousness, and the Evil Overlord gets a sword in the kidneys. Well, I'm not making that
mistake. Kill them."

"My lord, they . . ."

"Supervise it yourself, Cameray. The boys are good soldiers, but I don't want them getting softhearted when they
have to slaughter a helpless infant. Oh, and none of that 'cut
the heart out and bring it to me' nonsense either. They're liable to switch it with a pig's heart—you can't hardly tell the
difference. I'm wise to that trick. Cut the whole head off."

"My lord, they're gone."

"What!"

"There were so many of them," said Cameray. "And the
place is like a rabbit warren. Bolt-holes and side doors on
every wall. You couldn't turn a corner without running over
a laundress with a child in her arms, and we just couldn't
seal all the exits in time."

"You're telling me the heir got away? After all our careful planning, the heir to the throne escaped!"

"Seven of them."

"What!"

"The moment we crossed the drawbridge, the place
erupted with 'em. It was like kicking an ant mound, except
the mound was filled with old women carrying bedsheets.
The boys got a dozen of them. I thought they did pretty well."

"They killed a dozen heirs?"

"Right, Your Lordship."

"And there's still seven left?" Riddance looked at the bed. "This woman had nineteen kids? No, she's too young. She's his second wife? Or his third?"

"No, they're all hers. Three set of triplets, four sets of twins, and two singles. She had them in nine years."

"I can see why they needed all those laundresses."

"Yes, sire."

"Okay, so we've got seven more kids out there we've got to hunt down. Get on it right away."

Cameray cleared his throat. "Ah, begging your pardon, Your Lordship, but it's a bit more complicated than that. See, the rules of succession are pretty well established in Rockhadden. So even if you killed all the Duke's heirs, the line isn't ended. You just start with the next younger brother, and then his children. And when that line ends, you go to the next brother and his kids. Sisters, too, because women can inherit in Rockhadden."

"Yes, yes. I know how it works, Cameray. He has seven brothers and sisters and each of their homes was to be attacked when we attacked the castle. Now, don't tell me one of those attacks failed."

"No sire. They all went as planned."

"We got all the siblings?"

"Yes, sire. But, um, not all their kids."

"For goodness sake, man!"

"They all had huge families," said Cameray "And you know how kids are. You can't hardly figure out where your own are at night. Some were sleeping over at a friend's house, the older kids were slipping out to drink down at the quarry, we had a couple of runaways . . ."

"How many got away?"

"Well, for his brother Reginald, we lost three out of seven. For his sister Evelyn, we lost four out of nine. For his sister Bernice we did pretty well—killed eight out of the ten. The other two were at band camp. But then for his brother Art . . ."

"Just give me the final tally, Cameray."

"Thirty-four."

"Thirty-four including the seven here?"

"Yes, sire."

"I've got thirty-four rightful heirs to the throne of Rockhadden out there somewhere, waiting for the chance to ambush me?"

"Yes, sire."

There was silence for long minutes. Cameray waited, trying not to show the nervousness he felt. The Overlord's face went from pink to red to purple to red again. He clenched and unclenched his fists, and for a moment Cameray thought he was going to milk the giant cow. But he just exploded.

"Kill them," he screamed. He drew his sword and hacked savagely at a bedpost. "Kill them all! Let my edict go out. Kill every newly born child in the duchy of Rockhadden. My men will sweep through the town and villages like locusts, destroying every child they find, leaving nothing behind but corpses and grieving mothers. Death will spread from this castle like a poisonous cloud. I will not be thwarted, do you hear! Kill them all!"

Cameray cleared his throat. "Er, sire? They're not all newborns."

Riddance gave another whack at the four-poster. "Yes, right. I knew that. Kill all the children then."

"Some of them are pretty old."

"How old?" Riddance was looking speculatively at the bedpost, as if waiting for it to attack.

"They range in age from two months to nineteen years."

"Oh, damn it to hell," said the Overlord in a much calmer, and slightly exhausted tone of voice. He decided to let the bedpost escape. "And what's the life span here in Rockhadden?"

"The median life expectancy is forty-seven," said Cameray. Before becoming a minion, he had worked in insurance, so he knew all sorts of actuarial statistics. "So we'd have to kill . . ."

"Don't tell me," said Riddance. "I can work it out. Nineteen out of forty-seven, right? So that's—um." Cameray could see his lips moving slightly as he did the long division in his head. "So if we killed everyone under the age of twenty that would be forty percent of the population?"

"Roughly, yes."

There was a long silence while the Overlord thought this over. He looked thoughtfully at Cameray, but the Minion avoided his eyes. Even the bodyguards looked down and shuffled their feet. There was more silence.

"Well, it's doable," Riddance said finally. "I mean, it sounds like a lot, but it's really not that big a country. The trick is not to try and do it all at once. Just work at it steadily, you know, even if you just murder a few score a day, and over the long run, they add up. We could probably get it done in a year or so."

"Yes, sire."

"I mean, I wouldn't want people to think I was getting soft."

"No, sire."

"Nothing is worse for a man's reputation than to announce that he's going to slaughter forty percent of the population and then quit at, say, thirty-two percent. People lose respect for you. They say, 'Oh, you can't count on that guy. He starts projects and doesn't finish them.' "

"I quite agree, sire."

There was more silence. Cameray had been with Riddance for a long time. The Evil Overlord knew what his Chief Minion was thinking, and the Chief Minion knew that Riddance knew this. But he waited for Riddance to speak first.

"On the other hand, Cameray."

"Tax base," said Cameray promptly.

"Exactly. Wipe out forty percent of the population, and your economy goes all to hell. What's the sense of capturing a country, going through all that work and risk and expense, if you're going to impoverish yourself?"

"Especially if you take out the teens," said Cameray. "Sure, if we could stop at age twelve, maybe we'd be all right. But when you lose the teenagers, you lose your waitresses, your busboys, your salesclerks, your fry cooks—the whole service sector goes right out the window."

"You couldn't go out at night, either," put in one of the bodyguards. "How are you gonna get a babysitter?"

"We could expand our base of operations," said Cameray. "Attack another country and loot it."

Riddance winced. "Worse and worse," he said.

"Right," agreed his second bodyguard. "Because we'd have lost our draftees, you see. The seventeen-to-nineteen-year-olds, they're prime recruiting material."

"Exactly. It would be just the luck to draft one of those kids. Then we'd have an enemy right in our midst, and we'd even arm him. Now that would be cutting our own throats."

"I got it," said the first bodyguard. "We don't have to kill them all. We just check for the birthmark."

The other men stared at him. "What?"

"The royal birthmark. Or the noble birthmark, in this case. You see, when the rightful heir comes to claim the throne, how do you know he's the real heir? It's because he's got a birthmark in a special shape. All the noble families have them."

"That's just a myth," said the second bodyguard.

"The hell it is," said the first bodyguard. "What about Lady Wheatfell? She had a birthmark in the shape of the family crest."

"Probably a tattoo," said Cameray.

"No, it was a birthmark. It was on her bottom."

"Then how would you know about it?" said the second bodyguard.

"I was bodyguard for Duke Tencere. He told me she showed it to him."

"Yeah, right. Everyone knows Tencere was full of jackal kidneys. He'd have you think he made it with every babe from Rockhadden to Estervan, if you believed his stories."

The first guard bristled. "You think you're so goddamn smart . . ."

"Enough of that," said Riddance. He put a hand on each man's shoulder. "It's good to see you lads thinking outside of the box, but birthmarks are not hereditary. Cameray!"

"Yes, sire."

"Cameray, I am not a man who flinches from danger."

"Certainly not, Your Lordship."

"I fear no man. I set a course of action, and I stick to it. I don't let threats or intimidation deter me from my path."

"No, sire."

"And I do not worry about a handful of renegade heirs. So what if they're out there, thirsting for vengeance? I am the Lord of Rockhadden now, and no one will stop me in my ruthless quest for power! I'll take care of these heirs when the time is right. The first one that dares show his face will immediately suffer my wrath." He plunged his sword back into his belt and strode out the door, past Cameray and down the stairs, leaving his bodyguards behind.

"Very good, sire," Cameray called after him.

Riddance came back up the stairs. "Nonetheless, Cameray, double the guard around the castle."

"Yes, sire."

"Hire extra bodyguards. Change the locks. Repair the drawbridge, install bars on the doors and windows, and get some dobermans."

"Yes, sire. Anything else? Sharks in the moat, perhaps?"

"No, that ought to do it. No point getting paranoid about the situation. Oh, and get a food taster."

In fact, Lord Riddance did get progressively more paranoid about the situation—surrounding himself with bodyguards, looking over his shoulder constantly, and starting at sudden noises. Periodically he would hire private investigators to track down some of the missing heirs, and he actually found and executed a few, but eventually he gave up the job as futile. He grew to distrust his bodyguards and began spending more of his time locked in his study, passing written orders under the door. He became more and more suspicious of his food, ate less and less, and drank only rainwater he collected himself in a cistern on the roof. Eventually he left Rockhadden altogether. He had a castle specially built, a fortified stronghold constructed on the edge of a sheer cliff, hidden in a remote mountain valley, above a tiny village called Angst. It was a forbidding place, black and gloomy, designed to be as impregnable as the architecture of the day could make it. There he spent the rest of his reign, surrounded by soldiers and guards, until he suffered a fatal

stroke, a mere seven years after his conquest. The castle
passed into the hands of others, mostly rich families that
wanted a summer retreat. Some halfhearted attempts were
made to brighten it up with gardens. Or tapestry, artwork,
knotty pine paneling, and avocado green appliances. But
there was little improvement. The atmosphere of threatening and desperate hostility seemed built right into the stone,
and no set of matching end tables could change it. Eventually it was abandoned. For long periods of time the castle
sat empty. Occasionally there was talk of turning it into a
museum or perhaps a community college, but nothing ever
came of this. And then Lord Voltmeter arrived.

It was a furious young princess who stamped into the
Anxiety Armor Works of Angst that morning. She had
waited for Kevin to return. She had dawdled before her mirror, spending extra time brushing her hair so that she
wouldn't seem like she was waiting for him when he showed
up. She had lingered over breakfast at the inn, drinking a
whole pot of tea and eating an extra muffin, quietly seething
over the fact that he had gone without telling her. It was true
she'd had no intention of being left behind at the tavern.
And obviously he realized it. But that was no excuse. Becky
firmly believed that for a romance to succeed, a boy had to
be open, honest, and truthful to his girlfriend. It was all right
for women to deceive men, because they only did it to help
make the relationship better. Everyone knew that. Clearly,
Kevin was not playing by the rules.

Finally, she admitted he wasn't coming back that morn-
ing, picked up her shoulder bag, and went into the village.
As Kevin had predicted, there was an armorer not far away.
Despite her anger, she kept her voice under control when

she entered the shop. "I'd like to purchase a steel breast-plate, please. Nothing too heavy. Perhaps with a floral-pattern."

The proprietor sized up the situation and reacted instantly. "Right," he said, grabbing a measuring tape. "A breastplate. I'll just get a few measurements here."

Becky slapped his hands away. "I've already written down my measurements for you," she said sweetly. She handed him a slip of paper. "What have you got in this size?"

"I'll make any size you want, miss. Same for the design. We do custom lacquer, engraving, and even filigree, although that will take quite a bit longer."

"You don't have anything in stock?"

"Stock?" The armorer looked puzzled. "Miss, I don't know anybody who keeps plate armor on the shelf, except to display his handiwork. It's all custom-made to order. A plain steel breastplate won't take very long. Then I got a nice piece of bronze here. Excellent quality—feel the material. You can decorate it with strings of teeth and little skulls—gives it that barbarian look that's so popular nowadays. I can fit you this morning and you can pick it up in a fortnight."

"Ten days? I don't suppose you have dressing rooms either?"

"No, miss."

"You didn't happen to see a young man come by this morning. Tall, rather good-looking, nice clothes?"

"The stranger who rode into the village yesterday?"

"Could be."

"He didn't come in here. But I saw him riding to . . ." Here the armorer lowered his voice and glanced fearfully toward the door. "To the Fortress of Doom. They say he's scouting the place out for Lord Logan."

Fine, thought Becky. *Good for him. If that's the way the Prince wants to play it, then I can do the same.* Back at the inn she changed clothes. She decided against the boy's jacket and instead wore a divided riding skirt tucked into ankle boots, and a loose blouse that covered the Barbarian Swordswoman outfit. Then she slung her bag over one shoulder, Thunk's sword belt across the other, and took her horse from the stables. She was still seething when she approached the Fortress. There was no back entrance. The front gate was heavily guarded. So were the walls, which couldn't be climbed without special equipment. Becky forced herself to calm down and assess the situation. She hid her horse in a copse of trees and approached the Fortress on foot. This made for a hot walk, but she was rewarded with a series of signs that revealed the location of an unguarded ventilation shaft. A wide drainpipe led to the roof, so easy to climb it was almost like a ladder. On top, she slipped a tuppence into a turnstile and lowered herself into the shaft.

It wasn't difficult for an athletic young woman to work her way down the shaft. Nor did she feel any concern when the light above her faded. Quite the contrary; she regained her normal good humor as she sank into the darkness. So far everything had been easy. And she didn't expect the rest of the quest to be any more difficult. Most of the guards, she thought, would be on the outside of the castle. Or perhaps manning the walls. She was confident that once inside, she would have little problem searching for the Ancient Artifact.

This was the true beauty of her plan, the real reason she came to Angst. Her father had promised Becky's hand in marriage to whoever recovered the Ancient Artifact. But what if Becky brought the Ancient Artifact home *herself*?

What then? Becky knew the answer. She'd insist that she be allowed to choose her own husband.

That would still be Prince Kevin, of course, but she wouldn't let him know right away. Ha! She'd put him off, make him sweat a little, while she pretended to consider other guys. Maybe she'd flirt a little with Logan, or that other prince, Bigelow. Kevin would go crazy with jealousy. It would serve him right for deceiving her. Eventually she'd relent and marry him, but first she'd make it clear that he still *owed her a shopping trip*.

She became aware that the shaft was dimly lit. A red glow emanated from the bottom. That made climbing down even easier. In fact, she was amazed at how simple it was to get into this so-called Invincible Fortress. She had heard plenty of tales about this sort of thing. Getting into the fortress was supposed to be a big deal. Of course, she thought, it was just like men to say so. They were always trying to impress you with their feats of valor, making them seem more difficult than they actually were. They never realized that a woman could always do a better job. Becky figured she'd have this wrapped up in no time.

In fact, there was really no reason to go home right after it was over. She was rather enjoying this Barbarian Swordswoman gig. Maybe she'd stick with it for a little while. Recovering the Ancient Artifact would start her off with a reputation for daring. Then she could add to it with a quest or two. Before long she'd be famous throughout the country. *Rebecca the Bold, Barbarian Princess!* She drew a mental picture of herself striding into a tavern, clad in chain mail and leather, her sword in hand. All voices would stop when she entered. Instantly, a space would clear for her at the bar. Every eye would fix on the wild, fierce beauty, the one woman that all men desired but none could ever tame. The bravest would try to talk with her, but she would toss her head proudly and look right through them. She gave her head an experimental toss and banged it against the shaft wall. "Ow."

Maybe she'd better concentrate on getting out of this shaft first.

At the bottom was a piece of red glass set into the stone, a candle behind it, and some sort of map she couldn't read. The shaft branched horizontally in four directions, each extending out into darkness. She gave it a little thought, while catching her breath, but she couldn't think of any reason to choose one over the other. So she picked one at random and drew the sword, waving it in front of her to feel for obstacles.

Or whatever lay in wait.

She traveled only a few yards before the bottom dropped out of the shaft.

"Ooof." She landed on a pile of sand, hard enough to knock the wind out of her. It was some minutes before she was able to raise her head. She was in a small square room, lit by torches, with a door on each wall. Her sword lay beside her. She stood and picked it up. Above her head, the trapdoor was just out of jumping range. She tried a few jumps to verify this. She was about to try the doors when they all opened, simultaneously, and two armored soldiers, black visors pulled over their faces, swords in hand, entered from each door. The eight men spread out and surrounded her.

The Princess Rebecca said a most unladylike word. Then she swung the sword.

* * *

"Follow me." Valerie told Kevin. "The first thing we have to do is set you up with a pass. Then you can go to any room you want, except the restricted areas."

"Fine," said Kevin. He was pushing a circular cart filled with long-handled brushes and brooms. "I don't expect this to take too long. No more than a few days." He followed her down the hall. It was not an unpleasant task. She was wearing a very short black leather skirt and strappy patent heels, and her firm little bottom swayed when she walked. She was also wearing studded leather wristbands and a choker, but not a leather bustier. Today she wore a tight, cropped blouse with the words KISS ME, I'M EVIL embroidered in red across the front. Kevin had no problem following her. While her back was turned he quickly checked his mustache. It was still firmly glued in place.

From the inside, the Fortress of Doom was every bit as forbidding as it looked from the outside. It was dark, damp, and a bit smoky. The walls were mostly bare black stone, rough and unfinished, which swallowed the light from the oil lamps. The corridors were narrow and had only the minimum amount of headroom. The doorways were even lower and the stairs even narrower. You could tell it was a place that was built for strength, not comfort. Soldiers, always armed, passed them at a steady rate, although they always turned aside to let Valerie through. From time to time Kevin would look into open doors, to see officers sketching out maps and battle plans, working on makeshift tables cobbled together from boards and sawhorses.

Valerie was tossing out vague directions. "The kitchen and the mess halls are over that way. The officers' quarters are along this hall, and the barracks are that way. It's very confusing. Don't be afraid to ask directions. Everyone gets lost the first few weeks. There's no pattern to any of it."

"I've worked in plenty of fortresses," said Kevin. "They make the floor plan confusing on purpose, right? To slow down the attackers if the fortress is invaded?"

"Right. But this one is more confusing than most. The windows, for example. From the outside there are five levels of windows, because it is designed to look like it has five floors. But actually there are seven, not counting the levels underground."

Kevin nodded. But he was still surprised. At first glance, there *seemed* to be plenty of men in the fortress. Certainly there were enough to hold the walls against a well-planned siege. But if Kevin was any judge, the Fortress did not hold enough soldiers to mount an attack against any sizable army. Was there really a threat to Deserae here? What could Voltmeter be up to?

He pressed his mustache again. In front of him, Valerie knocked on a door, then opened it without waiting for an invitation. "Here's Stan. Stan will get you an ID badge. Stan, here's the man from the village I told you about."

Stan was a thin young man with an even tan, spectacles, and hair that was cut very short on the sides and kind of moppy-looking on top. He had a very tight, trim look, the body of a man who didn't do sports but spent a lot of time working his abs. He wore a uniform, similar to that of Voltmeter's soldiers, but without insignia. He was sitting at a desk in a small office, with an open copy of Ovid's *Metamorphoses* in front of him. Other books were on the shelves around him. He rose to shake Kevin's hand. "I'm the Chief Minion," he said. "So let me know if there's anything you need."

"You have a lot of books," said Kevin, looking over the volumes of Plato, Homer, and Aristophanes that were stacked on the desk.

Stan shrugged disparagingly. "I brought what I could. It's a nice little valley, but you have to admit it's pretty rural. It's hard to find intellectual stimulation out here in the sticks. You don't play chess by any chance, do you?"

"I'm afraid not," said the Prince. He actually played pretty well, but he didn't think it fit in with his disguise.

"Stan has a university degree," said Valerie. "And he doesn't like us to forget it."

"Two degrees," said Stan. "Alas, they were both in the liberal arts. History and classical literature. They didn't leave me much in the way of employment opportunities."

"History and literature?" asked Kevin. "I'm surprised. I thought there were plenty of jobs for waiters."

"Nah, the fine arts people snap them all up. We get the security guard jobs. That's what I was doing after I graduated. Then I heard that His Lordship was interviewing for an educated minion, and the rest is history."

"You're not a security guard here, then? The uniform had me confused."

"Well, the guards are better paid than minions, but minions don't have to work shift. Except we're on call one weekend per month."

Kevin turned to Valerie. "And you're a minion also?"

"No, I'm an Evil Assistant. So I don't have to wear a uniform."

"But you do have a uniform, Valerie," chided Stan. "And you're out of it right now."

Valerie glared at him. "That is not a uniform."

"Call it a dress code, then."

"His Lordship was merely making a suggestion."

"Sounded pretty much like an order to me."

"How about if you just worry about your job, Stan, and let me worry about mine?"

"Well," said Kevin, "I'll just get to work then." An argument seemed to be brewing, and he wanted to stay out of it. He was eager to get away from their sight so he could start searching the fortress.

"Fine," said Stan. He took a card from his desk drawer, quickly filled it out, blotted it, and handed it over. Kevin clipped it to the pocket of his coveralls and wheeled his cart away. Stan waited until Kevin had turned a corner before speaking to Valerie again. "By the way, we caught another one in the ventilation duct. A babe. She could be trouble."

"Oh?"

"She's a comic sidekick."

"Oh?" Valerie said again. "Whose comic sidekick?"

"Give me a break, Valerie. Who do you think?"

"Are you sure?"

"No, not really. Work her over and tell me what you find out. I didn't get much of a look at her. She was covered with dirt and dust."

"That's why we need this new guy."

"Yeah. Anyway, I commend her to your hot little hands. You can find out who she's working with. Oh, yeah, check these out." Stan stood up and unlocked a cupboard. A sword and scabbard were leaning up against the inside wall. He took them out and passed them to the Evil Assistant. "The guards took these away from her."

It was definitely a barbarian's sword. Valerie saw that immediately. She could tell just from the handle and the scabbard. But it also looked familiar. She slid the sword partway out of its sheath, turned it over in her hands, and studied it. Now she was certain she recognized it. "I'll see this woman right away."

She made her way down to the dungeon.

The dungeon wasn't much as dungeons go. The Fortress

of Doom did not have a lot in the way of locking up captives. It was not a palace, after all, which is a seat of government. (If the king has a penchant for taking political prisoners, a palace may contain numerous cells. The dungeons of King Bruno of Omnia were reputed to extend for miles underground, with block after block of cells, elaborate barred gates, multiple checkpoints, and mood lighting.) The Fortress of Doom had not been designed as a prison either, where criminals were going to be held for trial and tortured for confessions. Prisons, of course, are nothing but cells.

A castle, on the other hand, is merely a fortified personal residence, and a fortress is a military base. The Fortress of Doom had been built around a castle. It had only a single, short-term holding cell, and that was converted from a storeroom, one that had proved too damp to keep barrels of flour and sacks of beans. The Fortress of Doom didn't need dungeons because Voltmeter didn't believe in keeping prisoners very long. He preferred to execute them immediately.

Valerie walked down the final flight of stairs and along the short hallway at the bottom. Various lightweight wooden doors led into storerooms. She chose one that had been retrofitted with a heavier door, with a new brass lock, and opened it to enter a small, dirty chamber. There were spiderwebs in the corners and rat droppings on the floor. One wall held an old dartboard with a few darts, the feathers broken off, sticking in it. On the other wall was a faded calendar showing a busty girl holding a giant pipe wrench. The room was divided in half by a heavy iron grille. The grille had a small door, so low you had to crawl through it, and this was locked with an iron padlock around the bars. Outside the grilled area was a small table of unfinished wood, scratched and scarred, and a chair with one broken leg. Inside the grilled area, a disheveled young woman was standing against the wall, her arms chained over her head. Blond ringlets fell over her eyes. The chained arms forced her to stand with her breasts forward. Valerie felt her blood stirring. Unconsciously, she licked her lips.

A single guard was in the chamber, leaning up against the bars. "No, missy," he said. "It's clowns. Two cannibals are eating a clown and one of them says, 'Does this taste funny to you?'"

"No, it's clams," said Becky. "I'm sure I have it right. Two cannibals are eating clams, and one says, 'Do these taste funny?'"

"But if it's clams, the joke isn't funny."

"It's funny because cannibals don't eat clams. They eat people."

"They don't eat people all the time."

"Ahem," said Valerie. The guard came to attention.

"I'll be questioning the prisoner."

"Yes, ma'am." The guard watched Valerie hook one booted foot behind the table leg and drag it over next to the bars. He watched her put the sword down on the table. Then he watched her lay down her riding crop, so she could slip on a pair of search gloves, thin leather gloves that came to her elbows. She picked up the riding crop again. The guard looked from Becky's lush body to Valerie's slim one. "Whenever you're ready, ma'am."

"Wait outside."

"If you're going to do a strip search, maybe I better stick around," the guard said hopefully. "She might have concealed weapons."

"That won't be necessary. Wait outside."

"She could be dangerous."

"Out!"

"Right." The guard moved reluctantly to the door. "Well,

I'll be right here if you need any help." He took a last long look at each of the two girls and closed the door behind him.

Valerie took a ring of keys from her studded leather belt and unlocked the iron cage. She slipped inside and rose back to her feet in one single, sinuous movement, like a dancer doing a low dip, and stood so close to Becky that their bodies were almost, but not quite touching, staring into the prisoner's eyes. Becky returned her gaze warily. She knew, of course, that Evil Overlords had Evil Assistants. But she didn't have a clear idea of what an Evil Assistant actually did, besides look beautiful and evil. She did not expect, however, that being captured by an Evil Overlord was going to result in anything pleasant.

Without a word, Valerie slapped Becky across the face.

"Ow! What was that for?"

"Quiet!" Valerie reached out and tore open the front of Becky's blouse. This was done in a dramatic way, a common softening-up move that interrogators use before questioning. They believe that forcing a woman to expose her body increases her feelings of defenselessness. Thus Valerie was taken aback to find a chain-mail bra, and one that clearly was not going to be just ripped off. She recovered quickly, though. Stepping forward, she placed one gloved hand around Becky's throat and pushed her head against the stone wall. With her other hand she unbuttoned the blond girl's skirt and let it drop to the floor, at the same time kicking her ankles apart.

"What . . . what are you doing?"

With her head pushed up, Becky couldn't see Valerie's other hand, but she could feeling it sliding over her thighs. Valerie now had the whole length of her body pressing Becky to the wall. Her mouth was only an inch from

Becky's ear, and her breath was coming in quick pants. "Searching you for weapons."

"You're not going to find anything *there!*"

"No?" Valerie murmured. She pressed harder, and Becky squirmed beneath her hands, feeling the heat coming off the black leather. "I'll be the judge of that." She gave a sudden push that left the Princess weak at the knees. Then she stepped back suddenly and held up the sword. "Where did you get this?"

"Hmm? That sword?" Becky's voice was a bit faint. She strove to collect her thoughts. "I found it."

"Really? Where, pray tell?"

"Um, in a flea market." The Princess was also a girl who recovered quickly. "The dealer was asking ten crowns. I offered him five, because you know how it is, you never accept the first price in these places, and . . ."

Valerie slapped her again, harder this time. "This is the sword of Thunk the Barbarian."

"Right," said Becky. "Thunk the Barbarian. Yes. He gave it to me. I'm his comic sidekick."

"Of course you are. And where is Thunk?"

"Right around here, somewhere," said Becky. "Getting ready for revenge. You don't suppose a little beating will keep down a barbarian hero, do you? Ha! Now he's got this whole place figured out, and he's coming back to kick your butt."

"I doubt that very seriously," said Valerie. But she was thinking hard. So Thunk was alive. This was important news. Even a wounded Thunk was a dangerous man. He knew about the Diabolical Device. And the Ancient Artifact. It could change all their plans.

She left the prisoner and went to tell Lord Voltmeter.

When the plucky daughter of the kidnapped professor demands to accompany you on the rescue mission, grab her by the shoulders, turn her around,
and send her right back to that boarding school she
came from. It's okay to boff her first. She's not an
Evil Assistant, after all. But on no account should
you let her follow you into the Invincible Fortress.

—*HANDBOOK OF PRACTICAL HEROICS*
BY ROBERT TAYLOR

Kevin pushed his cart of brooms and brushes through
the narrow halls. He was wearing loose black coveralls,
black cotton gloves, and a black top hat. He'd had a busy
morning in Angst, collecting all this stuff, as well as making a quick trip to the local printer. It was worth it, though.
Now he was inside, and his Fortress of Doom temporary
ID badge, clipped to his breast pocket, was effectively giving him free rein of the Fortress. Of course, from what he
had learned in Angst, they might not be inclined to let him

go when he was finished, but the Prince was prepared for that. His sword, in a plain wooden scabbard, was in the cart. It was hard to see with all the other stuff, but Kevin had wrapped it loosely with dust rags to make it even more inconspicuous. He also had other tools, in deep pockets so bulges didn't show beneath the coveralls.

Rolled up and tucked under his arm was a sheet of foolscap. It held a rough sketch of the Fortress of Doom. He was searching the Fortress as systematically as he could, and when the halls were empty he would take out a stick of charcoal and add to the map he was drawing, putting in not only the hallways and rooms, but the chimneys and ventilation ducts as well. He tried every door he passed. Almost all were unlatched, but very few were empty. They invariably contained men who were preparing for battle—repairing and cleaning weapons, repairing and cleaning uniforms, repairing and filling packs, measuring out rations, or checking equipment lists. Uniformed guards were everywhere. Kevin would look the room over, putter around a bit with his brooms and mops, and say that he would come back later. This generally met with approving nods.

Before long, though, he was finding it hard to judge exactly where he was, as the hallways tended to twist and branch off, rarely going in the same direction for more than a few yards. Often they would dead-end. Even more often they would end at a short set of stairs that would lead up or down to another level. There seemed to be no end of stairs. Kevin estimated that he had gone up and down six levels, crossed the Fortress at least once, and was now close to the main entrance. He opened an unlocked door and found two surprises.

The first surprise was that the room was devoid of people. He had not come across very many empty rooms in the

Fortress—most of them were quite busy. The second surprise was that this room was considerably less gloomy than
the rest of the Fortress. It had a high ceiling and apparently
was built on an outside corner, for two of the walls had large
windows that let in plenty of light. At present the brunt of the
sunshine fell upon a shelf stacked with circular black ob-
jects. Kevin moved closer for a better look, then picked one
up. It was a coffee mug, cheap black ceramic with the words
FORTRESS OF DOOM painted in large red letters. Underneath
was the slogan ENSLAVE THE PLANET. And then he understood where he was.

He was in the Fortress of Doom gift shop.

He moved around the edge of the room, sliding past
counters piled with ashtrays, tee shirts, caps, fountain pens,
shot glasses, and commemorative Fortress of Doom beer
steins. He picked up a golf shirt with the Fortress of Doom
logo embroidered on the breast pocket. It was kind of nice-
looking. For a moment he considered getting it as gift for
Winslow, then smiled and shook his head at the thought.
Don't be ridiculous, he chided himself. *If you buy this you
know what will happen. Later you'll find the exact same
thing in the village, and the price will be lower.*

He concentrated again on his mission. There were a lot
of doors in this room. It had the shape of a rough octagon,
not quite symmetrical, with a door in each wall. He tried
each door in turn. Seven of the doors had simple latches.
They opened into hallways or stairwells. One was locked.

It was the door with the sign that said STAFF ONLY. It
looked like a ruse to Kevin. He was sure he was onto something. The door looked solid enough, but Kevin thought he
could force the lock if it came to that. He stepped back and
examined the wall. Above the door was the grille of a minor

ventilation duct. He pulled a table over to the wall, set a chair on top of it, climbed up, and removed the grille. It was tight, but his shoulders fit into the duct. He took a selection of brushes from his cart and tried them out, until he found one that fit the opening nicely. Then he pushed it into the duct and slid in behind it. The brush blocked his view of where he was going, but that was okay. It would trigger any booby traps, and it was too dark to see anything anyway. The brush also had the advantage of cleaning the duct ahead of him, so he didn't have to breathe a lot of dust.

Worming his way with his hips, and pushing with his toes, he slid along for some dozen yards before he came to another opening. Carefully and quietly he slipped the grille from its brackets and set it inside the duct. He stuck his head outside but found he couldn't see anything. He was facing a wall, and there was no room to change position inside the duct. He slid the brush out the opening and let it fall. Then he wiggled himself out until he was hanging by his fingers and dropped to the floor of the alchemist's lab.

He didn't recognize it. Kevin had never been in the laboratory of an alchemist, and this place didn't quite fit his mental picture of what a laboratory would look like. He expected to see a lot of flasks and beakers, with multicolored liquids boiling away. He expected mortars and pestles for grinding powders, delicate brass balances for weighing them out, bottles of acid and alcohol for dissolving them, and strange, cryptic texts in Latin and Arabic.

Instead he saw a place that looked more like a clock-maker's shop. The center of the room was taken up with a long, heavy workbench. It held a vise, a foot-cranked drill press, and a foot-cranked lathe. Scattered around them were a number of calipers and precision tools. There was a rack of shelves set against one wall, filled with technical manuals, with a couple of golf trophies serving as bookends. The top shelf held a very accurate mercury clock, and a spring-driven nautical clock. The rest of the wall space, every inch of it, was taken up with complex drawings, large sheets of vellum covered with numbers and blue lines, of some intricate piece of equipment. There was a large black boiler in one corner, with a scuttle of coal beside it. Iron pipes ran to it, and brass tubes radiated from it, and tiny valves on the tubes hissed puffs of steam.

At the other end of the workbench was a standard business desk. It held a few pens, an inkwell, some plotting paper, and a small portrait in a frame. The portrait showed a pretty girl with reddish brown hair and a scattering of freckles across her nose. A quite ordinary-looking man, of late middle age, was sitting at the desk, doing calculations on an abacus and writing the results in a blue exercise book. He had thin brown hair shot through with gray and a slightly unkempt beard of a similar color. He wore a long white lab coat, stained with grease. A pair of thick spectacles sat on his nose. He looked a little surprised when Kevin dropped from the ceiling. But thanks to the near-magical power of name badges, he accepted the intruder without curiosity.

Kevin waved his brush at the ventilation opening. "Dirty work."

"It's about time they did something about it," said the man. "Especially on rainy days when it gets that musty smell."

"We're getting rid of that," said Kevin. "It's all being taken care of. You're Professor Mercredi, right? Stan said I should talk to you. He said he wants me to work on the room with the—what did he call it—the Ancient Artifact?"

Mercredi brightened. "Ah, good thinking. Stan's a bright fellow. Yes, a clean, dust-free environment is essential for the workings of the phlogistocator. The tolerances are very close."

"Yes, that's what Stan said."

"Of course, the production model will be a sealed unit, so dust won't be a problem. But since this is the prototype, we constantly have to open it up and make adjustments."

"Yes, his words exactly. 'Make sure no dust gets into the Diabolical Device,' he said."

Mercredi stood up and fished a brass key from his jacket. "It's a restricted access area. I'll have to let you in." He opened the office door and led Kevin down yet another hallway. Since Kevin had come in through a ventilation duct, this left him even more disoriented. They went around several corners and by the time they reached a heavy set of double doors, the Prince was completely lost.

They were thick, solid security doors, oak reinforced with iron bands, with a heavy lock. The doors alone told you that something important was inside. Then, next to the door, a burly guard sat behind a desk. He looked at their ID badges, noted the time on a nearby clock, and wrote down the badge numbers on a clipboard. "We all have to log in and out of the phlogistocation chamber," Mercredi explained. He unlocked one side of the double doors, entered, and motioned for Kevin to follow him. But Kevin stopped in the doorway. For it took a moment to absorb what he was seeing.

He realized now that he was in the circular tower that could be seen from outside the Fortress. It rose some sixty feet from floor to ceiling. All around the base were tall windows, so that all of the surrounding country could be kept under observation. The inside of the room held a machine.

In his university days the Prince had been required to take a course in philosophy. The course had touched on Plato's discussion of ideal images. Chairs, for example, came in all shapes, sizes, and styles, yet people were always able to recognize a chair when they saw one. Plato said this was because the mind contained an image of the ideal chair, from which all other chairs were derived.

Kevin hadn't given this much consideration. Now he decided there must be some truth in it. He had never seen a Diabolical Device, not even a picture of one, nor had he even heard one described. Yet he instantly realized that the thing he was staring at—staring at with horrified fascination—was a Diabolical Device.

He blinked and looked away. *It's just your imagination,* he told himself. *The Device is not horrifying. It's just a machine, neither good nor bad in itself, a collection of innocent gears, cogs, and—um—those round spinning things.* And yet there *was* something evil about this machine, something in the streaky blackness of the cast iron, something in the glint of the polished brass fittings, something in the twisted array of copper tubes that told the observer, "This is a machine with a bad attitude."

"See what I mean?" Mercredi tapped an access panel. "How can you expect precision work with all this dust?"

"Yes, I can see that would be a problem. Dust, soot, cobwebs—I'll get them all cleaned out in no time at all. You can count on me. So where is this famous artifact that I've heard so much about?"

"Oh you can't see that." Mercredi had his back to Kevin as he twisted his key in the door. "It's kept locked up."

A firm hand seized his shoulder and turned him around. Mercredi found himself looking into the young man's eyes.

They were friendly eyes, yet the hand remained clamped to his shoulder, and the strong fingers were digging into his skin. "Ow!"

"I'm a diplomatic sort," said the young man with the smiling eyes. "Diplomacy is what I'm trained for. I think of violence as failure of diplomacy, a breakdown in communication. I'd much rather give people a chance to change, to reason with them, talk things out, try to come to an understanding before resorting to violence. Do you agree?"

"Ow!" The hand on his shoulder was squeezing really hard, pinching some sort of nerve. Mercredi felt his arm getting numb.

"Now I'm a man in the prime of life, somewhat taller than you and—if I may be so immodest—a good deal more muscular. Whereas you appear to be about thirty years older than myself, and I'm guessing that you haven't spent much of that thirty years exercising. Am I right? Yes? I don't expect you've had much recent experience in hand-to-hand combat. No? So don't you think it would be so much more comfortable for everyone involved if I took the Ancient Artifact without having to pound your face against this stone wall?"

"Ouch. Let go of me! Who are you?"

"I'm Kevin Timberline, Prince of Rassendas. *You* are an accomplice to a murderer. Cooperate with me, and maybe I won't kill you."

"This is your idea of diplomacy? Threatening to kill me?"

"You misunderstand. The diplomatic part is when I offer *not* to kill you in exchange for your cooperation."

"I can't help you! I didn't want to do it! I was kidnapped." Kevin gave him a skeptical look but removed his left hand from Mercredi's shoulder. At the same time he put his right hand around the alchemist's throat. "I swear to God," Mercredi choked. "Voltmeter forced me to work for him."

"Oh yeah." The Prince swung him around and made him face the Diabolical Device. "Yeah, I can tell how reluctant you are to work on *that*."

"He gave me no choice. You don't understand. He has my daughter!"

Kevin stared at him for long moments, trying to decide whether to believe the alchemist. Finally, he relaxed his grip on the man's neck. "Your daughter?"

"My daughter Laura."

"The girl in the picture. On your desk."

"Yes. He threatened me with her. He said if I didn't work for him, she would meet a terrible fate."

"He's kidnapped her, too?"

"No, she's away at school, thank God. But he showed me that he could get to her, no matter where we tried to hide. He has a tremendous organization. You have no idea how powerful he is."

"Yes, I do. I know he's powerful. I also understand he's a complete madman."

"Quiet, you fool!" Mercredi looked around in panic. "You don't call a man like Voltmeter insane."

"Sorry. I meant to say that he's working through a lot of complex personal issues."

"That's better."

"All right," said Kevin. He pushed Mercredi into a chair and released him. "I might be able to help you. You swear you only built this thing to protect your daughter?"

"Of course. I'm a quiet, placid man. I don't want to hurt anyone. I would never assist a fiend like Lord Voltmeter, except to protect my daughter."

"Okay."

"Also my grant money dried up."

"What!"

"Times are tough," Mercredi said defensively. "It's hard to get funding for research these days."

Kevin glared at him.

"But I didn't expect it to come to this. I wanted my ideas to be used for good and peaceful purposes, in ways that would benefit mankind."

"Like what?"

"Like what what?"

"The good and peaceful purposes." Kevin looked over the huge stack of tubing, valves, and gears. "I don't like the look of this. Just what, exactly, are the good and peaceful purposes for this kind of device?"

"Oh. Yes. Well," said Mercredi. "I haven't worked out the potential applications yet. Um, not precisely. There's all sorts of things, really tons of neat stuff, but it will take more work to bring them to the final product stage. Anyway," he continued more assertively, "that's more of a marketing issue. I'm just research and development."

"Uh-huh. Better start updating your résumé, because your device will not be activated. I'm here to defeat Voltmeter."

"You can't," said Mercredi.

He said this with an absolute certainty that Kevin found immensely irritating. "If you're going to tell me this job needs a professional hero, you're wrong. And if you're thinking about calling for help, I'll break your neck before you get out the first syllable."

"No, that's not what I mean. Good heavens, young man, do you think you're the first person who has wanted to kill His Lordship? Many hate him, and many have tried.

But Voltmeter possesses a magical power. I don't know how he obtained it, but it makes him invulnerable in single combat."

"I've heard of spells like that. It's a trick. You're invulnerable because your enemy thinks you're invulnerable, so he never really tries very hard."

"Nonsense like that has led better men than you to their deaths. It's no trick. Voltmeter has cut down professional heroes, barbarian swordsmen, and that sort. I have felt his power myself. But I gave you fair warning. Believe what you like. I tell you again that a single man cannot harm him, and a force of men cannot enter this fortress."

Kevin was pretty sure that a force of men led by Black Jack Logan could crack any castle they cared to try. That, of course, was the crux of Kevin's problem, disposing of Voltmeter *before* Logan arrived. "This fortress seems undermanned to me. What makes you so certain it's impregnable?"

"The phlogistocator, of course." Mercredi waved his hand at the Diabolical Device. "It saturates the air with phlogiston. It will, quite literally, take your breath away. Once powered up, it surrounds the castle with a cloud of death. One man or an army, it makes no difference. Suffocation is a matter of minutes."

Kevin took another long look at the machine. The brass valves seemed to wink at him with malevolent glee. But there was something wrong with Mercredi's story. It was too pat, too simple. He had to roll it over in his mind for a few moments before the flaw occurred to him. "If the machine suffocates everyone around it, then the people in the castle will die, too."

"Right." Mercredi looked approving. "Good thinking. That held us up for a long time. But I've come up with a

solution. When the machine is turned on, a separate compo-
nent neutralizes any magical field within the castle walls.
Inside the walls, we'll be safe. Outside, anyone within range
of the field will die."

"Okay, but you're still working on that, you say. So the
machine can't be used yet?"

"No, the machine can be used. The neutralization field
works. I just have to tweak it a bit. It isn't specific enough.
My goal is to only stop phlogistocation. Right now it will
neutralize any and all magical fields inside the Fortress of
Doom. But we'll still be safe and the people outside will
still be exposed."

"Okay, so much for that idea. I like this machine less and
less each minute. Where does the Ancient Artifact fit in?"

"The Ancient Artifact is a source of energy for the machine."

"Let's see it."

Mercredi looked as though he were about to refuse, indeed, as though he might summon the guards. Kevin had
to pick up a spanner from a workbench and tap it against
his palm in a meaningful manner to get compliance. The
alchemist then shrugged. Kevin followed him to the opposite side of the chamber, where a sturdy cabinet rested
beneath one of the large windows. Mercredi opened it to
expose a rugged iron strongbox with a puzzle lock. He
had to work on it for a couple of minutes before he was
able to swing back the heavy door. The Prince looked inside.

This time the strongbox was not empty.

"That's it? That's all it is?"

"What do you mean? This is the most powerful model
of any Ancient Artifact ever produced."

The strongbox contained something that looked like an

ordinary pottery bud vase. It was the length of a man's arm but thinner, just wide enough to hold a few roses, except that the top was sealed with a tin plate. It was painted in light blue enamel, with a thin line of gold filigree along the top rim. It had a handful of cryptic occult symbols running down the side, a few mysterious runes around the middle, and a nine-pin DIN connector at the bottom.

And it appeared to be brand-new.

"It looks brand-new," Kevin said.

"Factory rebuilt. Just as good as new, and you save about thirty percent. Of course that didn't make a difference to Voltmeter, since he stole it."

"I thought it was an *ancient* artifact."

"It is." Mercredi reached into the strongbox and turned the vase around, so Kevin could read the engraving on the other side. "JOHN B. ANCIENT COMPANY," it said. "MODEL 7 ARTIFACT."

"The John B. Ancient Artifact Company?"

"They made the best Artifacts of Power," said Mercredi. "Sturdy, reliable, powerful. Expensive, but worth the cost, in my opinion. The craftsmanship was second to none. They've been out of production for quite some time, you realize. They sold out to Sunbelt Sorcery Supplies, which was later bought by Universal Magic Equipment. Then Universal diversified into buggy whips, millstones, ladies toiletries, candlestick holders, porcelain chamber pots, boot polish, and embroidery thread, and changed their name to UnMaCo. Then they merged with National Necromancers—you've heard of them."

"I think so. Didn't they used to have that chain of stores called Spells 'n Stuff?"

"Right. Until the retail market got saturated, and they were absorbed by Wizard Systems, which was formerly

Wizard Products before it became the Wizard Group. After the merger they reorganized as National Wizard, which later spun off most of its acquisitions so it could focus on its core business."

"So the Ancient Company is gone?"

"Well, it's back now, because it was one of the spin-offs. But when National Wizard let it go, the parent company retained the rights to the artifact-manufacturing process, even though they don't make Artifacts of Power. So now the Ancient Company just makes party crackers and trick playing cards. Oh, and those birthday candles that keep relighting when you blow them out. Of course, John Ancient is retired, although he was pretty much just the designer. It was his wife that took care of the business end."

Kevin had a sudden flash of insight. "I think I've met her. Old woman, mysterious manner, given to prognostication?"

"You know her? Excellent! Did she make a prediction?"

"Yeah. She said I would not defeat the man in black."

"No, I meant did she say anything about convertible bonds, for example? Or long-term annuities? Pork belly futures?"

"I'm afraid not."

"Too bad. Anyway, if you're looking for an Artifact of Power, of magic power . . ." Here Mercredi's voice took on a tone of dramatic urgency. "If you want access to evil power, dreadful power, insidious power, power that corrupts by its very presence, a power that was meant for the use of no mortal man"—his voice rose until it was nearly a scream—"a *power* that is very nearly beyond the ability of any human to control, *of an awesome, terrifying, unearthly power,* then you must . . . then . . ."

His voice faltered. "What?" said Kevin. "What must you do?"

"Then you pretty much have to go to the used equipment market," Mercredi said matter-of-factly. "They don't make them like this anymore. We were lucky that King Calephon had one. In near-mint condition too."

"And it's the only thing that will run the Diabolical Device?"

"It's the most powerful of the Ancient Artifacts."

"Then there's no problem."

"I know what you're thinking, and the answer is no. I'm not going to help you steal the Ancient Artifact. Don't try to threaten me—I still refuse. The danger to my daughter is too great. The danger to myself is too great. You would never get away with it, and even if you did, Voltmeter would blame me, so I'd be dead either way. Leave the castle now, while you still can."

"He won't know you're involved. I'll take it tonight, after you've left. You'll have an alibi."

"He'll still hold me responsible."

"It won't matter. I've got news for you. Lord Logan is about to attack this castle."

"Let him try. He can't get past the device, and you can't defeat the man in black. If Mrs. Ancient said so, that's the way it is. She's got a very good track record."

"You're not thinking. I don't have to defeat the man in black. Logan will defeat the man in black. I'll be halfway back to Deserae with the Ancient Artifact when Logan attacks. The machine won't work, Logan captures Voltmeter, and you and your daughter are both free. Game over."

"No!" said Mercredi. "No. Absolutely not! My daughter's life is paramount. Never will I place her in jeopardy, no matter what the circumstances. I stand firm on this. Nothing—do you hear me—*nothing* could induce me to put her life at risk."

"That's too bad. Because my father is King Eric of Rassendas. I can easily get you a position at Rassendas University.

Mercredi opened and closed his mouth twice. Then he said, "A research position. No teaching. And I want tenure."

"Tenure track and six classroom hours a week."

"Two classroom hours. And a scholarship for my daughter."

"Tuition only. No meals or housing."

"That's fine. She can live at home."

"We've got a deal then. Can you come up with an excuse for leaving the Artifact out of the strongbox?"

"All right, let me think. Yes, I'll say I needed to leave it out of the case to let the field stabilize. But I can't give you my key to this laboratory. That would definitely place me under Voltmeter's suspicion. Anyway, the door is guarded night and day."

Kevin looked toward the ceiling. "Leave that to me. Just leave the Artifact out. I'll be gone by tomorrow morning. Don't try to leave the Fortress. When Logan attacks, just hunker down in your office until it is over."

Both men gave a start at the sudden sound of a key turning in the lock. Mercredi quickly slipped the Ancient Artifact back into the strongbox, and Kevin busied himself with a dust mop. Valerie entered.

Mercredi cringed a bit. It was a slight gesture, lasting only an instant, for he immediately straightened his shoulders again, but Kevin saw it. For the first time he felt a little sorry for the man. Mercredi did not have a whole lot in the morality department, but it was clear that working under Voltmeter had not been pleasant for him. Nonetheless, he managed to come up with a brief show of false bravado.

"Ah, Valerie," he said. "I see you're out of uniform."

Valerie gave him a cold, hard look, and Mercredi fell silent. "Do you have a problem with the way I am clothed, Professor?"

"Uh, no."

"Perhaps you would like to repeat your comment to His Lordship?"

"No!" said Mercredi, all traces of bravado evaporating. "Ah, no. I think you look fine, just fine. Very evil. It suits you." He opened the strongbox and took the Ancient Artifact back out as if he were just getting started with it.

"Professor, have you succeeded in neutralizing the magical fields yet?"

"Oh yes. Wrapping that up right now. It just needs a little fine-tuning."

"Then I expect you to pay more attention to your work and less to my clothing."

"Yes, of course." Mercredi blew on the Ancient Artifact and polished it with his sleeve.

Valerie turned to Kevin. "If you can break away from here for a moment, I'd like you to check the flue in my fireplace. It gets smoky when I try to build a fire."

"All right."

"It's summer," said Mercredi. "Why do you need to build a fire?"

"Ah, I want to be prepared for autumn."

"We won't be here. Lord Voltmeter is about to start his campaign of conquest."

"My room gets chilly in the evening, and anyway, I don't have to explain anything to you. Get back to work! And you," she said to Kevin, "come with me."

"Sure," said Kevin, who could always find time to aid beautiful girls in hot clothes. He followed her out the door and past the guard, but as he left, he turned back toward

Mercredi and saw the older man giving him a broad wink. And was it his imagination, or did the guard seem to be suppressing a smile?

It is the tendency of young men everywhere, when placed in close proximity to a sexy woman, to allow wishful thinking to substitute for reasoned judgment. They will interpret every glance as interested, every smile as encouraging, every movement as suggestive, despite the fact that no suggestion was meant. (Truthfully, this tendency is by no means confined to *young* men) Kevin was no exception. Mercredi's wink had started a train of thought, and once started that train was difficult to derail. The sight ahead of him, of Valerie's slim legs and gently swaying bottom, kept it firmly on track.

As usual in the Fortress of Doom, going from any one place to another involved wending through narrow passages and traveling up and down stairs. Every now and then Valerie would turn her head to give Kevin a flirtatious smile. Or at least it appeared so to Kevin. Several times she stopped, causing the Prince to bump up against her. Kevin was almost certain she was doing so on purpose. By the time they actually reached her room his expectations had risen to stratospheric levels.

The sight of her room did nothing to lower them. If anyone, upon meeting Valerie, doubted for a second that she was a Bad Girl, a few minutes in her room would have set them straight. The walls were covered in red flocked wallpaper. There were mirrors on the ceiling. The candles were colored and scented. There was a settee that was upholstered in black lambskin leather, and a bearskin rug lay in front of the fireplace. There was a very large four-poster bed, its satin sheets slightly tousled. The sheets were a deep burgundy color, and Kevin could understand why—such a bed would set off Valerie's black hair and pale skin like a diamond in a jeweler's case.

Now she leaned into the fireplace and poked at the chimney with a pair of tongs. Her key ring jingled as she bent over. "The smoke backs up in here. I think there's something blocking the chimney. I know it's summer, but we're in the mountains. It gets cold at night."

"Could be a bird's nest," said Kevin. *Okay,* he was thinking. *She's bending over from the waist. No one bends over from the waist like that, unless she's deliberately trying to show off her figure. She's definitely flirting.*

This immediately raised the next question: What was he going to do about it? Taylor warned about this in his book, Kevin remembered. He had an important mission to perform. The practical hero would put off sleeping with the Evil Assistant until the Ancient Artifact was secure. Kevin dismissed this without a second thought. Every young man knew that the possibility of getting laid, however slim, took precedence over all other factors. The Ancient Artifact could wait. It wasn't going anywhere that afternoon. The next issue was Becky.

Unofficially, Kevin and Becky were engaged. It was wrong, Kevin decided, for him to make it with another girl when he was engaged to Becky. Not quite as wrong as if they were actually married, but wrong nonetheless. A man who was engaged to be married should not even consider sleeping with other girls. There was no question in Kevin's mind about this.

He thought about it some more. The key word, he decided, was "unofficial." He and Becky were not *really* engaged. The truth was that Becky, at this point, was promised to Logan. Granted, she didn't intend to marry Logan if she could help it, but she was still promised to him. You could make a pretty good case that Becky was more engaged to Logan than she was to Kevin, and Kevin was therefore free to do as he pleased.

Kevin went through this whole line of reasoning in something less than an eighth of a second. It wasn't much time to spend on this sort of decision; but he knew it was a weak argument anyway and not really worth dwelling on. The important point, he felt, was that he didn't act like one of those lowlife guys who hopped right into bed with a girl without considering the consequences. A man who wanted to be honest and decent would think about the consequences before going to bed with the girl anyway. Now his conscience was clear. He was certain he was doing nothing wrong to Becky.

And hopefully she'd never find out about it.

Unfortunately, this exercise in protective rationalization was a complete waste of time. Yes, Valerie was indeed flirting. But Valerie, like any good Evil Assistant, was a Bad Girl, the kind for whom flirting comes as naturally and unconsciously as breathing. While it might not be one hundred percent accurate to say she'd flirt with a statue if no one else was about, she had on several occasions flirted with oil paintings just to keep in practice. And like most flirts, she had no intention of following through. In her case especially, it was part of the job.

Kevin, nonetheless, continued to make his move. "Have you been working here long?" he asked, which was by no means an original line but served well enough to keep the conversation going. Which is why it has been used by so many men for so many years. He took the tongs from her and peered up the chimney.

"About five years," said Valerie. "I started back in Angostura. Stan likes to think he outranks me, but I have more seniority than he does. I was hired first." She left Kevin by the fireplace and lounged back on the bed.

"This damper needs to be adjusted," said Kevin. "The hinges are rusted out." He turned around to see Valerie stretched languorously on the burgundy sheets, a sight that was every bit as enticing as it sounds. He couldn't help noticing, however, that she seemed to be stroking a long black rod. "Um, is that a whip?"

"Hmmm?" said Valerie. She looked at the object in her hands, which she had idly picked up from the side of the bed and begun playing with. It was a thin, pliable length of polished dark wood. "Oh, this? No, it's a switch. In my line of work, you do run into people who lack discipline. I think it's important to maintain discipline, don't you?"

Kevin's ardor cooled like gravy on a glacier. "Sure," he said.

"This one gives a nice wrist action." Valerie brought it down on the mattress, where it made a resounding THWAP! "But it won't break the skin. For that I like to use the cat."

"Right," said Kevin, backing in the general direction of the door. Any door, at that point, would have done as well.

"The cat-o'-nine-tails." Valerie was warming to her subject. She jumped down from the bed and rummaged around in a nearby chest, emerging with a short ebony handle, from which dangled multiple leather thongs. "I adore the pattern of red marks it leaves, especially on white skin. The knots on the end of each thong make lovely little circles. On dark or tanned skin it doesn't show up so well, though." She pouted, then reached into the chest again. "That's when I use this." She held up a narrow whip of stiff rawhide.

"Great," said Kevin, not taking his eyes off her. He was holding the fire tongs defensively across his body. His other hand, groping blindly behind him, found the doorknob. For the first time he noticed that the bed was equipped with broad leather straps, riveted to the frame. The straps had buckles that padlocked.

"It works better when it's wet." Valerie put the whip to her red lips and ran her tongue along its length. She let her breath out slowly. "Mmmm. This will raise a welt that will last for days."

"Sounds wonderful." Kevin was already halfway out the door.

Valerie leaned toward him, and he backed away another step. But her eyes were closed. "Lovely, lovely red welts," she murmured, rubbing the whip against her cheek. "All across their little backsides."

"I'll need some tools from the village to fix that damper. I'll bring them when I come back tomorrow. Well, back to work. Toodles." With not unseemly haste, the Prince turned to leave. Something caught his eye.

It was a sword.

It was by the side of the bed, leaning up against the head-board. It was still in its scabbard, but Kevin recognized it immediately. It was the sword of Thunk the Barbarian, and, until recently, it had been carried by Princess Rebecca of Deserae.

And that meant that Voltmeter had Becky.

Kevin did not let his eyes rest on the sword for more than a second. He stepped back inside the bedroom and closed the door behind him. "Getting drafty in here," he explained. "Makes it hard to judge how the flow is going through that chimney. I'll just take another look at it."

"Mmmm," said Valerie. She kept her eyes closed while she stroked the whip, gently running her red-tipped fingers along its length.

"I might be able to knock some of the soot loose right now with the poker."

"Mmmm," said Valerie again. Her eyes were open now. Kevin was bending over the fireplace, shoving an iron rod up the chimney, while he pondered his next move. Valerie found her attention drawn to his thighs. She tapped the switch speculatively against her palm. Loose soot rattled down into the fireplace. Clanging noises accompanied it.

"I can do a better job later, but if you want a fire tonight, at least you can have one without smoking the place up." Kevin straightened up to find that suddenly Valerie was standing right beside him.

"Forget the fireplace. Take care of it later. You've been working hard, and I think it's time for a break." She hooked her arm in his. She was standing very close to him, so close he could feel her breath on his cheek and the warmth coming from her slim body. The whip was gripped tightly in her other hand.

She tugged him over toward the bed. "Just sit down here. No, not way over there. Right next to me. I'll get you a glass of wine, and we'll talk a bit. I like to get to know the people from the village. Have you lived there all your life?"

"Yes," said Kevin. "And yes, a glass of wine would be nice. How did you come to be Lord Voltmeter's Evil Assistant?"

Valerie had her back to him. She was pouring wine into two silver goblets. "Oh," she said absently. "Angostura is a lot more traditional than Deserae." She twisted the top off one of her rings. "There's not many career options for a woman. You're either a nurse, governess, or Evil Assistant—that's

really about all there is. I just couldn't see myself as a governess." She was talking quickly to keep Kevin distracted.
Her hand passed quickly over one goblet. There was a fleeting glimpse of white powder. The wine bubbled briefly, then
she offered the goblet to Kevin.

He took it without drinking. "Yes, well I suppose if you
sign on with the right organization, and you're completely
lacking in compassion or moral scruples, then Evil Assistant is a good choice."

"Yes, exactly. And Lord Voltmeter offers an excellent
benefits package. What do you think of this wine?"

Kevin brought the goblet to his lips, then took it away,
again without tasting it. "Of course, the problem with being an Evil Assistant is that you have to be beautiful."

Valerie gave a self-deprecating little laugh. "Is that a
problem? I don't think that is a problem for me." She snuggled up to him. "Do you think that is a problem for me?"

The Prince let his arm slide around her waist. She
pressed herself closer to him, resting her head on his shoulder. Her black hair tumbled across his neck. One of her
hands strayed to a strap on the bed and began toying idly
with the buckle. "Oh no," Kevin said. "Certainly it's not a
problem now. You've got a few years left."

"What?" Her hand stopped toying with the buckle.

"Well, I mean, you can't be an Evil Overlord's Evil Assistant when you're old."

Valerie sat up sharply. "But I am beautiful. I am far
from being too old to be an Evil Assistant."

"Yes yes, of course. I didn't say that you *are* too old. I
just meant that someday you *will* be too old. I mean, we all
get old and gray eventually."

Valerie grabbed a hand mirror from her dresser,
knocking her whip to the floor. "I don't see any gray hair."

"No, you don't have any gray hair," said Kevin patiently. "That isn't what I meant. You look fine."

"Fine as in 'she's so fine,' or fine as in 'fine for her age'?"

"Your age is fine. I don't know what you're getting so excited about. You've got years before you need to worry about it. You're only—what—twenty-nine?"

"Twenty-seven!"

"See, there you go. Say, are these goblets solid silver? They're pretty nice." Kevin raised his to his lips again.

Valerie grabbed it out of his hand. "Don't you have work to do?"

"Um, I guess."

"Then get to it. What are you loitering here for? We're not paying you to sit around swilling wine." She took him firmly by the arm and led him to door. As soon as she shoved him through, she closed the door and bolted it.

Then she lit extra candles beneath her looking glass and spent the next half hour examining the smooth skin under her eyes for tiny wrinkles and her thick dark mane for gray hairs. She found neither, but she was still so upset didn't notice that Kevin had taken her key ring.

If there was one thing Deserae did not lack, it was good maps. Logan appreciated that. Because of Deserae's strategic position among the Twenty Kingdoms, enough armies had passed through it, or planned to pass through it, that accurate military maps were in abundance. He said as much to his cavalry officer. They were both looking over one such map, in Logan's tent, still a day's march from Angst.

"There are two roads south from the Valley of Angst."

Logan traced them on the maps. "We don't know which one he plans to take."

"We've gone up both of them," said the cavalry officer. "There's no sign of any troop movement. It seems he hasn't moved yet."

Logan nodded. "I didn't expect him to. But I want to cover all possibilities. We'll take the eastern road—it's slightly shorter. But there's a chance he might decide to come down the western road while we are on the east. I don't want to divide my forces and go up both roads. That would leave either half too weak if it encountered Voltmeter's army."

"Yes, sir."

"So we'll go up the eastern road and you take your cavalry up the western road. If you run into Voltmeter, send word immediately and fight a delaying action. We'll reverse course and intercept him back here."

"Understood, sir."

"The important thing is to force a battle while he's still in the mountains. I realize this contradicts the advice I was giving to the Council of Lords just a few days ago. But we don't want to let Voltmeter get his Diabolical Device near a heavily populated area."

"His Diabolical Device, sir?"

Logan reached for his glass of brandywine. He gestured toward the bottle, indicating the officer should pour one for himself. The officer did so. "His Diabolical Device," Logan continued. "All your up-to-date Evil Overlords have a Diabolical Device. I've led three military campaigns against Evil Overlords, and each one had some sort of weapon of mass destruction. Very nasty things, too. Or so they say. We never found out for sure what any of them was supposed to do, because we managed to destroy each one, in some heroic fashion, just at the last possible second."

"Yes, sir." The cavalry officer reflected on this. "Er, Your Lordship, how did you know . . . ?"

"That they were destroyed at the last second? They each had a timing device that counted down the seconds. Very convenient little gadgets. They let you know just when the last second was coming up."

An orderly entered, carrying a pair of polished boots and a pressed uniform. He set the boots beside Logan's cot and put the uniform away in a chest. A supply officer entered. "Sir, another mounted knight rode up and volunteered to join our force."

"Oh, for God's sake," Logon looked exasperated. "Unless he brought his own provisions, we can't take him."

"Sir, it's Prince Bigelow."

"And he has his own provisions." Bigelow stepped in behind the officer. "And his own horses."

"Does he have his own feed for his own horses?"

"As a matter of fact, I do. You can't keep me out of this one, Jack."

Logan shrugged in resignation. "No, I guess not. Okay, Sam, you're in. That means you're under my command, so you'll have to start calling me 'sir.'"

"Yes, sir."

"Pour yourself a brandy."

"Yes, sir."

"We're storming a fortress," said Logan. "Not breaking a line of infantry. I've got no use whatsoever for armored cavalry. But still they keep showing up, all those useless second and third sons of the nobility, desperate for a little bit of military glory, with their gleaming armor and fine chargers and servants that have to be fed. I've nothing for them to do, and they get in the way of the regular soldiers, but they're too well connected to keep out. Happens every campaign."

"Yes, sir," said Bigelow, who knew he fit that description well. He set the decanter back down on a folding wooden sideboard. The general's tent was sparsely furnished. The bed was just a military-style cot. He had a small desk, at which he also took his meals on a tray. There was the chart table and the sideboard, and several chests of clothing. Logan's sword hung by the bed. He did not wear armor. Bigelow took a swallow of brandy. "But it's been a long and fruitless stay in Deserae, and I'll be going home as a rejected suitor, with nothing to show for my time . . ."

"I'll see there's some sort of campaign ribbon issued to all the knights."

"That's all I ask. My servants can feed themselves, by the way."

"Good. There will be plenty of glory to spread around, but provisions are short. We did not get all our supply problems worked out before we had to leave."

"I thought Timberline was supposed to be good at that stuff."

"Timberline's not here."

Bigelow looked surprised. "No?"

"He's still back at the castle. Prince Kevin Timberline of Rassendas," and here Logan made no attempt to hide the dislike in his voice, "took to his bed at the first sign of danger."

"Beg pardon, sir?" Bigelow's voice was a careful study in neutrality. The other officers, well aware of the competition for the Princess Rebecca, and naturally on the side of their commander, watched Bigelow carefully. "The Prince is ill, then?"

Logan waved a hand. "Oh, all right, Sam. No disrespect

intended to Timberline. I know you like him. I'm sure he really is sick." Here Logan couldn't keep the smirk off his face. "Lovesick, perhaps."

"Which reminds me to offer my congratulations on the upcoming nuptials, sir."

"Thank you, Sam."

"So you get the glory and the girl."

"One usually follows the other."

"And how is the Princess Rebecca taking this? I got the impression she was rather interested in Timberline."

"I didn't get that impression myself." Logan said, a bit stiffly. "I am assured by her father, though, that she will do her duty."

"Oh, I quite agree, sir." Here Bigelow smiled. "Princess Rebecca certainly gives me the impression that she is a girl who will do her duty *as she sees it*. May I ask if you have spoken to her about it?"

"I have not seen her. For security reasons, she and her retinue decided to retire to their summer castle."

"Ah. Very sensible." Here Bigelow swirled his glass, held it to the lamplight, and studied it. "So the Princess is out of town and Timberline is closeted in his rooms."

"We're well rid of Timberline, I think. We don't need his sort on a campaign. He's too much the diplomatic type. Too willing to talk, too willing to negotiate, too late to strike."

"Oh, yes." Bigelow looked out, past the open flaps of the tent, out to where the bright sky met the deep green of the mountains, and the file of soldiers marching past kicked up little bits of gravel that went bouncing down the trail. "Too much talk, too little action. That sounds like Timberline all right."

* * *

Lord Voltmeter placed his ring on a blob of sealing wax and put the letter in his out-box. He pushed back from the desk, putting his arms behind his head to stretch the kinks in his back. "Paperwork, Valerie," he said. He looked ruefully at the pile that still remained in his in-box. "Can't run an evil empire without it."

"No, my lord." Valerie brought him a glass of wine. He took it from her hand and sipped it.

"It's the bane of the successful, Valerie. Now I give the orders instead of obeying them, and there are so many orders to give. When I first started it was just a question of following the rules. The dogs, for example."

"Dogs, my lord?" This was new to Valerie.

"Before your time, my dear. It was an axiom that evil men kicked dogs, and if you wanted to be accepted as truly evil, you had to kick a lot of dogs. It sounds old-fashioned today, I know, but the guilds were quite strict about it. It was no easy feat. Sometimes I'd have to chase a dog for half a league before I could get a good kick in, and often as not I'd collect a bite on the ankle. But I kept at it until I met my quota each month, then exceeded it."

"Admirable, my lord."

"It wasn't easy being evil, even as a schoolteacher. A lot of people think it's just a question of picking out your geekiest students and giving them the highest marks, so the other kids will hate them even more. But it gets more complicated than that. Especially when you start moving up the ladder. There's so much competition. There was the orphanage, for example. I suppose I've told you that story."

"Many times, my lord."

Voltmeter ignored her. "Even today, no man can be considered truly evil until he's foreclosed the mortgage on an orphanage. Oh sure, some men have to get by with foreclosing on a family farm or an old widow, but they'll never make it to the top. I knew that all the really famous Evil Overlords had foreclosed on at least one orphanage, and I was determined that I would join that elite group."

"Very noble, sire."

"The problem was getting my hands on an orphanage mortgage. The demand was high in the evil community, and speculators were bidding up the prices. I finally bought one at a horrendous price, a four percent premium over the real interest rate, and then what happened?"

The Great Influenza Epidemic, Valerie said to herself. "What did happen, sire?"

"The Great Influenza Epidemic. It mostly hits the very young and the very old, you see. I swear it killed off at least a third of the children in Angostura. So of course as soon as the parents got over their bereavement, they were snapping up orphans left and right. There I was, hemorrhaging cash, and the orphanage was making money hand over fist. It was two years before they started missing payments again. I tell you, Valerie, I nearly abandoned evil for good."

"Another glass of wine, my lord?"

"No, thank you." Voltmeter pulled his chair up to his desk again. "But you know, Valerie, some days I think those were the best times. Sure, I was young, and I was struggling, but I had a goal, a purpose in life. Every day was a new challenge." He drew a blank sheet of foolscap toward him, dipped his pen, and began to write. But he stopped almost immediately and continued his monologue. "Now there are so few challenges left. My enemies have been crushed, my plans are almost complete." He stared at the paper without seeing it. "Just one man, really, stands in my way."

He snapped out of his reverie. "What are you holding there, Valerie?"

"A sword, my lord. We caught another woman in the ventilation shaft today, and she was armed with this."

"A soldier?"

"She claims to be a comic sidekick, my lord."

Voltmeter brightened. He turned to face Valerie, who was standing very straight and tall in her high heels, not exactly at attention, but not relaxed either. "A comic sidekick? Lord Logan's comic sidekick, perhaps?"

"I don't think she's anyone's comic sidekick, my lord."

"Really? And what do you think she is?"

"A barbarian swordswoman, my lord. She was carrying a barbarian's sword." Valerie handed the sword to Voltmeter. "And she's wearing a barbarian swordswoman outfit underneath her riding dress. And finally, there is no way I will believe this girl is a comic sidekick. She can't tell a joke to save her life."

Voltmeter slid the sword partway out of its scabbard, glanced at it incuriously, and slid it back in. He gave the sword and sheath back to Valerie. "I have no use for a barbarian swordswoman. Kill her at dawn."

"Yes, my lord." Valerie turned to leave. But at the door she turned back. Voltmeter was bent over his desk and writing at high speed. "My lord, do all Evil Overlords have Evil Assistants?"

"I suppose so, Valerie." Voltmeter answered a bit absently. "Assistants and minions. Can't do the job without them."

"Is the Evil Assistant always beautiful?"

"Hmm? Oh, yes. I expect we always try to hire attractive young women. More status, you know. Impresses the other Evil Overlords. Anyway, it's traditional." Voltmeter folded the paper, picked up his stick of red sealing wax, and held it to the candle. "Remind me to order some black sealing wax."

"There's never been an Evil Overlord with an older, slightly gray Evil Assistant?"

"Not that I recall. What are you going on about, Valerie?"

"Nothing, my Lord." Valerie left, closing the door behind her.

Kevin tried not to waste time. He didn't know what Voltmeter had in store for Becky, or how she was being treated. He pushed his cart of brooms and brushes through the corridors, asking for directions as casually as he could, but it took him a long time to get to the dungeon. It wasn't hard to find. Everyone knew where it was, and everyone gave the same directions: Go down. It was just that in the Fortress of Doom, with its numerous short staircases and twisty halls, down was a difficult course to steer.

It was well into the evening before he found it. Outside, the stars were out. In the upper reaches of the Fortress, the lamps had been lit. In the sublevels, where the dungeon was located, the stairwells always had to be lit, with slow-burning candles set into niches in the walls. The door to the dungeon was guarded. Kevin passed by the door without paying attention to it, merely giving a nod to the guard, who nodded back. He went to the end of the corridor, turned the corner, and thought a bit.

The door was barred. There was one guard. He had a battle-ax, but unlike the guards on the walls, the inside guards did not wear armor. Kevin thought he could take him out. Voltmeter's men were reputed to be experienced mercenaries, but Kevin had the advantage of surprise. If it had just been a question of spiriting Becky out of the castle, he would have attacked right away.

But there was still the Ancient Artifact to recover. Mercredi would have it waiting for him tonight. And Kevin didn't know when the guards changed shifts. When the next shift discovered that Becky was gone, they would raise the alarm, and that pretty much precluded getting the Artifact back.

He could get the Artifact first, then come back for Becky. But that was too much to risk, especially when he didn't know how long they kept prisoners here. It would be terrible if he came back for her, only to find she had been taken away to be tortured, or even executed. Merely the thought of this made his throat constrict, and he pushed the idea out of his mind. Now that he was this close to Becky he was certainly not leaving her.

That left, of course, the tried-and-true ventilation shaft method. They were certainly big enough. Kevin had once asked an architect why so many castles and fortresses were honeycombed with ventilation ducts big enough to crawl through.

"They're inside the fortress walls," said the architect defensively. "It's not like they're a security risk. Once your enemy has breached the walls, you're already in trouble. A little ductwork isn't going to make a difference."

"Sure it will," said Kevin. "If they breach the walls, you're going to be fighting room to room. You still have locked and barred doors inside your fortress. What's the point of barring the door if you've got a ventilation duct right into the room?"

The architect took a deep breath and went into an involved lecture about minimum vent sizes, air velocities, pressure losses, convection currents, natural draft ventilation systems, and the Reynolds number for turbulent flow. Kevin privately thought he was making it all up, but didn't argue any further.

At least Voltmeter has the sense to booby-trap his ventilation ducts. If Kevin owned the castle, he would just have put locking grilles over the entrances. But he supposed that those would only slow your opponent down, not stop him. The enemy could still cut through the grilles. Booby traps gave Voltmeter a chance to show he was smarter than his adversaries, which was part of what being an Evil Overlord was all about.

In any case, it took a long time to get into the dungeon. Kevin started out from one of the storerooms. The sight of it worried him. It was filled with barrels of salt pork, salt beef, and pickles. Other storerooms were loaded with crates of hardtack biscuit, bags of salt, and sacks of dried peas. It was standard fare for an army on the move, and Kevin, with a former supply officer's experienced eye, knew that Voltmeter could either march a large force of men a considerable distance, or withstand a long siege.

At least the crates gave easy access to the ceiling vents. But getting into the dungeon, even though it was only a few rooms away, turned out to be complicated. The ventilation ducts were even more devious and twisted than the hallways, and Kevin had to feel his way slowly, checking for possible trip wires and trapdoors as he went along. It was close to midnight by the time he reached the grille in the ceiling of the dungeon room.

He got his first inkling of trouble when he heard voices coming through the grille. One was low and harsh. The other was high, sweet, and female. Someone was talking to Becky. That was good. It meant she was alive. It was also bad. It meant either the guard had come inside, or there was a guard outside and a second guard inside. Very slowly, with the utmost care, and in total silence, Kevin pulled the grille out of the ceiling and set it down inside the shaft. Very slowly, he lowered his head to the opening and peered out.

The dungeon was lit by a single torch, made of rags soaked in oil, with an iron handle wrapped with cloth for insulation. It was set in a bronze holder that was bolted firmly to the wall. In the shadows thrown by the torchlight, he could see Becky behind an iron grille. She looked dirty and disheveled, and her blouse was torn, but she seemed otherwise unharmed. Her arms were chained to the wall, with her wrists above her head. A burly guard in a black-and-green uniform was leaning against the bars, talking to her. He had situated himself so he could get an optimum view of her cleavage.

"No, missy," he said. "It's *rabbi*. Not rabbit. A priest and a *rabbi* walk into a bar."

"I'm sure the book said rabbit."

"It must have been a misprint. A priest and a rabbi. It's an old joke."

The door opened, and a second guard came in. "Good evening."

"Get lost," said the first guard. "I'm on duty here."

"I thought I'd give you a break. Let you leave early." The second guard edged up to the cage and smiled at Becky, showing a mouthful of yellow teeth.

"I'll leave when my shift is up, thank you very much."

"It's shift change now." The second guard was crowding the first guard, trying to get a better view. The first guard shoved him back.

"The hell it is. Midnight hasn't struck yet."

"Just trying to do you a favor."

"You can wait until shift change to do me favors. Outside. Wait outside."

"Listen, I hear the clock striking."

"You do not!"

The door opened and a third guard came in. He was carrying a dented metal tray with four chipped enamel mugs. "Tea anyone?"

"Get lost!" said the other two guards together.

The third guard was trying to peer between their shoulders. He caught Becky's eye and smiled. "Tea. You know, I was passing by the canteen, and I thought of you two down here in this damp, dank, dungeon, and I said to myself, 'Wouldn't those blokes enjoy a nice hot cup of tea.'"

"I'm fine without it," said the first guard.

"Me too," said the second. "Why don't you just go back to the canteen and drink it yourself? Then take the kettle and stick it . . ."

"Perhaps our prisoner would like a cup of tea?" interrupted the third guard, standing on his toes so he could look over their shoulders.

"Thanks," said Becky. "I'd love one."

"I'll give it to her," said the first guard.

"But I brought it down here!"

"Too bad. It's my shift, and I'm responsible for the prisoner." The first guard had his key in the lock already. He grabbed a mug off the tray.

"How is she going to hold a cup with her hands chained up?"

"Guess I'll have to hold it to her lips." The first guard had the door open. "Well, I'm sure you gentlemen are very busy, so you can just shove off now. Thanks for the tea."

"Wait," said the second guard. "Listen."

All three guards fell silent. And listened. So did Becky.

Up in the ceiling, so did Kevin. From the outside of the Fortress, on one of the battlements, a bell began to toll.

"Midnight," said the second guard. He grabbed a mug of tea, sloshing half of it on the floor. "My shift. I'll give her the tea."

"But I brought the tea," protested the third guard. "It was my idea."

The first guard gave a longing look at Becky. "Dammit. No, wait. I'm staying over."

"You can't stay over. It's my shift. I'm responsible for guarding her now. You two run along. You're not authorized to be here."

"I'm staying. You came in early, so I get to stay later."

"What? That doesn't make any sense!"

The door opened, and another soldier came in. Kevin immediately spotted him as the Captain of the Guard. His boots were polished, his jacket was tailored, his neck scarf was silk, he had bars on his shoulders, and officers' insignia on his tricornered hat. The three soldiers came to attention. "All right, what's going on here? What is this, some sort of fan club?"

Kevin had been wondering the same thing himself.

"We're guarding the prisoner, sir."

"It doesn't take three of you to guard one girl. Outside, all of you. You, too, Macomber."

"I'm on guard now, sir."

"You'll stand guard outside the door. She's not going anywhere, and it will keep your mind off her . . ." Here the Captain sneaked a quick look at Becky's breasts. "Keep you from being distracted."

"Yes, sir," said Macomber, disgruntledly. The two other guards followed him out, with the Captain coming up last, to keep anyone from going back in. The door closed with a solid thud. Kevin pulled back into the shaft, silently counted to one hundred to be certain that the guard wasn't going to return, then quietly dropped down into the room.

Becky's eyes widened in surprise, but she was smart enough not to speak loudly. "Kevin!" she whispered. "I'm so glad to see you."

"I'm glad to see you. Are you all right?"

"Yes, fine. I knew you'd find me. How did you get into the Fortress?"

Kevin was flipping through Valerie's ring of keys, trying each one as quickly as he could. He paused to show her his breast pocket. "I can go anywhere. I have an ID badge."

"You're working for Voltmeter?"

"Shush, not so loud. I told them I was here to clean the ventilation ducts."

"You're here in disguise?"

Something in her tone implied criticism. Kevin stopped trying keys. "What's wrong with that?"

"Well, it's not very heroic, is it?"

"What!"

"I know that one man can't assault a castle directly. So I can understand slipping over the wall and maybe slitting a few throats along the way. But walking in through the front door with a false mustache and a phony business card seems to lack daring, don't you think?"

"It certainly does not. What are you talking about? Heroes assume disguises all the time."

"As wandering minstrels. They disguise themselves as musicians. Sometimes jugglers. Carrying a broom isn't very heroic."

"Really?" said Kevin, who was more than a little stung by her accusation. "There's nothing heroic about being locked in a dungeon, if you ask me."

"I was about to escape," said Becky haughtily. "I was waiting for the right moment to get out of this cage, force open that door, overpower the guard, and make my way to freedom."

"You're also chained to the wall."

Becky turned her head to one side, then the other, examining the chains as though seeing them for the first time. "Okay, I hadn't quite worked out the details on that part yet."

"Uh-huh." Kevin got the cage door open. He gave her a quick kiss on the cheek and started working on the wrist cuffs. "Are you okay? You should have waited for me."

"You shouldn't have gone off without me."

"How did your blouse get torn? Was it the guards?"

"No, it was *that girl.*"

Kevin didn't need to ask who *that girl* was. "Count yourself lucky. She was about to go after me with a whip."

"The guards have actually been pretty nice. We'll need to be careful. They may talk like a bunch of goofballs, but they can fight. I was afraid some of them might try to molest me while I was chained up like this, but their discipline is good."

Kevin stopped trying keys and gave her a speculative look.

"Why are you looking at me like that?"

"Well, Becky, you do look pretty tempting all bound up and helpless like that."

"Kevin!"

The Prince gave her wicked grin. "And I've got a little time. I'm ahead of schedule. Who knows when an opportunity like this will come along again?"

"You're not funny." Becky kicked him lightly on the ankle. "Is there ever a time when boys aren't thinking about sex?"

"Of course there is." Kevin started trying keys again.

"It's when we're—wait a minute—let me think—no. No, there isn't."

"Why did I even ask?" The wrist cuff popped open, and Kevin tried the same key on her other arm. It, too, came open. Becky rubbed her wrists for a few seconds, then threw her arms around Kevin and kissed him. "Thank you." She kissed him again. "Now let's get out of here." She looked toward the door. "Can you take the guard?"

"Not so fast," whispered Kevin. "Taking on the guard will sound the alarm. We still have to get the Ancient Artifact, remember."

"The Ancient Artifact? You know where it is?"

"Yes," said Kevin, with just a trace of smugness. "And I've arranged for it to be unguarded."

Becky looked at him with respect. "Okay, maybe I was wrong about using an alias. How do we get to it?"

"Up here." Kevin led her out of the cage and pointed to the hole in the ceiling. "Through the ventilation ducts."

"Oh no," said Becky quickly. "We can't go through those."

"Sure we can. I just came in that way."

"Um, I think they might be booby-trapped."

"Of course they are. I'll take care of that."

The hole in the ceiling seemed very dark and very black. Becky looked at it with dismay, thinking of the results when she last tried crawling through the shafts.

"It's okay," said Kevin. "I've got a lantern. And I've spent all day mapping them out." He cupped his hands. "Come on. I'll give you a boost up."

"I think you should go in first."

"You'll have to go in first because you won't be able to reach without my help."

"But if I go in first, you'll be able to look up my dress."

"That's a risk I'm willing to take. Up you go." He boosted her into the opening, and while she was arranging herself inside the shaft, he went back into the cage and snapped the wrist cuffs shut. He took the keys to the cage and cuffs and searched for a crack in the stone floor, then covered them with dirt and straw. He left the door to the cage open.

"What's that all about?"

"I'm hoping they'll think you slipped your wrists through the cuffs. They'll think they left the door to the cage unlocked after bringing you the tea. They'll accuse the guard at the door of falling asleep, even if he didn't. So even if they are looking for you, they might not be looking for an accomplice."

"Good thinking. It's sort of convoluted, but it might work."

"Well, the better plan is to snag the Ancient Artifact and get out of the Fortress before the guard changes shifts. Then it won't matter what they think." Kevin jumped and caught the rim of the ventilation shaft opening with the tips of his fingers. He got his hands to either side of the opening and levered himself in. Becky scooted down the shaft a bit to give him room to work, while he carefully replaced the ventilation grille. "And that's about the best we can do."

"Here's your lantern. This is a strange lantern. I've never seen one this small."

"It burns distilled spirits. The flame is small, but it doesn't leave behind the telltale odor of lamp oil."

"What's the tube on the side?"

"Recirculates the smoke to be burned again."

"Clever."

"Thanks. Follow right behind me." He began worming his way down the shaft, with the young princess on his heels. "Watch out for this trip wire here. This whole ventilation system is rigged with trapdoors and snares."

"Really?" said Becky.

"Although I don't know who Voltmeter thinks he is fooling, leaving that outside shaft unguarded like that. It is so obviously a trap. A person would have to be three kinds of fool to go in through there. I'll show it to you after we get out of here. By the way, how did you get caught?"

"It's very dusty in here. Don't you think it's dusty in here? I've never seen so much dust. This is certainly a very dusty place."

"That's why they needed them cleaned. I got the idea from a team of duct cleaners we had in Rassendas last year. You should consider having your castle done."

"Yes. Good idea. So Voltmeter thinks you're from Angst?"

"I haven't seen him yet. I've been concentrating on getting the Artifact back. It was that girl Valerie and a minion called Stan that hired me."

They were following Kevin's map, moving through an alternating series of vertical and horizontal ducts, gradually working their way upward. A short time passed before Becky picked up the conversation again.

"Wait. You mean Voltmeter hasn't seen you at all?"

"No."

"Does he know what you look like?"

"I shouldn't think so. Why?"

"Do the other two know who you are?"

"Of course not."

"Then why are you wearing a fake mustache?"

"Oh this?" Kevin patted his lip. "Well I always wondered

how I'd look with a mustache, and this seemed like a good time to try it out."

"Ah, that explains it. I expected you to have a good reason for wearing a fake mustache. And I was wrong. Anyway, now you know. It looks awful. Don't grow one."

"You think so? I kind of like it."

"I'm not marrying a man with a mustache. They're wet. They get soup and beer and stuff in them."

"No they don't. There are special mugs for straining that stuff out."

"Would you marry a woman with a mustache?"

"Well, no but that's not . . ."

"See, there you go. Fair's fair." They eased around another corner, and she watched Kevin make a mark on the wall. "What is that?"

"Luminous chalk. For marking a trail in the dark."

Luminous chalk? Becky pondered on this while they ascended another vertical shaft. "Kevin, have you been holding back on me?"

"What do you mean?"

"You know what I mean. Keeping secrets about yourself. Tiny spirit lamps, luminous chalk, false mustaches, stolen key rings—is there something you're not telling me? You didn't have time to buy any of this. You must have brought it with you. Why did you come to Deserae equipped like a thief?"

"We always carry special equipment with us."

"We?"

The darkness hid Kevin's look of embarrassment. "The Corps. You see, in the diplomatic line of work, sometimes you need to read stuff that wasn't meant for you to read. Stuff that might be kept locked up."

"Kevin! You've been spying?"

"Not spying. Diplomatic intelligence."

"You haven't been reading Deserae's secret communiqués, have you?"

"Uh, maybe. Sometimes. Just a few."

"Kevin, that's terrible."

"It's just part of the job. Everyone does it. Maybe once in a while I pop open a desk. Deserae does the same thing to us. It's expected."

"It is not. We're talking about highly classified documents of vital importance to our national security. You're not supposed to steal them and read them. It's illegal, immoral, and highly dishonorable. You should do like everyone else and wait until they're leaked to the press."

"Shsssh," whispered Kevin. He uncovered his lantern, consulted his map, then covered the lantern again. "We're getting close." He stood up inside another vertical shaft, wormed his way to the next level, entered a horizontal shaft, and waited for Becky to catch up with him. "If my calculations are right, there should be a grille right here."

There was. The shaft dead-ended at a grille, set vertically into the wall. The black of the iron bars wove a pattern against the dark gray of the room beyond. Kevin lowered his voice to the barest whisper. "Let's be very quiet. This room has a high ceiling. I was in here today. The ventilation grille is above the door, and there will be guards outside the door. It's a pretty thick door, but we don't want to take chances."

"Right," Becky whispered back.

She helped him slide the grille off its hooks and gently lean it against the side of the shaft. Once again Kevin handed her the dark lantern. "I'll go out first."

She nodded, although he couldn't see her in the darkness.

He slipped out the opening feetfirst, gently probing with one toe for the door lintel. When he found it he balanced momentarily on his toes, bent his knees slightly, then dropped to the floor, almost without a sound. Becky handed down the lantern and followed the same way, except that Kevin caught her by the waist as she jumped. For a long minute they clung together, silently listening.

There was nothing to hear. The room was empty of people. No sound penetrated the door. Large windows were set high on the walls. Between the scudding clouds enough moonlight came through that Becky could see the shadows of high shelves, and stacks of equipment were dimly outlined. Kevin unwrapped a long strip of black cloth from around his waist. He handed one end to her. "We'll tuck this under the door so light won't shine through."

"Right."

They stuffed the cloth strip into the crack beneath the door, up the sides, and over the top, with Kevin using his knife to press it into place. Becky remained kneeling by the door. "Do you know where the Ancient Artifact is kept?"

"Yes. It was over there. It's being kept in a strongbox, but the alchemist said he'd think of an excuse to leave it out tonight."

Becky looked where Kevin was pointing. Her eyes had adjusted to the dark, but still she saw only dim, vague shapes. "I think you better uncover the light," she whispered. "We don't want to stumble into something and make noise."

"Right. I'll just do a quick flash to orient us."

He uncovered the lantern, swung it in a quick circle, just long enough to reveal shelves piled high with goods, and instantly covered it again. Then Becky heard him swear under his breath. The Prince stood up, uncovered the lantern, and

held it over his head so it lit up the room, revealing shelf
after shelf loaded with tee shirts, coffee mugs, and commemorative plates. They were in the gift shop.

"He's out there, Stan."

"Who, my lord?"

"Logan, of course. It's only a matter of days now. Perhaps hours." Voltmeter was looking out the window again.
The moon was rising against the mountains, and he stared
into the pale light, searching for the silhouettes of moving
dark figures on the rocky crests.

"You seem very sure."

"Of course I'm sure. I've been waiting for him, you
know. He knows we stole an Ancient Artifact. He'll guess
that we intend to power up a Diabolical Device. They've
already tried to take it back by stealth. Now they'll try by
force of arms. And, of course, he'll try to confront us here.
Here in the mountains. He'll try to prevent us getting the
Diabolical Device near a population center."

Stan tried to clear his head. Partly he was tired. It was
late, way past his normal bedtime, and Voltmeter did not
seem ready to retire anytime soon. Partly it was the feeling
of lethargy that Voltmeter could induce in anyone nearby.
"I meant that you seem very sure that it will be Lord Logan
and not some other general."

"It will be Logan. He was there at the capital, wooing
the King's daughter. He had a force of men with him. He's
capable and experienced. King Calephon would be a fool
not to use him, and Logan himself would never turn down
a challenge like this."

"True, my lord."

Voltmeter returned to his desk and picked up an invoice. "What is this, Stan?"

"Ventilation duct cleaning, my lord."

"We've brought someone in to clean the ventilation ducts?"

"They needed to be done, sire. You know how allergic you are to dust mites. He showed up at the gate this morning, my lord, and we decided to accept his offer."

Voltmeter studied the invoice. "Ventilation duct cleaners. In my day, Stan, we had chimney sweeps. Now they call themselves ventilation duct cleaners and charge four times the price."

"He offered us a good deal, my lord. He threw in three rooms of upholstery cleaning if we did the ducts for the whole fortress."

"Well, can't beat that, I suppose. Did you hire him yourself?"

"No, sire. Valerie hired him."

"Was this man a local?"

"Yes, sire. From Angst."

"From Angst," Voltmeter repeated. He studied the invoice. "Amazing that anyone from Angst would dare to come up here, after the way we've treated them."

"Perhaps he just moved into town, sire, and is not aware of the way we do things."

"Perhaps. Was this an old man, Stan?"

"No sire. A rather young man."

"Tall? Good-looking?"

"Um, I would say yes."

"Hmmm." Voltmeter drew back his cloak to reveal his sword. He drummed his fingers on the hilt while he reflected. "Stan, go wake Valerie up."

* * *

Kevin swung the lantern around, turned to examine the entire room, and finally met Becky's eyes. "I don't suppose," he said carefully, "there's any chance that you'll refrain from making a smart-ass remark."

"I was merely going to say that you owed me a shopping trip. Although I was actually expecting someplace a little more upscale. But any port in a storm."

"Shop away, my love. I'll study my notes and see if I can figure out where we are. I still think we're close to it, at least."

Becky wandered down an aisle, while Kevin sat cross-legged on the floor and studied his map. It took about half an hour, during which he mentally retraced their escape from the dungeon, looked out the windows to orient himself from the direction of the moon, wrote lots of notes on the back of his map, then rubbed them out and wrote more notes. Finally, he said, "Okay, I've got it this time."

Becky came back from the other end of the shop, holding a leather jacket with the Fortress of Doom logo on the pocket. She held it up for him to see. "How do you think I'd look in black leather?"

"Sleazy."

"I know that. But sleazy in a good way or sleazy in a bad way?"

"The Ancient Artifact is just a few rooms away. I'm pretty sure. But we don't have much time. We're getting close to dawn, and that means they'll change guards at the dungeon. The next watch is certain to check the cell and find that you're gone."

"So we'll need to move quickly." Becky tossed the

jacket down. "Give me a minute." She quickly pinned up her torn blouse with a couple of Fortress of Doom pins. "I'm ready when you are."

Once again he boosted her into the ventilation shaft, and once again he followed her in. Back at the vertical shaft he slid past her so she could follow him. They went up one more vertical shaft, past two rooms, down another shaft, then doubled back in the direction they had come. Becky picked up the conversation again. "Kevin," she whispered.

"What?"

"When you said you were reading diplomatic secrets . . . ?"

"Yes?"

"Were any of them about me?"

"Oh sure. Plenty of them."

"What did they say?"

"I can't tell you that. They're secret."

"Right, right. Of course. But since they're *about me,* I probably know them already, so you wouldn't be revealing anything by telling me."

"Sorry, no."

"Kevin! Tell me!"

"Shush." Kevin stopped at another grille. "This is it."

"Are you sure?"

"After the last time? No, I'm not sure. But I think this is it."

They were running out of time, so Kevin decided to take a little more risk. He put his head and arm through the ventilation grille opening, uncovered his lantern, and shined it briefly around the walls. There was a chance that a guard might see the flash of light from under the door, but Kevin didn't want to take the time to climb down and stuff the crack, only to find he was in the wrong room again.

But this time his careful mapping, his sense of direction, and no small amount of luck had him in the right place. He drew back inside and put his head close to Becky's. "This is it," he whispered. "This is where I saw the Ancient Artifact."

"Great."

They repeated their actions from the previous room— climbing through the vent carefully and blinding the door. When he was sure they could not be detected, Kevin turned Becky around and shined the lantern on the Diabolical Device. He heard her sudden intake of breath.

"I know how you feel. I had the same reaction."

"Oh my," she said. "That's really evil."

"Well, it's just a machine."

Becky shook her head. "No, it's more than that. Listen, when I was a young girl my governess took me past a church that had a big pile of wood next to it. The church had some sort of trial, and they were going to burn a man for heresy. Granddaddy was still King of Deserae, and he allowed that sort of thing."

"Uh-huh."

"See, that pile of wood wasn't just a pile of wood. You could tell it had a purpose. It was something horrible waiting to happen. And this machine is the same way. It's scary."

"It's a phlogiston machine."

"The stuff that makes things burn?"

"Right. Set fire to something and its phlogiston is released into the air. When the air gets saturated with phlogiston, the fire goes out. And Mercredi says if the phlogiston content of air is too great, you can't breathe it either."

"Sweetie," Becky said patiently, "you don't have to explain phlogiston to me. I took high school alchemy, too, you know."

"You told me you made a D."

"A D is a passing grade!"

"Sorry, you're right."

"Oh, Kevin, we've got to stop it."

"Don't worry. We will. The machine is useless without the Ancient Artifact. Come on, let's find it."

Their search took but a few minutes. The Ancient Artifact was sitting on a square metal plate, next to an open box of Thin Mints. The plate was hooked up to several instruments with gauges and dials, although nothing was hooked up to the Artifact itself. Kevin tried to work up some respect for an object that contained awesome power, or so he had repeatedly been told. But it continued to look like nothing more than an unassuming porcelain jug. Becky seemed to feel the same way. "That's it? The flowerpot?"

"That's what the alchemist said."

"It's a trick, right? That can't be it. It's a decoy."

"If it was a decoy, it would look the same. No, that's it. Valerie saw him take it out of the case, and she accepted it as the Ancient Artifact."

"Then let's get it."

But Kevin hesitated, and Becky made no move to pick it up either. They both studied the metal plate and the gauges. Finally, Becky spoke. "Is it booby-trapped, do you think?"

"I don't know. Mercredi said he was making some measurements. But look here, all these gauges are showing zero. They don't seem to be measuring anything."

"Maybe the Artifact has weakened over the years."

"Maybe he finished his measurements and disconnected it. Or . . ."

"Or what?"

"Or maybe we're being tricked, and it really is booby-trapped."

"What are you going to do?"

Kevin looked at it some more. "I don't have any ideas. We don't have much time."

"We still have a few hours until dawn."

"Yes, but we still have to get out of here. We'll have to risk it." He took a long, deep breath, stepped forward, and put his hands around the Ancient Artifact.

Then took them away. "Stand back, Becky, in case something happens. No, back farther, all the way against the wall." When he was satisfied she was at a safe distance, he snatched up the Ancient Artifact and stepped away.

A sound behind them went "TAP TAP TAP."

Kevin and Becky both jumped. In unison they whirled around. A very tall man, dressed in black, was tapping his gold pinkie ring against a table. Behind him, in the open doorway, stood Valerie and Stan, and behind them the corridor was full of guards, heavily armed with spears, swords, and crossbows. "No booby traps," said the man in black. "Although I couldn't help but wait for the right dramatic moment to make my entrance known. Please forgive my theatrics."

Kevin and Becky just stared.

Voltmeter turned away. The soldiers in the corridor parted to let him through. "Put them in the torture chamber," he called back. "And send for me when they are ready."

Logan stood at the top of the pass, observing the valley through a spyglass. He swept it over the darkened fields, ran it quickly along the streets of the village, moved it more

slowly up the cliff face, then focused for a long time on the
Fortress, carefully examining the torchlit battlements, the
windows, and the soldiers moving along the walls. When
he was satisfied that he had seen everything that could be
seen, he put the spyglass away and looked at the sky. The
moon was bright when it was out, but the sky was dotted
with dark clouds. He wet a finger and tested the wind. On
the plains a north wind generally meant clearing skies, but
here in the mountains there was no way of predicting the
weather.

He walked back to his horse and the knot of officers that
waited for him. "All right," he said. "There's enough moon.
Move into the valley now. Muffle the harnesses. No lights
and no fires. Give the men a cold meal and get them in for-
mation. I want them to be ready at dawn."

There was a low chorus of yessirs. Someone asked, "Will
they see us?"

"There are men watching from the walls. They'll know
we're here, but they won't be able to tell much more than
that until the sun comes up. So be ready. We'll give them as
little time to prepare as possible."

The officers murmured their assent. Logan held up a
hand. His hands and face showed ghostly pale in the moonlight, while his body, clad in his black uniform, faded into
the night. "All right, then. You all know the plan, and you
have your orders. See to it."

The officers moved quietly down the line. Bigelow
started to walk away also, but Logan put a hand on his shoulder to restrain him. Bigelow followed the general back to the
top of the pass, where Logan unsnapped his spyglass and
handed it over. He waited until Bigelow fixed it to his eye.
"Over there. See the lights?"

Bigelow looked. "It appears to be a tavern."

"It looks like there is a good bit of activity tonight. I want you to take an orderly down there. Dress in mufti, take a room, eat dinner, and have a few drinks with the locals. See if you can learn anything about the Fortress. Then send the orderly back with a report."

"Yes, sir." Bigelow did his best to sound neutral, but there was no disguising the disappointment in his voice. "Sir, you're not cutting me out of the battle, are you?"

Logan sighed. "No, Sam. Not at all. I'm putting you with my own guard unit. You're to rejoin the ranks at dawn and engage in the charge up the cliff trail. Feel free to act as heroic as you like. I just want some corroboration that Voltmeter is actually in the Fortress. We'll look like a bunch of damn fools if we attack the place and find he's already slunk off with the Ancient Artifact."

"Yes, sir." Bigelow returned the spyglass. "Drinking in a tavern for my king and country. I always knew my gentleman's education would someday stand me in good stead."

It is one of life's ironies that successful people rarely have time to enjoy the fruits of their success. Many a wealthy merchant spends more time filling in his ledgers and counting his money than he ever spends enjoying his wealth. Many a king or cardinal, overscheduled with meetings and inundated with paperwork, wishes for a few free hours to take a stroll down by the river, to attend a concert, or catch up with the latest novel. Lord Voltmeter was no exception. In the early days he had delighted in personally torturing his victims; but as his criminal enterprise grew larger, he was more and more often forced to delegate the job to his minions. Nowadays, it was only for the most important captives that Voltmeter supervised the torture himself.

Kevin was not flattered by the attention. He was standing on the stone floor in the center of a windowless room. This was Voltmeter's torture chamber. There was a blackboard in front of him. The wall in back held a faded map of the world, with the names of many of the countries out-of-date. A row of small desks lined one side of the room, and Kevin knew, with one glance, that the legs were uneven and the desks would wobble. He stood with his hands crossed in front of him, manacled at the wrists. A guard stood on either side. Each guard was armed with a spear, and each held it with the point pressed against Kevin's neck. There was a plain wooden stool next to Kevin, but the guards had kept him standing motionless for several hours. Behind him, Becky was strapped down to an oak torture table, the kind with grooves along the edges for blood to collect. The Prince could turn his head from side to side, though, and watch while Stan directed the activities of a handful of minions. They were hurriedly trying to straighten the place up for His Lordship's visit; sweeping the floor, trimming the lamps, putting the scalpels and gouges back in their trays, oiling the thumbscrews, and replacing last month's safety posters with new ones. Two more minions brought in an armchair and a small table, and a third set the table with a cup, a pot of tea, and some lemon biscuits. Valerie stood next to Becky's table, stroking the leather straps that held the beautiful girl immobile, and looking thoughtful.

That was what worried Kevin the most. His army training had taught him about modern torture methods. He knew that everyone broke down eventually. But he also knew that nearly any soldier could hold out for at least two days, and most lasted for longer than that. In two days Logan's army would have this fortress under siege.

The problem was Becky. Kevin didn't think he could stay silent if they started hurting Becky, and it was Becky that was strapped to the torture table. It didn't take a genius to figure out who was in trouble here. Fortunately, they'd made the mistake of cuffing Kevin's hands in front of him instead of in back of him. He resolved to attack the moment the Evil Overlord entered the room.

It didn't work that way. Voltmeter came in with a breezy air. Tall, black-clothed, booted, wearing a black cape lined with scarlet satin, good-looking in a brutal sort of way, he walked right up to the Prince and stood in front of him. His throat was in easy reach of Kevin's hands, but Voltmeter was unconcerned. He wanted Kevin to try to attack, to experience for himself the impossibility. He saw Kevin give the little headshake that so many people used when the spell was on them, and nodded with approval.

Then the Evil Overlord favored the Prince with a benign smile. "My dear fellow," he began genially, "I have been so looking forward to this. I can't tell you what an honor it is to finally meet you face-to-face."

"Um," said Kevin. "Thanks." He was still a little distracted. He knew that Voltmeter had a spell that made him invulnerable in single combat, but this was the first time he'd felt its effects. His mind was still clear, but his whole body seemed enveloped in a curious lethargy. His muscles seemed overly relaxed, as though he had just awoken from too sound of a slumber.

"I was hoping you would come," Voltmeter continued. "I remarked to Valerie only this evening that you were just about the only man who could prevent me from putting my

Diabolical Plan into action. You are famed throughout the Twenty Kingdoms for your bravery and daring, so I am eager to test my skill against yours. Once you get to my level, there are so few worthy opponents."

"Uh, really, you are too kind." The Prince was a bit surprised. He'd always had good opinion of himself, but he didn't think he had that much of a reputation. Voltmeter must have a pretty fair intelligence-gathering system, he decided.

"I note that you avoided my little traps and ventilation system snares. That doesn't surprise me. Such childish devices are merely for the chumps and wannabes. A hero of your stature found them no challenge, of course."

"Of course." Kevin tried to look at Becky, hoping she was getting all this.

"And now you are in my clutches, and only the interrogation remains. This is the true test of caliber, Lord Logan. Physical bravery is admirable, but all too common. For men like us, the ultimate challenge resides in the mind. Without the use of your army, your weapons, or your strength, using only your intellect and wits, you must contrive to deceive me as to your military plans, while I attempt to extract the truth. Prepare yourself, Lord Logan, for only the . . ."

"Excuse me, my lord," interrupted Stan. He handed Voltmeter a dossier. "This isn't Lord Logan. I am quite certain that this is Kevin Timberline, Prince of Rassendas."

To his credit, Voltmeter didn't so much as blink. "Of course, Stan. I knew that. I was just testing you. Yes. Prince Kevin of Rassendas. Right. Son of—Eric the Good?"

"The other one, my lord."

"Yes, of course." Voltmeter was hastily leafing through the dossier. "Well, Prince Kevin, prepare to meet your fate.

You bit off more than you could chew when you elected to tangle with me, even if your skill and daring . . ." He broke off and stared at the dossier. "Aren't you a little inexperienced for this sort of thing?"

Kevin ground his teeth. "I had this book," he admitted. "By Robert Taylor."

"Taylor?" Voltmeter shook his head. "Young man, you have made a grievous error by coming to this valley. If you were following the advice in that handbook, you have been seriously misled. The fishing here is terrible. Oh, you might hook a few brookies and maybe some German browns, but for really good fly-fishing you need to go . . ."

It was Stan's job to interrupt again. "My lord, I believe he's referring to the *Handbook* . . ."

"*Of Practical Heroics*. Yes, Stan. I was toying with him."

Valerie leaned over Becky, and whispered, "A prince? He's a prince?"

"Prince or pauper," said Voltmeter. "It matters not. The point is that he shouldn't be here at all. I am Lord Voltmeter, dammit! I am the greatest criminal mastermind in history. The most dangerous man on earth! I have stolen the Ancient Artifact and used it to power the deadliest device known to mankind. My army is poised to sweep across the Twenty Kingdoms in a tidal wave of destruction. I will crush their Lords and Ladies in my fist like ripe grapes, I will stomp their populations beneath my heels, and the blood will flow like red wine! The sky will blacken with the smoke from their funeral pyres. And yet King Calephon scorns me by sending this—this dilettante!" His voice rose. "I will be revenged against this insult!" he screamed. He raised his fists to giant cow position, looked around at the staring throng, then self-consciously brought them down. "I really am a pretty dangerous fellow," he told them in a lower voice. "The Ancient Artifact model seven renders me undefeatable."

"I prefer the model three myself," said Kevin coolly.

"The model three is a collectable. If you use it, you depreciate its value."

"Well, that's true."

"Sit down," commanded Voltmeter.

"I prefer to stand," said Kevin. Every military officer knew that the basic rule of resisting interrogation was not to cooperate in any way. If they offer you a chair, remain standing. If they give you a drink, tell them you're not thirsty.

Except that even as the words came out of his mouth, he found his legs were disobeying his brain. He sat down, trying to conceal his look of surprise.

"Outside," Voltmeter told the guards, and Kevin knew that trick, too. Voltmeter was showing how confident he was in his control of his prisoner. Inwardly, Kevin seethed.

"Now then, Timberline." Voltmeter selected a wicked-looking blade from a pewter tray and laid it against Kevin's head, just above his right eyebrow. "I suppose I could waste time asking a bunch of specific questions, but really, why must you and I go through such a tedious game? You know what modern torture methods can do. You know that everyone talks in the end. You know what I want to know."

"I don't know anything."

Voltmeter made a motion with his hand. Stan brought over a small wooden desk and set it in front of Kevin. He set an inkwell down on it and put a pen in Kevin's hand.

"You will spare yourself and your friend a lot of pain if you cooperate."

"If I talk, will you release my companion?"

"Kevin!" said Becky. "Don't do it!"

"I'll release you both," said Voltmeter.

"Yeah, well okay then."

"Kevin!"

"Keep her quiet," Voltmeter told Valerie. If he was surprised at Kevin's quick acquiescence, he did not show it. He produced a blue examination booklet from under his cloak and laid it down in front of Kevin. "You have ten minutes to write down everything you know."

Kevin raised his hands. "Does spelling count?"

"Certainly. You may open your booklet . . . now."

"Right." Kevin took a deep breath and began writing at top speed. Voltmeter sat down in his armchair, poured himself a cup of tea, and watched him with increasing smugness. Becky watched with increasing dismay. The Prince stayed focused on his task, dipping his pen at regular intervals and filling page after page. There was no clock in the room, so he had no way of telling how much to write or how much time he had. He suspected Voltmeter didn't know either, and the man was just toying with him. A drop of sweat formed on his forehead, slid down to the end of his nose, and dripped onto the paper. He was still writing when Voltmeter held up his hand. "That's enough. Close your booklet and pass it to the front."

There was no one to pass it to, but Stan took the booklet away from Kevin. Voltmeter, Valerie, and Becky waited expectantly. Stan cleared his throat. The corners of his mouth quirked momentarily, but he made his face expressionless as he began to read. "Civilization began seven thousand years ago in Mesopotamia, at the junction of the Tigris and Euphrates Rivers, an area known as the Fertile Crescent. With the invention of agriculture . . ."

"You said everything I know, right?"

"Fool!" A blade flashed in Voltmeter's fist. A red slash

appeared on Kevin's forehead. Blood ran into one eye. "I want to know Logan's battle plans!"

Kevin closed the eye and looked at Voltmeter with the other. "Battle plans? You want to know about battle plans? That's a relief. I was afraid you were going to ask me about quadratic equations. I hate math tests. Sorry, I don't know anything about battle plans. How about you, Becky?"

"Logan?" mused Becky. "Did you say Logan? The name sounds familiar—but you meet so many people in this business." She shrugged. "Sorry, can't place him."

"Fine," said Voltmeter. "I believe you. In that case, you are of no further use to me and you will die." He yanked open the door, letting in a bevy of heavily armed men. "Kill them," he told Stan. He swept his cloak behind him and turned away.

"Whoa! Wait!" Kevin started to rise. The guards forced him down with their spears. "Wait. Aren't you forgetting something? Before you kill me, you're supposed to explain your Diabolical Plan."

Voltmeter stopped. When he turned around his face was composed again, and his voice was back under control. "My dear Timberline, you are completely correct. Rest assured that I fully intended this morning to explain my Diabolical Plan." He paused for a moment to give Kevin a tight-lipped smile. "Explain my plan, that is, to Lord Logan. I've wasted too much time here already. I do not explain myself to mere apprentice heroes." He started for the door again. "Only a man like Lord Logan can fully appreciate my genius."

"Yeah, well you can't be all that smart." Voltmeter was almost gone when Kevin called out again. "Thunk escaped from your clutches."

"Thunk cheated!" This time Voltmeter's voice was high

and shrill, a man barely on the edge of control. He strode back to Kevin's table and slammed his fist down on the oak. "Cheated, I tell you." He took a deep breath and brought his voice back down. "Very well, Timberline, you know the game. Here you are, locked in a torture chamber, deep in a fortress, your death ordered by an Evil Overlord. Instead of sticking around to make sure you are dead, he then leaves the room. What do you do? How can you possibly escape? Come on. You've read Taylor's book. You know the answer."

Kevin considered this. "Well," he said carefully, "I guess there's two things to try. Traditionally I would either trick the Evil Overlord's dim-witted minions or seduce his Evil Assistant."

"Exactly right. Trick the minion, seduce the assistant. I knew that, of course, so I prepared for it. My Chief Minion graduated from a top-notch university with full honors. I searched for an Evil Assistant who didn't like men. I had it all set up, and then we captured Thunk, the foremost hero in the Twenty Kingdoms."

Voltmeter picked up a lemon biscuit from the tray, frowned at it, then crushed it in his fist. Yellow crumbs trickled on to the floor. "I tortured him a bit. He didn't have any information I wanted, but I felt in need of amusement. And then I let slip my Diabolical Plan. I wanted to give him vital information to take back to Deserae, so he would have an extra strong incentive to escape, beyond merely saving his own life. Right in front of him I gave the order for his death and then I left the room, enjoying the thought that behind me his attempts at trickery and seduction would prove futile." His voice rose again. "And do you know what that barbarian half-wit did?"

There was silence in the room. Stan and Valerie studiously avoided meeting the Overlord's eyes. Voltmeter answered his own question. "Instead of trying to trick my minion or seduce my assistant, Thunk tricked my assistant and seduced my minion!"

He picked up a scalpel and jammed it into the table. Stan looked at the ceiling. Valerie looked at the floor. Becky was the first to break the silence.

"I am so heartbroken," she said. "I had such a crush on Thunk when I was a girl. I had no idea he was that way."

"We were just experimenting," Stan said immediately.

"Silence," roared Voltmeter. "Get out!"

Stan left the room quickly.

"And you," Voltmeter told Valerie. "You should have known better."

"Excuse me, Lord Voltmeter," said Becky again. "Not to sound self-righteous or anything, but when you decided to hire an Evil Assistant who was seduction-proof, weren't you assuming that the hero would always be a man? Surely that's a bit old-fashioned."

Voltmeter smiled at her. "Spoken like a true barbarian swordswoman, my dear. I thought of that also." He switched his attention to the other girl. "Valerie, why aren't you wearing your outfit?"

Valerie winced. "But, my lord . . ."

"Don't argue with me. You know the rules. Change your clothes. Now!"

Valerie opened her mouth again, but was silenced by Voltmeter's glare. She pouted and left the room.

"Wait until you see this," Voltmeter told his unwilling guests. Valerie was gone only a few minutes. When she returned she looked completely different.

The bright red lipstick and dark eye makeup had been washed away, and she had done something to her long black hair to make it hang limp and flat against her skull.

She was wearing a bulky wool sweater that effectively disguised her bust and a long tweed skirt that concealed her legs. She wore clompy brown shoes with white anklet socks, and a Star of David on a chain around her neck. She stood by the torture table and crossed her arms sullenly.

"There, you see," said Voltmeter. "Clothes make the man, they say, and the woman also. Have you ever seen a more unattractive outfit in all your life? There is nothing, absolutely nothing, about Valerie now that anyone, *man or woman,* would find the least bit sexy."

"I'm not wearing panties," Valerie whispered to Kevin.

"I heard that!"

"Also, I shaved my . . ."

"Quiet!"

"Hey!" said Becky. "I thought you weren't into guys."

"I didn't know he was a prince. Besides, everyone looks good when they're in handcuffs."

"Nothing you do here matters," Kevin told Voltmeter. "Suppose you do conquer Deserae? Suppose you do gain control of the throne? So what? The Twenty Kingdoms are full of guys who won't rest until the legitimate throne is restored. You'll spend the rest of your life dodging assassination attempts, surrounded by bodyguards and hiding behind walls. What kind of life is that?"

"Right," said Becky. "Unless you marry the Princess, you're going to be miserable."

"What?" said Voltmeter.

"What?" said Kevin.

"See, if you marry the Princess and have a son, then you have an heir. So there's no point in anyone knocking you off, since rule would pass to your son anyway."

"Um, Becky," said Kevin. "Maybe you'd better be quiet."

"Go on," said Voltmeter. It was clear that this was an angle he hadn't thought of. "But then they would try to kill our son."

"Probably not. Her son would have legitimate right to the throne, since in Deserae the line of inheritance can run through either the son or daughter. Of course someone might still try to kill him, but he'd be at no more risk than any other king."

"Say, how about this weather?" said Kevin desperately. "Boy, it sure cools off here in the mountains at night, doesn't it?"

"But a marriage made under duress isn't legal," said Voltmeter.

"Sure it is," said Becky, warming up to her theme. "This is royalty, remember. You're right, you can't grab some milkmaid right off the farm and force her to marry you. But for nobility, arranged marriages are a fact of life. No one will question it, even if the girl is unwilling. So if Lord Voltmeter marries the Princess Rebecca . . ."

"Be quiet!" Valerie suddenly slapped Becky across the face, cutting her off. Kevin looked at the Evil Assistant with surprise. There was some dynamic here he wasn't aware of.

"Um," said Becky. She seemed to realize what she had been saying. "Of course, none of this matters to me, because I'm a barbarian swordswoman. And a comic sidekick. So why should I care what happens to the Ice Princess? I was just babbling."

"All right, that's enough of that." Voltmeter was finished. "I'm a busy man, and it's time to wrap up this session. Timberline, you may be a novice, but I must admit that you did manage to penetrate my fortress and get your hands on the Ancient Artifact. I respect that. Normally I'd torture your girlfriend to death in front of your eyes before starting on you, but I'm going to take it easy on you and kill you both quickly and cleanly."

"Thanks," said Kevin. "If I can ever return the favor, let me know."

"Gloves," Voltmeter told one of the guards. The man brought a pair of loose black leather gloves that stretched up Voltmeter's arms. "Apron," he said. "I'm going to cut his throat. Stand back. The blood is liable to spurt quite a distance." The guard brought a long leather butcher's apron. "Scalpel." A second guard put a blade into his hand. Voltmeter placed it against Kevin's throat. "Any heroic last words, Timberline?"

"No, dammit," said Kevin. "I should have thought something up ahead of time."

"Too bad." A drop of blood appeared at the tip of the scalpel.

There was a brief knock, and the door to the torture chamber opened. Stan stuck his head back in. "Er, Lord Voltmeter? I thought you should know this. We just caught a plucky girl in the ventilation shaft."

If you find yourself confronted by a group of armed guards, be warned that they will attack you in mass. No matter what you have been told by other sources, rest assured that they will not line up to attack you one by one. Trust me on this.

—HANDBOOK OF PRACTICAL HEROICS

BY ROBERT TAYLOR

To the surprise of no one, the plucky girl turned out to be Mercredi's daughter Laura. The two prisoners were released from the torture chamber and thrown back into the dungeon while Voltmeter pondered over this new development. "It will give you a chance to think of a slick exit line," he snapped at Kevin, as the guards dragged them away. "Bring this new girl to me," the Evil Overlord then told Valerie. "Search her thoroughly first."

Valerie smiled. "Yes, sire."

"And search Timberline's duct-cleaning equipment.

Confiscate any weapons or fishing tackle he might have."
He stalked back to his office.

Kevin and Becky were marched at sword point back
to the dungeon, chained to the wall, and the cage door
slammed shut before them. Becky gave Kevin a worried
look. "Are you all right, sweetie? There's blood all over
your face and shirt."

"It was different from the exams I took in school. Usually *I* ended up okay, and my papers got covered with red
marks."

Becky smiled at this display of bravado. She said, "I'm
scared."

"Don't worry. We'll get out."

"That's not why I'm scared. I was just thinking—I
guess it's the same for you—that being a princess and all,
I've spent most of my life around politicians, lawyers, and
nobles."

"Right."

"But I know there are a lot of honest, decent people in
Deserae, even though I rarely get a chance to meet them.
They're the ones I'm scared for. What will happen to them
if Voltmeter brings his Diabolical Device into the city?"

"The game isn't over yet. That reminds me of a question. How do you manage to get away from your chaperones so often?"

"All my chaperones and ladies-in-waiting come from
the very best of the noble families. So you can bet they've
got plenty to hide. I just find out what it is and we come to
an agreement."

An hour later the two met with a surprise. Mercredi
was thrown into the cell with them. However, there were
only chains enough for two people. There was a huddled
discussion among the guards as to whether Mercredi

should be chained up instead of Becky, because a grown man was more dangerous than a young woman, or whether Becky should be left chained up, because they thought girls looked really hot that way. Unfortunately, professionalism overcame salaciousness, and Becky and Mercredi were both chained with one arm each, while Kevin was chained with both arms. This, alas, did not allow Becky to reach the key hidden in the floor.

"How did Voltmeter know you switched sides?"

"How does Voltmeter know anything?" said Mercredi. "He always seems a step ahead of everyone else. I should never have tried to double-cross him. What's wrong with his plan for world domination anyway? I could have had my own university. Named after me, too. Even better, a research park. One of those places with big lawns and automatic sprinkler systems."

"He would have killed you eventually," said Kevin. "It's in Taylor's book."

"Who?"

"*The Handbook of Practical Heroics* says the Evil Overlord always kills the mad scientist. To keep him from revealing his secret to anyone else."

"I expected you to realize by now that Lord Voltmeter is not your run-of-the-mill Evil Overlord. And I am hardly a mad scientist. Phlogiston theory is well developed and accepted, with many practical uses and benefits. It's just that no one has thought to apply it to genocide until now."

It was only a few minutes later that Laura was brought in. She was a pretty teenage girl, with red hair tied back in a long ponytail and a scattering of freckles. She wore stockings, a plaid skirt, a plain white blouse, and one of those uniform blazers with the emblem of some private school that Kevin didn't recognize. Right then her clothing was in disarray, and she looked like she had been crying. A smirking Valerie brought her into the dungeon and stood by while the guards chained her up. Laura waited, grim and stone-faced, while the guards unchained one of Kevin's arms and applied the manacle to Laura's wrist.

"All right," Valerie said when they were finished. "Up on the walls. Prepare for Logan's attack."

The guards exchanged glances. "Shouldn't someone be guarding the prisoners?"

Valerie tested the cage door. It was solidly unmoving. "They don't need guarding. They're chained and caged. They're not going anywhere."

One of the guards pointed at Becky. "This one got away before. She's a slippery one."

Valerie let her eyes linger on Becky and seemed about to make a comment. But instead she turned back to the guards. "I'm sure that if I were in your place, I'd also rather be down here cowering inside a nice safe dungeon than upstairs facing Logan's army. But your officers say the major threat comes from outside this fortress rather than from within, and they want every man on the walls. If you have a problem with that, argue with them."

The soldiers greeted this last remark with glaring hostility. Mercenaries all, they did not like having their professionalism called into question. However, they were also professional enough to keep silent and obey the order. They left, with Valerie taking up the rear and slamming the door behind her.

The moment they left, Laura burst into tears.

This was followed by an exchange of hugs with her father and an emotional reunion that Becky thought was very sweet and Kevin thought could have been put off until a more appropriate time. Finally, Mercredi said, "What are you doing here? I told you to stay in school."

"I was trying to help you."

"What sort of help is this? I'm only doing this for your safety."

Laura pouted. "You're always telling me what to do. You never let me make my own decisions."

"Of course not, when you keep making dumb decisions like this."

Laura's voice rose. "Don't call me dumb!"

Mercredi's voice also rose. "I didn't call you dumb. I said you made a dumb decision. You should have stayed in school. Do you know how much I'm paying per semester to put you into a nice safe school?"

"A fat lot you cared about that school! Did you ever come to any of my field hockey games? No, not even when I was captain of the team."

"How could I come to a hockey game? I'm being held prisoner in an Invincible Fortress, forced to work for an Evil Overlord!"

"You always have an excuse! You just care about your stupid phlogiston stuff more than you care about me."

"Excuse me," said Kevin, loudly but calmly. He waited until he had their attention, then touched each of them on the shoulder. "Professor Mercredi," he said kindly, "You've got to realize that Laura is no longer a child. She's a grown woman and ready to take responsibility for her own life. You need to give her space to make her own mistakes."

"And Laura," he continued soothingly, turning to the girl, "you need to understand that your father's work is very important to him. You should try to respect that and realize that his time is not his own."

Mercredi looked embarrassed and Laura looked con-
trite. "I'm sorry, Daddy. I just wanted to . . ."

"I'm being sarcastic!" yelled Kevin. "I want the two of
you to put your bickering on the back burner until we get
out of here. We need to warn Logan about the Diabolical
Device and tell him to hold off the attack until we can devise a counter to it. Otherwise, Deserae's entire army will
be dead."

"Not quite," said Mercredi. "Logan's army will be fine.
We'll be dead."

All eyes turned on the alchemist. Mercredi gave an embarrassed cough. "I took a little precaution in case our plan
went wrong. Or in case Lord Voltmeter decided to double-
cross me." He quickly explained the phlogistocator to Becky
and Laura. "The machine will suffocate anyone within
range, but that includes everyone in the castle. So to protect
Voltmeter and his men, it also creates a second field inside
the castle that neutralizes all magical forces."

Kevin nodded. "And now you're saying you turned that
protective field off?"

"Correct. I adjusted the machine so now it will kill
everyone *inside* the castle, but the people outside will be
unharmed."

The three young people digested this new information
in silence. Becky spoke first. "It's not so bad, then. At least
Voltmeter will be killed. And Deserae will be saved."

"I'm not afraid to die to protect innocent people," said
Laura nobly. "Good work, Daddy."

"I had intended to flee the castle before the machine was
turned on," said Mercredi. "I didn't intend to die for anyone."

"I'd prefer to avoid it myself," said Kevin. "What did
you do to the machine? Reverse the polarity?"

"Reverse the polarity!" snapped Mercredi. "Reverse the

polarity? Where did you get that idea? I'm sick of hearing it. That is such an overworked cliché. Every time a powerful piece of equipment goes out of control, you can be sure some nitwit will snap his fingers, and say, 'I've got an idea—let's reverse the polarity.' They don't even know what they're talking about. It's just some phrase they picked up, the all-purpose solution to every technological problem. Ridiculous!"

"Sorry," said Kevin. "You're right. It *is* just a phrase I picked up. What *did* you do?"

Mercredi was silent for a long time. "Well, as a matter of fact, I reversed the polarity," he finally admitted. "That wasn't my point. My point was that people act as though it's a simple change. It's not. It requires a lot of calculations and delicate adjustments. It's not just a question of switching the T-leads."

"Right."

"This is all your fault anyway. If you had taken the Ancient Artifact when you said you would, the issue would never have come up."

"*Mea culpa.* Okay, so we've got to get out of here before Logan attacks and Voltmeter switches on the Diabolical Device."

"Logan won't attack if he thinks I'm here," said Becky. "He won't take the chance of harming me. I don't think he knows I followed you, but if someone from the village described me, he might suspect. He's clever enough, for a soldier."

"I think you're right. He won't lose any sleep if I'm killed; but if we can get to him with a message from you, he'll call off the attack."

"Why?" said Laura. "I mean, why should Lord Logan care if you are harmed in the attack?"

Mercredi looked interested in this question also. Kevin didn't answer, leaving it to Becky to decide how much about herself she wanted to reveal. Becky finally shrugged, and said, "Because I'm Princess Rebecca of Deserae."

Laura's eyes widened. She looked as if she was about to curtsey. "You're Princess Rebecca? Really?"

"Oh, come now," said Mercredi. "Yesterday this young man told me he was Prince Kevin of Rassendas."

Laura looked at Kevin's dirty hands, grimy coveralls, and soot-streaked face. "Yeah, right."

"It's kind of a long story," explained Becky, "but if we don't recover the Ancient Artifact, I'll have to marry Lord Logan."

Laura frowned. "Isn't Lord Logan supposed to be a big, handsome, brave, heroic sort of guy?"

"Yes."

"And you *have* to marry him. Well, I can see that would be a problem all right."

"He's a jerk. I don't like him."

"There are also lives at stake here," put in Kevin. "Not that I'm criticizing your sense of priorities."

"If it's cloudy outside, Logan will attack at dawn," said Becky. "I learned that much before I left. But if it is sunny, he'll wait until midmorning. The men on the walls will be in the sunlight and make clear targets, while the men in the valley will be in shadow. So I don't know how much time we have."

Laura asked "Does Lord Logan know that Lord Voltmeter has a phlogistocator?"

"No. He knows that he has the Ancient Artifact, and of course he suspects that it is being used to power a Diabolical Device. But he doesn't know what sort of Diabolical Device it is."

"I heard that Thunk the Barbarian told him."

"Thunk never talked to Logan," said Kevin.

"He talked to us," said Becky. "But he died without going into much detail."

"Thunk is dead? The poor man. That is so sad."

"The best time to escape," said Kevin, "will be right at the beginning of the attack. We'll have to time it carefully. Too soon, and the guards will shoot us as we flee the walls. Too late, and we'll be caught in the phlogistocation field."

Laura looked around at her fellow prisoners, each with one wrist in a rigid iron cuff. She looked at the cage, with its massive padlock and iron bars set solidly into the hard stone wall. She looked at the thick oak door, with its own lock and heavy iron hinges. She said, "I think we have a hard task ahead of us to get out of here at all, without worrying about the timing."

"Oh, we have keys," said Becky.

"What?" said Laura.

"What?" repeated Mercredi.

"They're in that crack in the floor," said Kevin. "I got them from Valerie."

"From Valerie," said Laura. She gave him an odd look.

"Right. That crack by your foot. See if you can work the keys out."

Laura seemed doubtful, as though she thought Kevin and Becky were losing their grip on reality, but she slipped off one shoe and tried working her toes into the crack. "No," she said after a while. "The crack is too deep and too narrow. I can touch one, but I can't move it."

Becky, with a long stretch of her legs, could also reach the crack, but she also failed to make any progress with the keys. "We'll wait for our chance," said Kevin. "Don't be discouraged. Eventually they'll unhook us to feed us, or move us, or something."

The little group fell silent, as each person thought that, in all probability, they would simply be ignored until after the battle and then it would be too late. "How long have we been here?" said Laura. "It seems like we've been here a long time already. There's no window, so you can't see the light change."

"Time always passes slowly when you're in a dungeon," her father told her. "We haven't been here an hour. If you listen carefully, you can hear the clock strike in the Fortress tower."

Reflexively, they all fell silent, listening. They did not hear the clock strike. Instead, they heard the key turn in the door, then Valerie entered with a guard. "This one," she said, pointing to Laura. "Bring her to Lord Voltmeter. He's ready to interrogate her."

The guard unlocked Laura's wrist. Immediately she dropped to her knees. "No, not that," she screamed. "Anything but that!" She wrapped her arms around the guard's legs. "Please, have mercy. Don't take me to Lord Voltmeter." She pressed her face to the stone floor and sobbed out loud. "Please, I beg you."

The soldier grinned. Guarding prisoners was generally pretty dull work, but moments like this made it all worthwhile. Valerie was merely annoyed.

"Oh, for goodness sake." She grabbed Laura by her ponytail and yanked her to her feet. "Get a grip, will you? He's just going to question you. He doesn't have time for serious torture today."

She shoved Laura over to the guard, who twisted one arm behind her back and frog-marched her out the door, behind Valerie. They heard the key turn again, and the sound of Laura's wailing and sobbing gradually diminished as she was taken away. The remaining three prisoners continued to listen, until silence convinced them that no one else was coming. Then Kevin turned to Becky. "Did she get it?"

"Yes," said Becky. "They're both under my feet." She lifted her sandal and showed them the two keys, where Laura had slid them across the floor after snagging them from the crack.

"That was quick thinking," said Kevin. "She's a clever girl."

"That's my daughter," said Mercredi. "Her school gave her top marks for deportment and pluckiness."

Becky had slipped her foot out of her sandal and managed to wedge the key to the wrist cuffs between her toes. She swung her leg up and passed the key to Kevin.

"That was graceful."

"Thank you."

The Prince unlocked his wrist, rubbed it for a second, and freed his fellow prisoners. Becky took the second key and unlocked the cage. Mercredi tried the door, which was still locked. "We're a little better off, but we still have a problem."

Kevin pointed to the ceiling. "Ventilation shaft. It's only a short slide to the outside corridor. Becky will go first."

"Not yet," said Mercredi. "We have to wait until they bring back Laura."

"We can't wait. We'll have to come back for her."

"By the time they are done with her it may be impossible to come back."

"Right. So by the time she gets back it may also be too late for us to escape. That's why we have to leave now. When they bring her back they might put us under guard again."

Mercredi folded his arm. "I am not leaving without my daughter."

"He's right," said Becky. "We can't leave her behind. We'd be dead already if she hadn't come in."

"She'd want us to leave. She said she was willing risk her life."

"No!" said Mercredi.

"We can wait at least for a while," said Becky.

"All right!" said Kevin. "All right. Let me think." He paced around the small room. "No. Listen. We have to get you out of here. You're the Princess of Deserae, and there's too much danger for you to stay. Mercredi, if Voltmeter somehow defeats Logan, Deserae will need you to devise a counter to the phlogiston device. Once I see you two over the wall, I'll go back and rescue Laura. I've got the keys, and I know my way around the fortress somewhat. I won't leave without her, I swear."

"That's good," said Becky. "Because I won't leave without you, I swear."

"And I won't leave without Laura," said Mercredi.

Kevin sat down with his back against the stones. "Everyone wants to be a hero these days. That's why no one can."

"Keep your ears open," said Becky. "As soon as we hear someone coming, we need to get into position. What are you going to do to the guard?"

"Hide behind the door and hit him over the head as he comes in."

Mercredi said, "That doesn't sound very sporting. I thought hero types could just knock out a guard with a single punch to the jaw."

"Taylor doesn't recommend it. Even if you're built like Thunk the Barbarian, there's a good chance you'll just get a pissed-off guard with a broken jaw. Damn! I just thought of something. When the fortress fills with phlogiston, we won't be able to get back in and get the Ancient Artifact. The prophecy was right."

"What prophecy?" asked Becky.

"An old woman made a prophecy in the garden outside your castle. She said I wouldn't defeat the man in black or return the object I sought."

"Oh, those prophecies are always nonsense. Kevin, I'm surprised at you, paying attention to seers and soothsayers. It's nothing but a bunch of carnival show hokum. Only the gullible are taken in by that stuff. Who was it, anyway?"

"Mrs. Ancient," said Mercredi.

"Oh. She didn't happen to mention precious metal futures, did she?"

"No."

"Well, don't worry about it. Voltmeter isn't even wearing black clothing."

"What? Yes he is."

"Are you sure? I think it's more like a charcoal gray."

They waited. Then they waited some more. It was hard going for Kevin. Even under such dire circumstances, there were few men in the world who would object to spending time at close quarters with the Princess of Deserae, especially when she was wearing a torn blouse. Had there been but the two of them in that cell, Kevin could have passed the hours in fine good humor. Unfortunately, there was Mercredi. Mercredi was a professor of alchemy. That is, he was not one of your progressive, liberal, bohemian professors. He knew exactly what standards of decorum were expected of a princess in a fairy-tale kingdom, and he was one of those adults who considered it their responsibility to help young people ward off temptation. Furthermore, he was the father of a teenage girl. This meant he tended to treat all young men with the same benevolent warmth that a shepherd displays to a ravening wolf.

So Kevin sat well away from Becky and waited, while Becky gave him smoldering looks, and Mercredi shot him glowering stares. They heard the clock strike the hour. They told each other jokes. They told each other stories. They heard it strike another hour. They sat with their backs against the wall. They rose and paced around the room. They sat with their backs against the cage. They lay stretched out on the floor. Eventually the clock struck another hour.

"It must be broken," said Becky. "It must be more than an hour since it last struck."

"I wonder what he's doing to her," said Mercredi.

"Take a nap," said Kevin. "I'll stand watch." He took the torch down from the wall and gave it a few experimental swings, throwing a fast, flickering pattern of shadows against the wall. "I'll rouse you when I hear someone coming."

"I think not," said Mercredi. "I have responsibilities, too, you know. I can't allow you to take advantage of this young lady."

"Oh, you can trust Kevin."

"Right. I'm an honorable guy. And Becky and I have met before."

"I'm sure you have. And I can't help noticing that her bodice is ripped."

"Hey! That wasn't me!"

"Of course not. Now get back to your own corner."

"I can't sleep on this stone floor," said Becky. She rested her head on her arms. "Where do men like Voltmeter come from, anyway?"

"He's not even the worst," said Kevin. "Remember old

King Cravatte of Omnia? The guy before King Bruno?"

"Sure," said Mercredi. "I have a friend who was there. He told me about it."

"About what?"

"Cravatte somehow got into demonology and that sort of stuff," explained Kevin. "He announced that he was going to sacrifice a beautiful virgin to the Dark Gods."

"And what happened?"

"The largest bacchanal in recorded history," said Mercredi.

"Right. I mean, what did he think was going to happen? They say it was one hell of party. The night before the sacrifice, every babe in Omnia made sure to lose her virginity."

"And every woman who already lost it decided to lose it again," said Mercredi. "I'm told some of them lost it four or five times that night, just to be on the safe side."

"You two are making this up, right?"

"No, it's in the history books. You can look it up."

"So what did the King do?"

"Nothing. Lord Bruno saw his chance, and the next day Cravatte woke up dead. All his bodyguards, you see, were in town celebrating with the girls. Bruno correctly figured no man could stand to miss a debauch like that."

"It didn't hurt," added Mercredi, "that Bruno was passing out free beer and wine to the girls."

"For some reason my history tutors failed to mention this. That's a drawback of going to an all-girls school." Becky brushed some of the dirt off the floor. "I know some people can sleep anywhere, but I never could get comfortable on a hard surface," she said, and immediately fell asleep. And then woke up to the sound of a fight.

At first it was hard to see. The room was darker, and she was disoriented. The torch was lying on the floor. A thin line of flaming oil trailed across the stones, marking where the torch had rolled, so the struggling men were now lit from below, and their shadows traded blows across the ceiling. Mercredi was hunched in a corner, with his hands over his head. And Laura was back, standing in the open doorway, openmouthed, dumbfounded, and frozen. A burly guard had Kevin backed against the wall, holding him by the throat with one huge fist and hitting him with the other. For his part, Kevin had his fingers dug into the man's windpipe and was matching him blow for blow. But the guard was a professional soldier, one who had seen many fights and had long ago learned to shrug off injuries. His punches were brutal and methodical, while he didn't seem to even notice Kevin's fist.

All this Becky saw in an instant. It took her even less time to react. She sprang to her feet, seized the torch, and swung it against the guard's helmet with a resounding crack.

It didn't faze him in the least. He batted her away with an irritated look and resumed punching Kevin. Becky hit him again, and the third time had the presence of mind to hit him on the back of the neck. At which point the guard actually did topple over, though whether from Becky's blows, or Kevin's chokehold, or a combination of the two, it was hard to say. Kevin leaned against the wall, rubbing his throat and trying to speak. "Thanks," he panted.

Becky hugged him. "Thank you. You were very brave."

"Apparently you didn't notice I just got my face punched in."

Becky touched him lightly on his bruised lips. "That was why it was brave. Any man can jump into a fight when he knows he's going to win. Tackling someone who outweighs you takes more courage."

"She's a princess," Kevin told Mercredi and Laura. "They teach them to say supportive stuff like that."

Mercredi was already at the door. "That solves the problem of getting out of this room, anyway." He and Laura eased out warily, looking up and down the corridor. "This is the first time I've been down this far. I think they brought me this way."

"No," said Laura, "I'm sure the stairs are the other way."

Becky looked out the door also. "I'm not sure. I was surrounded by guards when they brought me down. I couldn't see where I was going."

"Actually, I couldn't see much either."

"Follow me," said Kevin. "I searched out all these levels when I was looking for Becky. The stairs are right over here."

He led the way, left out the door, taking a right turn, and going to the end of the corridor, where a narrow stair was set in a niche in the wall, not visible more than a few feet down the corridor. The stairwell was so narrow that Kevin's shoulders brushed the wall on both sides. The rest of the group followed him up, waiting while he paused at the top and looked cautiously around the corner. The coast was clear, so they followed him into another set of corridors, turning first left, then right, then left, and onto a broader set of stairs that opened into a somewhat wider corridor. "No guards so far. Where is everyone?"

"They're all out manning the walls," said Becky.

"Right. I forgot. We need to go up some more."

He opened a door marked AUTHORIZED PERSONNEL ONLY and went through, which brought them into another hallway with lamps hanging from the ceiling, then led them around a narrow, curved passage and down a half flight, then up a flight of stairs to another hallway with lots of doors leading into rooms of various sizes. "This is good. We are back at ground level."

"Are you certain? There are no windows."

"I remember going through these rooms."

"Then which is the way out?"

"We're getting there, Becky." He led them through one of the doors, into a passage with a ceiling so low they had to duck their heads. But presently this brought them to a much broader passage, one with parquet floors and tapestries on the walls. It had a door at the far end. Kevin stopped with his hand on the wood and the rest of the group piled up behind him.

"Okay," he whispered. "We're on our way. This door leads to the entrance hall and beyond that are the front doors, which open into the front courtyard, with the gate beyond that. Now once we're outside, we'll be targets for the archers on the walls; but I'm guessing they'll save their arrows for Logan's attack."

"Will there be guards in the courtyard and entrance hall?"

"I don't know about the entrance hall, Becky. We can expect the courtyard to be defended, but they'll be looking the other way, expecting danger to come from outside. So we'll move quickly. If there are only a few men here, we should be able to just rush past."

Becky, Mercredi, and finally Laura, just nodded.

"Okay," said Kevin. He twisted the knob. "Let's go." And then he shoved the door open and all four of them tumbled into the next room.

Which happened to be the gift shop.

Becky looked at Kevin. "It's like *déjà vu* all over again."

"Oh, look," said Laura. "This blouse is on sale."

"Damn, I wish I still had my notes." Kevin picked up a paperweight, a glass globe with a small model of the Fortress of Doom inside. He studied it while the flakes of artificial snow settled around the Fortress. "Okay, I think I know where I went wrong. We're not too far off. The entrance is really close to here."

"I'm sure," said Becky. "And I know just how to get there. Follow me."

Kevin eyed her doubtfully. "You said they hauled you straight off to the dungeon. When did you get a chance to learn your way around the fortress?"

"I didn't," said Becky. "But now we have this." She plucked a large, gaily colored brochure from a counter. She unfolded it so the rest of the group could see the title—printed in a hokey, gothic sort of script—that read *Tourist Guide to the Fortress of Doom*. Then she flipped it over to show the back. "It has a map in it."

"Great! Just what we need. Let me see it."

Becky held it out of Kevin's reach. "It's mine. I found it. I get to lead us out of here."

"I just want to take a look at it."

"Ha! You just think a girl can't read a map."

"I didn't say that."

"Just follow me, and you'll find out."

"If we don't get a move on," said Mercredi, "you two won't have any breath to argue with. Your Highness, I would follow you anywhere, but preferably out of this fortress."

"This way," said Becky. She chose one of the doors, pulled it open, and checked the hallway. It was still clear. She consulted the map. "Left."

She led them down the hallway, into another hallway, up a long flight of stairs, along another hallway, down a short spiral of stairs, and into a large room. She pointed at one wall, painted in a pastoral scene with a handsome shepherd tending his flock. "That's south."

"How can you tell?"

Becky read from the brochure. " 'Pause to admire the fresco on the south wall, one of the earliest known works of Antonio Calivetti.' There's the fresco, so that must be the south wall."

"Okay. But now we're off the ground floor?"

"Right."

"Where do we go to next?"

"First we have to pause to admire the fresco."

"Sure, Becky. Maybe after the battle we can check out the artwork. Right now I think our top priority ought to be getting out of here."

"Stop telling me what to do, Kevin Timberline!" Becky's voice was high and edgy, on the brink of hysteria. Kevin realized the strain of the past few days was catching up with her. "These are my directions, and they say to *pause to admire the fresco!*"

"Right, right. Pause to admire the fresco. What a lovely fresco. Note the depth of color, the chiaroscuro, the almost impressionistic interplay of light and shadow. Magnificent."

"I like horse pictures," said Laura.

Becky read again from the brochure. "The shepherd was modeled after the son of Calivetti's patron, the Duke of Fortescue."

"His eyes are really pretty," said Laura. "They seem to follow you around the room."

"Because the artist made the eyes the center of perspective," said Mercredi.

"I'm deeply moved by this painting," said Kevin. "Now, Becky, could we please move on?"

They moved on to the next exhibit, because Becky insisted on doggedly following the map step by step. "If we follow the tour, it will end at an exit. If we deviate from it, we'll only get lost again." There was no choice but to follow her. And Kevin had to admit he was totally lost. None of these rooms looked familiar to him. Laura had not been inside the fortress before. Mercredi, though he had been working there for several months, had only been allowed in the area around his lab. Even then he had often been under guard, with little chance to explore.

So they trailed behind the Princess, dutifully admiring an elaborately carved banister, twenty steps high, yet built from a single piece of bird's-eye maple. They nodded respectfully at a pair of antique mirrors in gilt frames (work of an unknown craftsman), gazed upon several stained-glass windows (impossible to see out of, unfortunately) and did a quick critique of a floor-to-ceiling depiction of— according to the brochure—the Diet of Lohengrin-Fatima, which showed several dozen cardinals in red robes gathered around an altar.

Mercredi let his eyes drift across the portly figures. "Just the types you'd expect to find at a Lo-Fat Diet."

"Cute," said Kevin. "If we could go on?"

The next stop brought them back down to a lower floor. Kevin looked around. "Are we back on the ground floor?"

"It all looks the same," said Laura.

Becky looked up from the map. "Yes, it's the ground floor. Just one last pen-and-ink, and we're out of here." Kevin was doubtful at first. All the halls on this section of the castle tended to look the same, and after the last sketch (*Portrait of the Countess de Werque* by Francois Delouard) there were no more tourist points of interest to orient themselves to the map. Then they had to hide in an unlocked room to avoid a group of soldiers moving through the fort-ress. When this happened for the third time he became con-vinced that Becky was right, and they really were on the ground floor, or at least a floor with access to the outer walls. Eventually their path was clear of soldiers. Becky brought them to another door. It was unmarked, heavy and solid. She waved for them to gather close by.

"Now *this* is the door to the entrance hall," she whis-pered, tapping the map. "And the plan is the same as Kevin said before. There will probably be guards inside, so our best chance is to rush for the door. Keep running and don't stop. Everybody with me on this?"

They all nodded. Becky's hand tightened on the door handle. "Let's go."

She flung the door open and they all rushed through. And stopped. They were back in the gift shop.

"The map is wrong." Becky threw it on the floor. She stamped over to a table and sat down to scowl at a rack of postcards.

Kevin sat down next to her and put his arm over her shoulders. "I'm sure it is," he said gently.

"Well it is, dammit! I read the map right. It's just wrong. I'll bet that isn't a genuine Calivetti either. Calivetti never used tempera."

"Never mind," said Mercredi. "I have it figured out. Fol-low me." He turned and went back out the door.

Becky pouted and didn't move. Kevin had to drag her by the arm. "Mercredi, wait," he said. "How do you know? Where are we going?"

"I'm a fool," said the alchemist, striding briskly, his fin-gers gripping the lapels of his laboratory coat. "I should have seen it the moment we started." He turned left around a corner. "I've been here for months, but mostly they kept me in the area around my lab, so I didn't realize it. But after taking that tour it becomes obvious." He turned another corner, going left again.

"What does?" The Prince was exasperated.

"The layout of the Fortress of Doom. We've all noted how it feels like we're living in a maze. All these turns and blind hallways and dead ends. Well, I maintain that it *is* a maze. It was probably built that way to confuse invaders. The floor plan is patterned on a maze and like any maze, all we have to do . . ."

"Is keep turning in the same direction," Kevin finished with him. They went around the next corner together, the two girls trailing behind.

"Exactly. Come in the front entrance, keep turning in the same direction—it doesn't matter whether it is right or left—and eventually you will come back to the front entrance. Similarly, put your hand against any interior wall"— here he paused to slap his palm against the stone—"and keep turning right or left from there. Trace the same hand along the wall, and you will trace the entire perimeter and reach the center."

"But we don't want to get to the center," objected Becky.

"Continuing from the center will bring you back to the entrance. But I believe we were already past the center when we started—we've been moving outward, not inward—so we'll reach the door to the Fortress next." Mercredi was completely sure of himself now, speaking in his college professor's lecturing tone. He was also walking faster and faster as he spoke, until he simply broke into a run. "Left." The others hastened to catch up with him. "Left, and another left." He skirted a staircase, breathing heavily. "And left again."

"Aha." A door appeared in front of him. He slowed his

pace. "And here is our way out. There's no need for maps
or memorization to escape a maze. A simple knowledge of
design and a little bit of common sense is all it takes." He
grabbed the door handle and pulled it open. "Quickly
now." And with Kevin at his side, and Becky and Laura
right behind him, he strolled boldly right back into the gift
shop.

This time it was not empty. It was half-filled with soldiers, and they were armed. There were at least four of
them covering each and every door to the room. They had
pushed back the shelves to give themselves space to fight.
Sunlight came in through the high windows and showed as
gleaming white lines on the finely honed steel blades of
their drawn weapons. They did not look as though they
were in any sort of a good mood.

"Um," said Mercredi. "We must have missed a turn."

The guards stepped forward. Kevin felt pinpricks as the
points of a dozen swords and spears penetrated his clothing.
He looked around the circle of brutal, unsmiling men.
Slowly and carefully he raised his hands over his head.
Becky, Laura, and Mercredi all did the same; but once again
the guards seemed to identify Kevin as the most likely
source of trouble. They closed in with their weapons until
Kevin was backed against a wall. And then they held him
there while a thin, ascetic figure pushed his way to the front.

"Really, Prince Kevin Timberline of Rassendas," said
Stan, "I am surprised at you. Surely you must have visited an
historic old castle before. Have you never realized they're all
designed the same way? It's impossible to exit without going
through the gift shop."

> If an opportunity comes to stab the Evil Overlord in
> the back, you must do so without hesitation. When
> innocent lives are at stake, the practical hero does
> not "give him a sporting chance."
>
> —*HANDBOOK OF PRACTICAL HEROICS*
> BY ROBERT TAYLOR

Logan rode his horse up and down the lines. The men
were at attention, but as he approached, they straightened
their shoulders just a little bit more, and after he passed
by they would start talking to each other from the sides of
their mouths. That was good. It meant morale was high.
Depressed men didn't chatter much.

"Have you ever been in battle before, Sam?"

"No, sir," Bigelow admitted.

"Nervous?"

"Not at all, sir."

"You look like you spent a sleepless night."

Bigelow was wearing his breastplate and metal gauntlets,

but he still had his helmet under his arm. His hair was tousled and his eyes were bloodshot. "Ah . . . I was . . . I'm fine, sir."

"That was a good report you sent. You were up late writing it?"

"Um, yes, sir. That was it, sir."

"Hmm." Logan looked up at the Fortress. To other people it reeked of evil and despair, but to Logan it was merely an obstacle. A man sees the world differently when he has an army behind him. "The townspeople are quite certain he's up there?"

"Oh, yes, sir. See that round tower, the new one? They say he often stands at one of the windows and looks over the valley. They see him all the time, dressed in a black cloak. Or possibly midnight blue. They weren't sure."

"Really? All right, Sam. Thank you. You may rejoin your unit now." Logan didn't wait for Bigelow to leave. He reined his horse around, gave it a little spur, and trotted it over to the lines of archers. He summoned the fire control officer. "You see that line of windows on the tower? No, don't point to them, just glance casually over."

The officer let his gaze sweep across the walls and the men massed atop them. "I see them, sir."

"Take half a dozen of your best archers and set them to concentrate their fire on those windows. If anyone appears at one of those windows, especially a man in a black cloak, I want him taken out."

"Yes, sir."

Logan wheeled his horse around again and resumed his inspection. The men were in full fine fettle. The ground was damp but firm, perfect for maneuvering. A light wind made the regimental banners flap. The band was tuning up. The townspeople were gathering on the hillside, where they would be in a good position to watch the fighting, then come down and loot the bodies afterward.

Logan looked up at the Fortress again. The sky was absolutely clear. The sun was over the mountains, and the tower was catching the rays. It didn't illuminate it, for it seemed no amount of sunlight could escape that flat black stone, but it did glimmer off the windows. In a short time it would be shining on the walls and into the faces of the soldiers who manned them. Then Logan would start the attack.

He smiled. It was a lovely day for battle.

"Damn. I knew that stuff about the exit," said Kevin. "I don't know why I didn't remember it."

Stan was being careful with his prisoners now. A full dozen of Voltmeter's soldiers, their weapons drawn, surrounded the escapees. Stan led them back into the depths of the fortress, with Kevin reluctantly at his side and four guards behind them. Then came Becky, Laura, and Mercredi, prodded along at spearpoint by the remaining eight soldiers. The constant jabs kept them all moving briskly, while adding insult to the injury of being captured once again. They wended their way through the wide halls and up the narrow stairs of the fortress. The mazelike design became more and more obvious. Stan didn't have a weapon himself. Instead he carried a clipboard. He talked to Kevin as they walked.

"By the way, that trick of always turning in the same direction doesn't work either. It works on the classical designs, but in a newer maze it will only keep bringing you around to the same spot."

"Thanks, I'll keep that in mind for future maze running."

"I don't see why you keep on trying to play the hero, Timberline. Why should you care who rules Deserae?"

"I have an aversion to seeing innocent people slaughtered."

"They won't be slaughtered if they surrender without a fight. After what you see here today, you can persuade Calephon to abdicate. Put that diplomatic training to good use."

"If you're counting on my help, you're going to be disappointed."

"I've studied your dossier, Timberline. You're being forced by your father to marry Princess Rebecca. I suppose you're trying to win her hand with these heroic antics."

Kevin's silence confirmed his guess. Stan looked smug. "The Princess Rebecca. She's the one they call the Ice Princess, isn't she? Frankly, I should think you would be glad to be out of it."

"It's complicated," admitted Kevin.

They reached the forbidding oak door of the central chamber. Stan paused to look back over the other prisoners. "If I were you," he said quietly, "I'd forget about the Ice Princess and make a play for that barbarian babe. She seems more your type. And it's obvious she likes you."

"Stan," said the Prince, "you're a smart man. But you don't know as much as you think."

Stan shrugged. "Too late now." He opened the door.

The soldiers pushed them through. This was unnecessary, as they made no resistance, but pushing people around is part of the job when you're a soldier to an Evil Overlord, and Voltmeter's guards were well trained. The prisoners stumbled inside. Immediately, Kevin felt the curious lethargy, the inability to resist, that he had previously felt in the Overlord's presence. Once they were inside, Stan dismissed the soldiers. "They are under Lord Voltmeter's power. There is no need to stick around. Go and man the battlements. The attack is about to begin."

The guards disappeared. Kevin willed his body to make a run for the door, but it continued to carry him forward, and Stan closed the door behind the soldiers. In the center of the room, the phlogistocator sat silently. On top of the gleaming stack of copper and brass tubing, astride a massive black iron boiler, almost at the ceiling, rested the Ancient Artifact. Next to it was a small round platform that held only a large T-switch. A metal ladder led up to the platform.

At Voltmeter's back was a long table stacked with swords, knives, crossbows, arrows, bolts, and other assorted weapons. Kevin suspected Voltmeter laid them out as some sort of psychological torture, knowing that the Prince would long to grab a sword and slice off the Overlord's head. Indeed, Kevin tried to do exactly that. But the four captives could only look at the weapons helplessly.

The Evil Overlord was staring out one of the casement windows, squinting into the bright sunlight. He spoke without turning around, and without a trace of surprise. "So glad you could join us, Your Highness. I believe your friend Lord Logan is about to make his move. Would you care to have a look?"

The Prince stepped sluggishly forward and looked down. Becky looked over his shoulder. Below her, Voltmeter's mercenaries were massing on the Fortress walls. Yesterday Kevin had told her their ranks were thin, but today there seemed to be plenty enough. Beyond them, in the valley below, were the neat lines of Logan's army. They had crossed the stream and were assembled on the fields before the cliff, flying the flags of Deserae and Angostura. From the tower they seemed small and vulnerable. Her heart went out to them. The path that switchbacked up the cliff face was long and steep, and the attackers would be exposed to a constant rain of arrows. Upon reaching the top, they would be confronted by the heavy doors and sheer walls of the Fortress itself. Even if those were breached, there would still be Voltmeter's well-trained and well-armed soldiers to contend with. The attackers had no siege engines or rams—it would be pointless to try to get them up that cliff.

The door opened, and Valerie entered. She had changed back into her black leather bustier, then added a pair of calf-high boots over skintight leather pants. She had also touched up her hair and reapplied her red lipstick. In one hand she carried Thunk's sword. The frumpy dress was draped over her other arm. Stan looked the leather clothing up and down and gave her a disapproving frown. The two girls, who appeared pretty bedraggled after their night in the cell, stared at her resentfully. Valerie ignored them all. She put Thunk's sword on the table, gave the Prince a calculating look, and stood beside the Chief Minion.

A flicker of something black moved in Kevin's peripheral vision. He turned back to the window. An armored knight was riding along the ranks of archers. His shield and breastplate were lacquered in deep, glossy black, and a plume of rich black feathers sprang from his helmet. His horse, draped in black silks, was massive. And more riders were circulating through the massed troops, calling out orders, assigning positions, directing movements. As their paths crossed back and forth it was impossible to get an exact count of them. Kevin did not have to be told who they were. He recognized them immediately, as did every man on the Fortress walls. They were the Black Guards.

He felt like cheering for them. This battle would not be one-sided. He could see down to the field, where Logan had assembled his archers. Already the men were fitting arrows to their longbows. Despite the cliff, the Fortress walls were within reach of those weapons. They would lay down a continuous barrage, keeping Voltmeter's men under cover while Deserae's soldiers stormed the Fortress. The foot soldiers were strong, fast, and efficient. The trail up the cliffs was steep all right, but men carrying siege ladders would rush it under the protection of the longbows. Once at the base of the walls, short bows and crossbows would drive the defenders away from the battlements, while the infantry scaled the ladders. They would go over the top with swinging swords and axes. Blood would flow.

Logan was an experienced commander. Kevin knew there was a very good chance the Black Guards would take the walls successfully.

"What a lovely day for battle," said Voltmeter. And he laughed again, that staccato, patented, Evil Overlord's laugh. "The sun glinting off all their bright little buttons, their banners fluttering in the gentle breeze. I almost wish I could pack a hamper and go out for a picnic." There was not the least trace of concern in his voice. Kevin turned his head and saw that Becky was looking at the Diabolical Device. It filled the tower, not only with its actual bulk but with its malevolent presence, like a huge predator waiting to feast.

Logan, on a black charger of his own, paraded before the men, giving his prebattle speech. The soldiers cheered. The band struck up a bright marching tune—the incongruously cheerful "Whiskey in the Jar." Voltmeter's men were looking distinctly nervous. When a man knew he was about to fight the Black Guards, it tended to sap his confidence.

"Music, too. How very pleasant." Voltmeter turned. "Stan, go downstairs and join the defenders. I want you to collect data for the calibrations. Girls, please step to the windows. Today history will be made. I should hate for you to miss it. Professor Mercredi, would you be so good as to mount the ladder and prepare to throw the switch on my command?"

Mercredi was no more capable of refusing than Kevin was. The fear showed plainly on his face as his body made him climb the ladder. He pulled himself onto the platform and crawled over to the switch. Voltmeter waited until his shaking hands were curled around the switch handle before reassuring him. "Oh, no need to worry, Professor. I took the liberty of switching the polarity back to its original settings. We're quite safe here from the phlogiston field."

Kevin gave Mercredi a look. Mercredi returned it. "Well, of course *he* can do it," the alchemist called down defensively. "He's an Evil Genius. I never said it was impossible. I just said it wouldn't be easy."

"I didn't say a word," said Kevin.

Mercredi stood by the ladder. Stan left to rejoin the soldiers. Laura stepped forward and stood to one side of Voltmeter. Becky summoned every ounce of will she had to resist Voltmeter's command, but slowly her feet dragged her to a window. Outside, Voltmeter's archers nocked their arrows. Down in the valley, Logan's archers released their first round. But not at the Fortress. Instead, the arrows struck the cliff wall, broke, and fell upon the trail. Black smoke issued from them.

Smudge pots, thought Kevin. *Logan is trying to create a smoke screen along the trail, so his men will be harder to hit.*

There was a sudden clatter outside the windows. A second flight of arrows had struck the battlements. Voltmeter's men ducked behind the parapets. Logan's men began to flow up the cliff, a double file that moved with surprising speed against the steepness of the trail. Dispersed within the column were the Black Guards, letting their armor block the arrows to protect the men behind. Even Voltmeter was impressed.

"Strong men," he observed. "And well disciplined."

Another flight of arrows struck the Fortress of Doom, and more followed. Rising from the shadowy valley, they were nearly invisible until they suddenly flashed into sunlight, then they were lost in the glare. Voltmeter's men stayed down behind the walls, holding shields over their heads. One of them, less careful than the rest, suddenly staggered back with a narrow shaft of oak protruding from his left shoulder. Voltmeter leaned out the window to get a better look. "Can't see a thing down . . . GET DOWN!"

Compelled to obey, Kevin, Becky, and Laura dropped instantly to the floor. Voltmeter spun away from the window just as four arrows came through simultaneously—one even passing through his cloak—to miss him and clatter on the stone floor. Two more came through Kevin's window and zipped over his head, breaking harmlessly on the Diabolical Device.

Voltmeter laughed. "Very nice, Lord Logan. Very nicely done indeed." Still another arrow came through the window and struck the floor at his feet. "Well, I think that's enough of that. Professor Mercredi, be so good as to activate the phlogistocator."

Mercredi responded with a hostile look but reluctantly threw the switch.

Nothing happened.

Well, of course nothing appears *to be happening,* Kevin told himself. *Phlogiston is invisible, after all. You can't see phlogiston, you can only see its effects.* Still, he expected the machine to do *something.* Hum, click, whir, rattle, make high-pitched beeping noises, emit puffs of steam, or at the very least, glow with an unearthly green light. The massive machine made no more movement than a pile of scrap metal. Any activity was on the inside, and apparently very quiet. There were a few dials at the top that Mercredi seemed to study, but Kevin couldn't tell what they showed, if anything. Voltmeter wasn't looking at the Diabolical Device at all. He had returned to the window, apparently with no fear of another arrow.

Kevin went back to the window himself. Logan's men were fast. The first of them had nearly reached the top of the cliff path. They were breathing hard, gasping for breath, but did that mean anything? They had just charged up a steep trail with weapons and siege ladders. Of course they would be out of breath.

Then the smudge pots went out.

The smoke cleared away. And down in the valley, the archers began breathing hard also. The barrage of arrows had already stopped, and the men were putting down their bows. The officers were exchanging puzzled looks.

On the Fortress walls, Stan told the officers to hold their fire. The officers relayed the command to the men, and the shouted orders traveled along the battlements.

Now all the men along the cliff path stopped their charge. Swords, axes, and ladders dropped to the ground. Most men put their heads back, mouths open wide, drawing great breaths, desperately trying to suck in air that just didn't seem to be there anymore. Others frantically tore open their collars. A few clutched their throats. The man closest to the

Fortress walls took a step forward, tripped over the ladder he had just dropped, and fell to the ground. He didn't get up. A moment later his partner was lying beside him. The scene was repeated down the line. Even the horses swayed and fell.

"Excellent results," said Voltmeter. He clapped his hands lightly. "Just what you predicted, Professor Mercredi. It's rather a shame they broke ranks, don't you think? It would have been so nice to see them all topple in a row, like dominoes."

They were too brave, thought Kevin. *If only they had retreated. If only they had fled.*

The Evil Overlord was hanging out the window, shielding his eyes with one hand. Becky casually drifted to one side of the table of weapons, where Thunk's sword lay. Laura noticed her. She looked at Voltmeter and Valerie, both preoccupied with the battle outside, and she, too, edged away from the Overlord, to the other side of the table. Kevin was careful not to look at the girls at all. Instead he put his head out of his window and kept Voltmeter's attention. "You fiend, you'll pay for this."

"How trite, Timberline. Was that phrase in your little book?"

"Yeah, it was. But my dad has plenty of sorcerers and alchemists of his own. And so do Deserae and Angostura. They'll devise a counter to your damn machine, and the next attack will succeed."

Becky wrapped her fingers around the hilt of Thunk's sword.

"They won't have time," said Voltmeter. "This is the prototype. We have also built a portable phlogistocator, small enough to fit on a wagon. We only need this test to calibrate it. Then my legions will march forth from this castle, the phlogistocator leading the way, pushing before it a wave of death that no plague could ever match. Deserae will be mine within days. Angostura will be next, then Rassendas. In a month I will control the Twenty Kingdoms. Your armies will be helpless to do anything. Except bury their dead."

Carefully, silently, Becky slid the barbarian sword out of its scabbard. Across the table, Laura eased a crossbow from the pile of weapons and fitted a bolt to it.

"Oh, look at this," said Voltmeter. He pointed over the walls. A lone knight, not one of the Black Guards, was staggering up the cliff trail. He had discarded his helmet, and the agony on his face was plain to see. His chest heaved with the effort of drawing each breath—Kevin could hear his labored gasps even from the tower—but still the knight kept coming. His hair was soaked with sweat and beads of it stood out on his forehead. He had thrown his sword away. In one hand he held a short bow he had picked up. The other hand held a single arrow. At the top of the trail he looked to the tower windows, and clearly he recognized the Evil Overlord, for he fitted the arrow to his bow.

And in a single horrifying moment, as the knight raised his eyes to the tower, Kevin recognized him. *Oh my God,* he thought. *It's Sam Bigelow.*

The Evil Overlord made no effort to move from the open window. He stood motionless, a fully framed target, with a slight smile playing on his face. His mercenaries stood up, looking at the knight at the base of the wall, at Voltmeter in the window of the tower, and back to the knight again. And Bigelow, swaying on his feet, his vision swimming, tried to take aim. Twice he raised the bow, and twice he lowered it.

Please, thought Kevin. *Do it, Sam.*

Bigelow dropped to one knee and in that position was able to steady himself. He drew the bow and aimed again.

And then he collapsed, falling to one side, the arrow skittering harmlessly along the wall.

"What a commendable display of courage," said Voltmeter. "I did enjoy that. You may be familiar with the saying, 'A single death is a tragedy, a million deaths is a statistic.' I can say truthfully that the valiant death of that lone soldier has amused me more than the destruction of all the rest of Logan's forces."

"Die, you bastard!" screamed Becky. Voltmeter swung around just in time to see the blond princess leap at him, the barbarian's sword high over her head and swinging downward. There was no time for him to move. The heavy steel blade was but an instant away from cleaving his skull. Becky's face was red with fury, but triumph was shining in her eyes.

Laura shot her in the heart.

Kevin's world ended.

His brain screamed, "Becky!" but he didn't hear the word come out of his mouth, didn't hear her short gasp of pain, didn't hear the hero's sword slip from her hand and clatter to the floor, didn't hear anything but the rush of blood pounding in his ears. He saw her knees buckle and her body pitch forward as if in slow motion. He caught her before she hit the floor and cradled her head in his arms. The blue eyes were rolled back in her head. The beautiful lips were slack. There were drops of water on her face, and Kevin only dimly realized that they were his own tears.

"Such language," said Voltmeter. "So unbecoming a princess."

He waved a hand dismissively and turned back to the window. Kevin looked up dully. Valerie stood still, too surprised to react, the absurd wool dress still draped over her arm. "Princess?" she said. She heard a clicking noise. Laura had calmly braced the crossbow against the table and ratcheted back the cocking lever.

"You."

"Me," said Laura. She fitted another bolt into the crossbow.

"You've changed sides."

"Not at all. I've been with Stevie all along. He just put me in the dungeon as a trick, so the others would reveal what they knew about Logan. There wasn't time for torture, you see. Learning that Daddy switched the polarity of the Diabolical Device was a nice bonus."

"Stevie?" Valerie was doubly stunned. "You call Lord Voltmeter Stevie?"

"I've been with His Lordship ever since he first heard of my father's invention. That's when he offered me the job of Evil Assistant."

"*I'm* Lord Voltmeter's Evil Assistant!"

"Ah," said Laura. "We do have a problem there, don't we?"

"You can't be an Evil Assistant. You're spunky! You have freckles! An Evil Overlord can't have a spunky, freckled Evil Assistant!"

"He can't have a disloyal one either."

"He doesn't!"

"Doesn't he, Valerie? You know what I'm talking about." Valerie shut up.

"Up to now," Laura continued smoothly, "I'm afraid that Stevie hasn't been quite satisfied with my devotion. He insisted that I prove my loyalty. You know how Overlords feel about loyalty. And I'm sure you know the penalty for disloyalty." She sighed theatrically. "Trust. So important to

a relationship, so difficult to earn. Now I wonder what sort
of test will make him happy?" She put a finger to a pretty
cheek in thought. Then her smile brightened. "Ah," she
said again. "This should satisfy him."

And in a second she swung the crossbow to her shoulder,
turned toward the ceiling, and fired. The quick shot was
deadly accurate—Mercredi fell almost instantly. His face
showed only a fleeting expression of surprise, an equally
fleeting grimace of pain, and he toppled off the platform,
his body turning over once before it hit the floor with a wet
thud.

"My God!" said Valerie.

"He betrayed Lord Voltmeter. You know the penalty."

"You killed your own father! That is so . . . so . . ."

"Evil?" Laura cocked the crossbow again. "You're too
old for this game, Valerie. You lost your edge, went soft on
us. The killer instinct has faded, I'm afraid. You even allowed Thunk to escape. You thought His Lordship didn't
know. But he did." She reached for another bolt.

If there was one thing that could be said about Valerie,
one rule that described her life, an epitaph to be engraved
on her tombstone, it was that she was a girl who saw her
chances and took them. The wool dress slipped from her
arm. Underneath was Kevin's sword.

"Your Highness," she screamed, and flung the sword.
Without even looking at her, Kevin caught it with one
hand. Gently he laid Becky's head on the floor. Carefully,
he stood up. His eyes burned with hatred. Voltmeter had
already turned away from the window. The Evil Overlord
swept his cloak back, drew his saber and waited, with a be-
mused expression, for Kevin to make his move.

Kevin drew his sword.

Voltmeter's expression changed.

* * *

Laura locked her eyes on Valerie while her hand
scrabbled on the table for another bolt. *She's trying
to stare me down,* thought Valerie. *Trying to fix me rigid.*
She spun and threw a kick at the younger girl's head.
Laura dropped the bolt and calmly stepped aside, let the
spiked heel whip past her face, then reversed the crossbow, stepped in, and slammed the butt into Valerie's stomach. Valerie doubled over. Laura knocked her down with a
blow to the head. Valerie's vision blurred as she hit the
floor. Then it cleared, and she saw the crossbow bolt in
front of her face. She reached for it. Laura's foot smashed
down on her hand.

"Not bad for your age," said the redheaded girl. She
pried the bolt from Valerie's nerveless fingers. "Not much
of a fight, but at least you tried. I expected you to make a
run for it."

Valerie swung at her face. Laura blocked her fist with
the crossbow, then kicked her twice in the side, causing her
to curl up in pain. When she looked up again Laura had the
crossbow loaded and cocked and aimed at her face. "Get
up," said Laura.

Valerie lay still. "Get up," said Laura again. "This is too
easy." Slowly, sullenly, Valerie stood up. "There's the door.
Run for it. I want a moving target this time."

Valerie didn't even look at the door. With a great show
of disdain she bent over and dusted the knees of her leather
pants. Then she planted her feet firmly on the floor, crossed
her arms, and glared at Laura defiantly.

"Go on," said Laura. "You might make it."

Valerie didn't move. She stared into Laura's eyes and
her expression radiated pure disgust, but she said nothing.

"Suit yourself." Laura's finger was tightening on the trigger when she felt a surprise tap on her shoulder. She snapped her head around quickly, but not quickly enough. She had time to catch only a glimpse. A glimpse of a fluid mass of blond curls, surrounding a pair of very angry blue eyes. And a glimpse of a fist, a small fist, clenched very tightly, coming very fast, straight at her chin.

Who the hell, she thought—and it was her last thought before blackness closed in—*wears a chain-mail bra?*

"That," said Voltmeter, "is not a hero's sword."

Of all weapons of single combat, there is perhaps nothing quite so nasty as the dueling saber. It's the preferred weapon of Evil Overlords everywhere. Voltmeter was an expert with it. The dueling saber is not like the cavalry saber. The cavalry saber is a heavy piece of rigid steel, designed to run an opponent through at high speed, curved so the blade can be withdrawn easily from horseback. The dueling saber, on the other hand, is a straight piece of light metal with a thin, ultrasharp blade. In action, it can accurately be compared to a flying razor. The dueling saber is not meant to kill an enemy quickly and cleanly. It's best used to slash an opponent and let him bleed to death. In the hands of a master, it truly becomes the death by a thousand cuts.

It was also the weapon that Kevin drew now. He held it point down, in a low guard, and faced Voltmeter full on. "I guess I'm not a hero then. But everyone has been telling me that anyway."

"It is the type of sword an Evil Overlord uses."

"Glad to hear it. When you're dead I'll have a matching set." Voltmeter, with his sword arm held at side guard, was moving in a wide circle, forcing Kevin to keep turning to face him. Kevin was ready. He stepped forward with each turn, gradually closing the distance between himself and the Overlord.

"You miss the point, my young friend. A man's choice of weapon says a lot about his character."

"Oh, stow it," said Kevin. "This is all in the book. Standard practice before we begin the final duel, eh? This is when you say something like, 'We are not so different, you and I,' and suggest that I join you. That's what you were about to do, right?"

"As a matter of fact, yes. But there is a reason why the standard practice becomes the standard practice. You have a lot to gain by joining me." In truth, Voltmeter really did have a "we are not so different speech." But he wrote it to use on Logan. He had little use for Kevin and no intention of sparing him. He was just trying to keep his opponent distracted with talk.

Kevin wasn't fooled. He attacked.

Becky kicked the crossbow away from the fallen girl. She took Valerie by the shoulder. "Tie her up," she said, pushing her at the feebly stirring Laura. "I'll take care of the phlogistocator." She seized the hero's sword, shoved it into the scabbard, and ran for the tall ladder.

"But Lord Voltmeter?"

Becky looked toward the windows, where the two men were squaring off for combat. "Kevin will deal with him." She slung the sword over her back, kicked Mercredi's body aside, and started up the ladder. A faint blue spark snapped her hand when she touched the metal. This close to the machine, she could hear a faint hum, and some sort of power was making the hair on the back of her neck stand up.

Halfway to the top she looked down. "Valerie, what are you doing? Just tie her hands."

In the short space of time, Valerie had somehow managed to bind Laura's arms with leather straps, lock a collar around her neck, and was now trying to force a rubber ball gag into the girl's unwilling mouth. "You play your way," she told Becky, "and I play my way."

Becky gave a mental shrug and kept climbing. The faint hum was slightly louder at the top, and the needles on the dials were slowly creeping upward. Her hair floated wildly around her head and made crackling sounds. She clambered across the platform and grabbed the giant T-switch with both hands. Then she hesitated. From the platform, she could see out all the windows to the outside grounds, where soldiers were still struggling and gasping like cod on a hot deck. Forty feet below, Kevin and Voltmeter were clashing swords.

"Throw the switch," called Valerie. "What are you waiting for?"

"I can't," said Becky.

It is not impossible for a swordfighting novice to beat a master swordsman. In fact, it is possible in any sort of martial art, be it swordfighting, boxing, wrestling, karate, or jujitsu. The pros don't like to admit it, but it does occur; and it's not even particularly rare. That's why they tend to stick to tournaments and not let themselves get drawn into street fights. The expert knows a great many advanced techniques. Experience and training have made every motion fluid and precise—and sometimes deadly—but in any given match the expert may only use a few moves. Often a single move is all that is needed to win.

The beginner will only know a few moves. But if he

knows them very well, and when he's young and very fast—well, more than one master swordsman has gone down in private duel.

Unfortunately, this did not happen with Kevin.

In truth, Kevin was not very good with a sword. He was indeed young, and quite fast, and what little he knew about saber technique, he knew very well, and that was all that kept Voltmeter from killing him in two strokes. From the first stroke he was on the defensive. Within minutes he was cut in a dozen places. Blood ran down his arms and spattered on his face. He ignored it, as he ignored the pain. His hands were a blur of motion as he sought to parry the Overlord's blows.

"You cannot defeat me," said Voltmeter.

"Don't have to," said Kevin. "Becky, pull the switch!"

Becky stood motionless, watching in horrified fascination. Down below, the two men were surrounded by arcs of glimmering light, reflected from the flashing blades. Valerie watched, too, half-hypnotized by the twirling action and rapid, dancelike footwork. (Saber duels are great for impressing babes—that was why Kevin chose to study it.) The ringing of the blades, echoing off the bare stone walls, filled the room.

Valerie tore her eyes from the two men and looked up at the platform. Becky was looking from the men to the windows, back and forth. "Becky, pull the switch."

"I can't," said Becky. "He'll die."

Valerie realized what she meant. The phlogistocator neutralized any magical power inside the castle walls. That was why they could still breathe. But it also meant that Voltmeter's defensive spell wouldn't work. If Becky turned it off, the men outside would be saved, but Voltmeter could paralyze Kevin with a thought. He'd kill the Prince in a second.

She ran to the windows. Most of the soldiers were still

struggling on the ground. Some of them were completely motionless. Stan was leaning over the parapet, taking notes, unaware of the battle going on in the central chamber. Voltmeter's own men had sheathed their weapons and were simply watching in silence. "Becky, there's no time left. The soldiers are almost dead! You've got to shut down the machine now!"

"But Kevin!"

"Yes, throw the switch," sneered Voltmeter. The tip of his blade drew a line of red across Kevin's chest. "It matters not to me. You'll be dead either way."

"You won't live to see me buried," snapped Kevin. He redoubled his efforts, and to the surprise of both men, managed a shallow cut to Voltmeter's shoulder. "Your little protection spell might help you against one or two soldiers, but you can't hold off an entire army. The Black Guards will chop you into hamburger."

"I'll kill you all."

"You're bluffing." Kevin blocked a cut, dropped down to one knee, and slashed at Voltmeter's legs. He missed, then bounced back up in time to parry a thrust to his heart. "I'll bet you're working around to your trapdoor right now."

"Trapdoor? What are you talking about, you young fool?" Voltmeter drew a cut across Kevin's forehead. He smiled as blood began seeping into the Prince's eyes.

"All Evil Overlords have a secret trapdoor that leads to an escape route. There's a hidden switch somewhere in this room. Everyone knows that. It's even in the book."

"You are an idiot who reads too much. I'll kill you, then I'll kill your little princess, and I'll reset the machine and kill your army." With a final angry blow, the Overlord knocked aside Kevin's parry and slashed his blade across the young man's wrist. A fountain of blood erupted. Kevin dropped his sword and clamped his hand across the wound. He stood straight up, panting, looking at Voltmeter, smiling with clenched teeth.

"Now," said the Overlord, "I've made this offer before, and I'll make it again. This is the last time. Tell your friend to get down from there, and I'll spare both your lives."

"Becky," called Kevin, not taking his eyes off the Overlord, "did you hear that?"

"Yes."

"Are you afraid?"

"No!"

"Then throw the damn switch!"

Becky threw the switch.

The machine stopped humming. She drew Thunk's sword and chopped the handle off the switch, rendering it unmovable.

Silence filled the room. Becky shifted from one edge of the platform to the other, trying to see what was happening outside. Valerie remained by the window. Even Laura stopped struggling and stayed still. Voltmeter halted with his sword raised, about to make a cut that would separate Kevin's head from his body. Kevin ignored him, straining his ears, listening for sounds from the windows.

The silence outside was broken by concerned voices. Voltmeter's men were nervous. Stan was saying something unintelligible. Then there was the crisp sound of drawn swords, and a few twangs of bowstrings being let off.

Then, from outside the castle walls, they heard a familiar voice. It was Logan, shouting commands. Other voices joined in, officers re-forming their ranks, soldiers swearing. There was the clatter of hoofbeats on stone, and the band started up with a cheerful hornpipe. A flight of arrows struck the windows. And then there came the roar of a thousand voices, joined in one great long battle cry. The attack was back on.

Voltmeter turned and ran.

Becky slid down the ladder at top speed and ran to Kevin. "Are you all right?" She knew, of course, that he wasn't, but she wanted to be reassuring, and phrases like "You look awful" or "Oh my God!" weren't going to do the job. She took off her blouse, tore a strip from it, and started binding up his wrist.

"Fine," said Kevin, who clearly wasn't. He was bleeding from a score of cuts and swaying on his feet. He ran his free hand over her chain-mail bra. With her blouse off, he could see the bright scar on the metal where the crossbow bolt had struck and glanced off. "You almost gave me a heart attack. For a minute there I really thought you were dead."

"You were very sweet. I was so touched when you cried."

"Yeah, well don't expect me to do it all the time."

"Kids," said Valerie. "I hate to interrupt this romantic tête-à-tête, but are we getting out of here or what?"

"Where did Voltmeter get to?"

"Down here, of course." She was kneeling by a trapdoor, set into the floor on the opposite side of the Diabolical Device. She peered into its black depths. "The hidden switch is over there."

"Don't go in," said Becky. "It's probably booby-trapped."

"He's getting away."

"Where can he go? The castle is surrounded."

"It doesn't matter," said Kevin. "The phlogistocator is going to explode. We've got to leave now to escape the fireball."

"What?" said Valerie.

Becky looked the machine over. It was just sitting there, a silent, inert mass of tubing, crystal, and cast iron, with a scattering of stickers that read NEMA 7 and UL APPROVED. "What makes you think it's going to explode?"

"The Diabolical Device always explodes after the Evil Overlord is defeated."

"It isn't going to explode," said Valerie. "The insurance people inspected it just last month. It's rated for a Class One Division Two area."

"The book didn't say anything about explosions," said Becky.

"Are you two crazy?" yelled Kevin. "When you defeat an Evil Overlord, the Diabolical Device *always* explodes! And you have to outrun the giant fireball, see, and then you throw yourself . . ."

"Where's the Ancient Artifact?" said Valerie.

They all looked to the top of the phlogistocator. The Ancient Artifact, which a few minutes ago had been sitting on its pedestal, was gone.

"Where is it? Did he get it?"

"I don't see how."

"Did he sneak back in while we were talking?"

"Maybe the machine is hollow. Maybe there's another trapdoor on top."

Becky leaned over the entrance to the secret passage. "We'll have to go after him now. With the Ancient Artifact, he can start all over again. Or he might sell it to another Evil Overlord. There's no telling what kind of damage he might do."

"Wait," said Kevin. He bent over and picked up his sword, swaying a little as he did so, and sheathed it. "The gift shop. No one can leave without going through the gift shop. That's where the secret passage leads. Valerie, can you take us back to it?"

"Yes, but . . . what are you going to do to Lord Voltmeter? You're not going to kill him, are you?"

"I will if I can."

"Then I can't help you. I still owe him loyalty."

"What? Valerie, he's a psychotic murderer with no regard for human life, a madman who has killed countless people and is trying to kill more. He tried to kill us."

"True, but I feel there's still good in him."

"He also wanted to kill you."

"Of course, there's not very much good in him," said Valerie thoughtfully. "Come to think of it, the bad certainly outweighs the good. Okay, follow me."

The black-haired girl took off, with Becky close behind. Kevin, who was getting weaker and more light-headed from loss of blood, tried to keep up. Valerie led them on a path that was even more twisted than the route they took in, up one flight of stairs and down another, through hallways and passageways. Occasionally soldiers crossed their path, sometimes Logan's men, sometimes Voltmeter's men on the run. Then Valerie opened a door and they found themselves in the gift shop once again, next to a shelf of Fortress of Doom bubble bath marked fifteen percent off. Becky pointed to an open trapdoor in the floor, but Kevin saw a flash of scarlet-lined cloak through one of the doors.

"That way," he pointed. "Past the cash register."

They piled through. They were at one end of a wide entrance hall, and at the other end, the giant main double doors of the Fortress of Doom. Set in one of the large doors was a smaller door. Voltmeter was pushing it open. The Ancient Artifact was under his arm. He turned once, just long enough to give them a look of hatred, and Kevin dimly felt the same lethargy he'd felt in the central chamber. Then Voltmeter disappeared through the door.

"He's getting his power back. The machine is turned off, so he's getting his power back." Kevin pushed past the two girls and was the first out the door. But he needn't have hurried. Voltmeter was standing only a dozen paces outside. His path was blocked.

It was blocked by the biggest and blackest horse Kevin had ever seen, a giant stallion with a jewel-studded bridle. In the saddle sat a tall man with bulging biceps and massively broad shoulders. He had a curly black mustache, a head full of tight black curls, and black eyes that glittered in a ruggedly handsome face. He looked down on Voltmeter and flashed his white teeth in an expression that was partway between a grin and a snarl. Black Jack Logan was in battle. Black Jack Logan was in his element.

Kevin looked over his shoulder. The two girls were standing in the doorway, looking at Logan with rapturous admiration. "That's Logan?" whispered Valerie. "What a hunk!" Becky nodded.

"Oh for God's sake," muttered Kevin. Aloud he said, "Logan! Be careful! He's got some sort of protective combat spell." He drew his sword again and prepared to charge into the Evil Overlord's back.

Both Voltmeter and Logan ignored him. Logan swung himself off his horse and patted the animal on the neck. His hand was on the hilt of his sword, but he left the blade in its scabbard. Instead, he walked without concern toward the Overlord, still with that same grim half smile. "So we meet again, Voltmeter. This time we finish it."

"Sure," snapped the Overlord irritably. "So we meet again. This time we finish it. You never were much of an original speaker, Jack. Now get out of my way. Go off and hire a speechwriter somewhere. I don't have time for you now."

To everyone's surprise, Logan burst out laughing.

He pointed to the Ancient Artifact under Voltmeter's arm. "That's it? That's the terrible source of magical power that you stole to feed your Diabolical Device? A model five?"

"You're a fool, Jack. This is a model seven! The most powerful Ancient Artifact in existence!"

Only Kevin noticed that Logan's knuckles were white around his sword. *He's bluffing,* the Prince thought. *He's trying to draw his sword, but he can't. Voltmeter has him under his spell.* With both hands, the Prince lifted his own sword. It was like swimming through thick molasses, but he got the point above his head. *I can do this,* he told himself. *Voltmeter is using all his concentration to hold Logan. He can't stop us both.*

Logan was laughing so hard he had to step back and lean on his horse. Finally, he gasped out, "That's not a model seven. It's just a cheap model five with the chrome etched off. You idiot, you've been taken in by one of the oldest swindles in the book."

"It's a model seven!" screeched Voltmeter. "What are you talking about? A model seven!"

Kevin got the point of his sword aimed at Voltmeter. His arms were trembling with the strain of fighting the protective spell.

"Check the serial number," said Logon. "It's under the lid." He laughed again and slapped his horse on the flank. "It's a model five. The junk shops in Angostura are full of them. Your fiendish plan would never have worked."

Voltmeter was livid with rage. He braced the Ancient Artifact against his hip and clawed at the lid. "The hell it wouldn't! You muscle-bound moron, I've forgotten more about Ancient Artifacts than you ever knew!"

Kevin stepped forward. With every ounce of his remaining strength, he drove his sword toward Voltmeter's back.

"Get down," yelled Logan, and flung himself into the dirt.

In a brief instant Voltmeter's spell evaporated. Kevin let the sword go and jumped back. He shoved the girls back inside the Fortress and dived for the gravel himself.

The lid to the Ancient Artifact popped off in Voltmeter's hand.

For one short, final moment he stood there, staring at the inside of the Ancient Artifact, the look of horror on his face plainly showing that he realized he had made a ghastly mistake. And then he was enveloped in a sphere of intense blue light.

It was a light that seared Kevin's brain even through his closed eyes, while the heat flowed over body like molten steel. He dug his fingers into the gravel and pressed his face to the ground and tried to keep from screaming. It seemed like ages before he could look up, and even then he saw nothing but spots. Eventually they faded. But Lord Voltmeter was gone.

The door opened behind Kevin. Becky said faintly, "What was that?"

Logan was already standing. He took his hand off his sword, looked at it, and flexed the fingers a few times. Then he began brushing the dirt from his uniform. "Oh well," he said, "I guess Voltmeter was right. It *was* a model seven after all." He approached a small pile of ashes and stirred them with his foot, uncovering a fused, twisted piece of steel that might once have been a dueling saber. "Of course, it's very dangerous to open up a model seven like that."

Becky looked at the door. It was coated with a fine layer of soot.

Kevin picked up a charred disk of metal, the lid from the Artifact. He brushed away the ashes and read the underside. *You are not a winner,* it said. *Please play again.* He threw it away and slumped against the Fortress wall. "Good trick, Logan. Very clever."

Logan ignored him. More of his men began coming up to the gate, or descended from the Fortress walls on their siege ladders. Some marched prisoners before them. He waved them over. Then he looked past Kevin with a startled expression. "Good Lord! Is that the Princess Rebecca?"

Everyone—Logan, Logan's soldiers, Voltmeter's guards, Valerie, and even Prince Kevin, stopped to look at Becky. She threw back her shoulders. "Yes," she said with icy dignity. "It is I, the Princess Rebecca of Deserae. And no, you cannot see my nipples through this chain mail. I checked before I bought it. It's just your imagination, so you can go back to whatever you were doing."

Logan's men went back to gathering up the prisoners, with a few backward glances at Becky. "What a putz," Logan told her. "I've wanted to get even with Voltmeter for years. Ever since I was a schoolboy. Can you believe he actually made us do book reports over the Christmas holidays?"

Logan's horse had run off. One of his soldiers brought it back to him. A young officer reported that the Fortress of Doom was now secure. The remaining prisoners were marched out the door. Four of Logan's men found Laura. A captured Stan identified her as Voltmeter's Evil Assistant. They brought her to the general, but Logan had eyes only for Becky. He favored her with a triumphant smile.

"Your Highness," he said, "permit me to accompany you back to your palace. I believe we have wedding plans to make."

"I do indeed," said Becky. "I am most grateful for your attention to duty, Lord Logan. My father the King, and the Council of Lords, shall see that you and your men are suitably rewarded. I shall be sure to send you an invitation to the wedding. The Prince of Rassendas and I are so honored that you can attend."

Logan's smiled slipped a tiny bit. "Are you forgetting your father's agreement, Your Highness? You are promised to whoever defeated the Evil Overlord."

"I was promised," said Becky firmly, "to whoever returned the Ancient Artifact. And since the Ancient Artifact is no more"—and here she pointed to the pile of ashes—"I believe I am free to marry whom I choose. And I choose Kevin."

Logan was not so much smiling now as baring his teeth. He was not used to being crossed, and especially not by a woman. "Princess Rebecca, I am not a man to be trifled with."

"I agree."

"I know what is due to me."

"I'm sure."

"Now, even among the nobility, marriage is an intimate and personal matter. I'm sure you don't wish this affair to be contested in open court, but I will seek the reward that is due to me."

"I'm sure you don't wish to go public with this either," said Becky. "Especially as I'd have to describe how you and your entire army were flopping around on the grass, gasping for air like fish out of water."

Logan's smile had completely disappeared now. For a

long time he was silent, trying out various responses in his head. "I admit the attack suffered a delay while the units regrouped," he finally said. "But my men rallied around me . . ."

"Oh, yes, your men were flat on their backs right with you," said Becky. "I watched the whole battle. You were not a heroic sight, let me tell you. In all truth, Lord Logan, you looked like—how did you put it— a complete putz?"

"Oh very well," snapped Logan. He knew when he was defeated. "I will not contest your marriage with Timberline." But he was determined to salvage something from the affair. "But I want complete credit for Voltmeter's defeat. Complete credit, do you hear! With no mention of his—er—defensive measures."

"It's a deal" said Becky. "I look forward to your presence at the wedding, Lord Logan. Oh, and if you're in mind to bring a gift, I could really use some additions to my silver."

"I usually ask my mother to pick out that stuff. You're registered, right?" Logan swung himself onto his horse. "Your Highness, these are dangerous roads for a young lady. I shall assign some men to accompany you back to Deserae." To Kevin he paid no attention.

"Thank you, Lord Logan, but that is not necessary. I'm not sure I will return home immediately. Perhaps I'll take a few lessons in swordfighting. I'm thinking about becoming a barbarian swordswoman."

Logan frowned. "And wear a fur thong? With all due respect, Princess, you don't have the figure . . ." His eyes widened as he saw Becky's hand tighten around the hilt of her sword. "That is to say, I'm sure you'd look perfectly lovely," he amended hastily. Searching for a change of subject, his gaze fell on Laura. "And you," he told the girl, "you will return with me, to face Angosturan justice." Still bound and gagged, Laura could only look back with unrelenting hostility.

"What does that mean?"

All heads turned to the Fortress door. In the shadows beyond, a slim figure moved forward. A few stray beams of sunlight reflected off highly polished black leather. Valerie stepped through the door. She gave Laura's helpless form a long, appraising glance, sucked in her breath, and ran a pink tongue over glossy red lips. "What does that mean *exactly,* to face Angosturan justice?"

"Um, actually I'm not sure. It's just something I say when I take prisoners. You know, to sound dramatic. When I get home I just turn them over to the courts. Generally they're thrown in a dungeon or something like that."

"Ooo, yes!" Valerie's breath came in quick pants. "Yes, locked in a dungeon." She ran her hands across her breasts and down to her slim waist, her eyes fixed on Laura the whole time. "Yes! Stripped naked . . . chained to the wall . . . and spanked . . . ooo!"

"What?" Logan frowned at her. "Chains? Spanking? All I said was . . ."

"Yes, yes," Valerie interrupted. She grabbed his horse's mane and in one quick motion swung herself into the saddle in front of Logan. "How do you feel about threesomes?"

"Threesomes?" Logan was distracted by the way Valerie's pert, leather-covered bottom squirmed against his thighs. "Um, when you say threesomes, do you mean two girls and a guy, or two guys and girl?"

"Two girls and one guy."

"Two girls and one guy *only,* right? Not like, the first time it's two girls, but then the next time I'm expected to bring another guy?"

"No no. Two girls and one guy only. That's all."

"Oh well, that's okay, I guess. Why do you ask?"

"I'll explain on the ride to Angostura." She took the reins from Logan, swung his horse around, and the two of them started on the trail back down into the valley. Logan's officers followed, then his soldiers, and within a remarkably short time his entire army, prisoners and all, had packed up and was marching away from Angst. The last to leave was Sam Bigelow.

He looked nearly as bad as Kevin, his hair dirty and matted, and he had taken a cut himself going over the wall. He limped over to the two of them. "Are you all right, Timberline? Can I give you a hand?"

Kevin shook his head. "Thanks anyway, Sam."

"Yes, thank you, Sam." Becky hugged him.

Bigelow looked embarrassed. "Um, Your Highness, I have a favor to ask. Um, I spent the night at this inn, you see. And there was this barmaid."

"Really?"

"Yes. I can't remember what I said to her *exactly,* but she swears I told her I could get her an invitation to the royal wedding."

"Sam, you shouldn't make promises like that," Becky said teasingly.

"I know, Your Highness. I'm sorry."

"But I'll see your invitation goes to her. I'm sure you and Cherry will make a lovely couple."

"No, I didn't mean that . . . I meant that . . . I just . . ." Becky gave him a severe, Ice Princess stare. Bigelow swallowed. "Yes. Thank you, Your Highness." He directed one more sympathetic look at Kevin, who was sitting against the wall with his eyes closed. "One more thing." He reached under his tunic and pulled out a tiny scroll, tied up with a pale ribbon. "An old woman gave me this message to pass on to His Highness."

"I'll take it, Sam." She watched him go, then unraveled the scroll and read the contents:

> *"You shall not defeat the man in black*
> *That which you seek, won't be brought back*
> *The guards will falter when they attack*
> *But you'll marry a babe who's really stacked."*

She made a face, opened her hand, and let the wind carry the scroll away. Then she knelt next to Kevin, took his hand, and said cheerfully, "Not a bad day. Voltmeter is dead, his army is taken prisoner, the Ancient Artifact is no longer a danger to anyone, Logan got his victory, and Sammy got a date. It all worked out well for everyone, don't you think?"

"No!" snapped Kevin. He climbed back on his feet, but in an unsteady way. "No, I don't think. Why does Logan get to be the hero again? His attack was a complete failure. Without us, Logan and his whole army would be food for the crows. But he gets to be the hero, and what do I get? Nothing!"

"You get to marry me," Becky pointed out.

"Oh. Right. Well, there's that. But still, look at me. I'm a bloody mess! I'm going to go down in history as Kevin the Bloody Mess."

"Maybe they'll call you Bloody Kevin for short. That's not too bad. It sounds kind of fierce."

"Fierce, ha! Everyone who saw me like this is going to report back that Voltmeter beat me. And that's not true. I fought him to a standstill. He ran away from me!"

Becky was about to point out that, technically, Voltmeter

ran away from the threat of Logan's Black Guards. But she caught the words before she spoke them. Because he was a hero, she realized. He had rescued her from the prison cell, even though she'd been caught again. He found the Ancient Artifact, although it had been taken from him. He'd held fast under threat of torture, but Voltmeter got the information he sought anyway. He had fought the guards and been beaten up, and he had battled the Evil Overlord and been trounced. He had done all of the things a hero should do and succeeded at none of them. Yet because he had done them, he and Becky had saved Deserae's army, and only then could Logan defeat Voltmeter. She threw her arms around him and hugged him with all her strength. "It's okay, sweetie," she murmured. "You're an unsung hero."

"I don't want to be an unsung hero," grumbled Kevin. "I want to be a sung hero. I want to have songs written about me. Grand operas."

"Grand operas are tragedies. You'd have to be killed first."

"*Opera buffa,* then."

"But those would make you look like . . ."

"Even a couple of madrigals would do."

"I think you should . . ."

"A ballad at the very least."

"Will you shush? Listen, sweetie, you're not looking well. Here's what I think. I think we should go back to the village and give you a bath and get all these cuts cleaned and dressed. And then we can have a nice, quiet dinner. And then we'll go up to my room and light some candles and maybe open a bottle of wine and then . . ." Here Becky put her chin on his shoulder and whispered hotly in his ear. "You can do *anything you want to me.*"

Some color returned immediately to Kevin's cheeks. "Anything?"

Becky looked at him with wide blue eyes and wetly parted lips. "Anything."

"How do you feel about threesomes?"

"I prefer foursomes, actually."

"Two guys and two girls?"

"It's more exciting that way, don't you think?"

"We're talking about golf, aren't we?"

"I was thinking of bridge."

"All right," said the Prince. "I could go along with a quiet game of cards." He put his arm around her waist. "But I get to cut."

"Then let's go."

"No," said Kevin. He took hold of both her hands. "Sometimes a man just has to put his foot down. I am the Prince of Rassendas, and I have made my decision. I'm not going anywhere until I get a kiss."

"Oh, you're not?"

"No."

"Then," said Becky, "I am the Princess of Deserae, and I guess I have no choice."

The kiss that followed was long and moist and soft and sweet. It started when the sun was high in the sky and lasted until the shadows lengthened in the valley. It was a tender and touching and extremely romantic kiss, for the air was warm, the breeze was soft, the sky was clear, and the quiet of the afternoon was disturbed only by the gentle rustle of the trees, the chirping of crickets, the occasional snatch of birdsong, and a thunderous roar as Voltmeter's Diabolical Device exploded in a giant fireball.

"I knew that was going to happen," said Kevin.

John Moore is an engineer who lives and works in Houston, Texas. He authored the novel *Slay and Rescue* and numerous short stories.

Coming October 2004 from Ace

For More Than Glory
by William C. Dietz
0-441-01214-0

Legion General Bill Booly has just crushed one uprising, and a new rebellion is already brewing in a remote world light years away—spawning a web of terrorism close enough to catch the Confederacy in its grasp.

The Merlin Effect
by T.A. Barron
0-441-01222-1

To save her father's life, Kate Gordon must enter an undersea world of bizarre creatures and terrifying foes, and succeed where Merlin failed.

Also new in paperback this month:

The Nimble Man
by Christopher Golden & Thomas E. Sniegoski
0-441-01215-9

Dracula in London
edited by P.N. Elrod
0-441-01213-2

Available wherever books are sold or at
www.penguin.com

**From the *New York Times*
bestselling author of the
Phule's Company series**

ROBERT ASPRIN

**Follow apprentice magician Skeeve, his scaly
mentor Aahz, and beautiful ex-assassin Tanda in
their high *myth*-adventures.**

**Available wherever books are sold or at
www.penguin.com**

B519